MURDER
AT THE
MANOR

MURDER
AT THE
MANOR

COLIN WADE

The Book Guild Ltd

First published in Great Britain in 2024 by
The Book Guild Ltd
Unit E2 Airfield Business Park
Harrison Road, Market Harborough
Leicestershire, LE16 7UL
Freephone: 0800 999 2982
www.bookguild.co.uk
Email: info@bookguild.co.uk
X: @bookguild

Web: www.colinwade.com
X: @CPWADE1
Facebook: @colinwadeauthor
Instagram: @colinwadeauthor

Also by Colin Wade: *The Lost Years*
Also by Colin Wade: *Plutus*
Also by Colin Wade: *Deadly Connection*
Also by Colin Wade: *The Sins of the Father*

Typeset in 11pt Minion Pro

Printed on FSC accredited paper
Printed and bound in Great Britain by 4edge Limited

ISBN 978 1835740 477

British Library Cataloguing in Publication Data.
A catalogue record for this book is available from the British Library.

To all my lovely readers. You are the reason I carry on writing.

Prologue

He stood on the path on the opposite side of the road from the bank. The biting February wind prickled his skin. He pulled the collar of his coat up around his neck to keep out the cold as he stared at the entrance. The constant stream of London traffic stood between him and his destiny.

He continued to watch the entrance and the steady flow of people going in and out of the bank. He blew out a breath. Doubt began to fill his mind. Could he really pull this off? The biggest score of his life. He'd learnt his lessons when jobs had gone south. Prison was not an option, and his mistakes had nearly cost him his freedom. He wasn't going to let that happen today. Every part of the plan had been triple-checked. The steps had been walked through and the variables considered. He was ready.

The narrow path he was stood on meant he was causing an obstruction. The heavy footfall along the street meant his presence was met with the occasional bump, a few tuts and the odd expletive from stressed city workers. He ignored them all. He waited a few more minutes before moving to the crossing. The high-pitched beeping signalled it was time to cross, and he pulled the collar of his coat up around him again, trying to minimise the chances of anyone remembering his face. As he got to the entrance to the bank, he put on some glasses with a slightly tinted frame. Just enough to make facial recognition difficult if someone examined CCTV. He adjusted the trilby hat he was wearing to add to the security countermeasures.

He strode into the entrance with a confident air, like someone who was meant to be there. No hesitations. Nothing that would make him look immediately suspicious. He walked up to the VIP counter.

"Good morning," he said, "my name is Mr Deveraux, and I wish to access my wife's safety deposit box."

The lady behind the desk was trussed up in the company business suit, set off by a fully made-up face that he surmised must have taken her some time to apply. As she blinked, he noticed the false eyelashes, a pet hate of his. These, together with the plumped-up collagen lips, made him think that she looked like one of those expensive sex dolls. Her attempt at a smile didn't seem to reach the contours of her face, and he wondered whether this creature was also a slave to Botox.

"Please can I see the key you have to the box, sir?"

He handed the key over to her, and she examined the security information on the fob, scanning the security chip into her system. A few seconds passed before her tight face attempted a frown.

"Oh, I'm sorry, sir, but you do not have approval to access this box. Our security settings only have your wife as a registered key holder."

"My apologies. I should have given you this." He took a letter out of his briefcase and handed it to the woman.

She scanned the letter and attempted to frown some more. "This is most irregular. We would not normally accept this type of authorisation."

"Can't you check the signature on your system?" he replied.

She didn't look at him, just flicked her attention from the letter to the banking system that held the records on the safety deposit boxes. He tried to remain calm as she compared the signatures.

"Well, I can see that the signatures match, but we are still not able to accept this as a sole form of authorisation."

"What else do you need?" he replied, keeping his tone calm and unthreatening. He was prepared for this and had to keep his composure.

She turned around without comment and walked into an inner office. He could see her talking animatedly to a guy, whom he recognised as one of the branch managers he'd identified on one of his reconnaissance missions. The phone was picked up. "Good," he muttered under his breath. They were going to call her.

A few minutes passed. He kept his head low to minimise the chances of his face being fully picked up on CCTV. The phone call was still going on. A bead of sweat formed on his brow as he tried to control his increasing heartbeat.

"Sir." A voice from the back. It was the guy. The manager. He walked up to the counter. "I'm sorry for the delay but you do understand that we must exercise the most stringent security checks when it comes to our clients' assets."

"Of course," the man replied. "Does that mean my wife has given you authorisation for me to access her safe deposit box?"

"Indeed she has, sir. Though, as my associate told you, this is most irregular, and I have made Mrs Deveraux aware that she should really add you as a permanent key holder to avoid this type of…" he paused for dramatic effect, "… inconvenience."

"No problem. I will talk to her about it when I get home."

The manager flashed a false smile. "Please follow me, sir."

He followed the manager, continuing to keep his head low. They went down a flight of stairs to a steel-gated entrance. The manager fobbed through the door, entering a wide, carpeted lobby. A wide, solid steel door faced them across the room. The manager fobbed another reader and then twisted a large wheel that was in the centre of the door. There was a loud click, and the manager pulled at the heavy door, which opened out into the lobby space.

They walked in, and the manager handed him the key to the safety deposit box. He walked over to where the box was stored and inserted his master key. One of the lights on the box turned from red to green.

"There you go, sir. Just insert your key and the box will be released from the cage. You can either use the desk and tables in here to inspect your box or go outside into the lobby and use the seating there. Please take your time and press the buzzer by the outer door when you are done."

He muttered a thank you and waited for the manager to leave. He inserted the key and the second light turned green. He pulled the box out of the cage and placed it on the table in the centre of the room. He wasn't going into the lobby. That area felt much more exposed for what he was planning to do.

He stopped for a second, staring at the box. This was it. Was the intel about the contents of this box going to be solid, or was he about to have his world collapse around him? He pulled the lid upwards and peered inside. He caught his breath. There was one single item in the box. A velvet bag, with a drawstring pulling the opening tight shut.

He picked the bag up and felt for what was inside. His heart felt like it was going to burst out of his chest. He could feel something.

He placed a finger in the small hole at the top of the bag to release the drawstring. As he looked inside, he saw what he had come for.

This was it. This was the moment he'd been waiting for.

1

The Lexus purred as it navigated the twisty roads that led out of Chipping Campden, the beautiful Cotswold countryside stretching out as far as the eye could see. Angela Walker smiled to herself as she revelled in the amazing views. After a couple of miles, the entrance to the driveway of the Cotswold Manor Hotel, which would be their home from home for the weekend, appeared on the left.

The long driveway snaked uphill. Fenced-off fields with sheep were evident on each side of the driveway. Numerous wildlife, including industrious blackbirds, a regal pheasant and lots of busy squirrels, bounded around the grass verges and tree-lined driveway. It was early April, and the trees were showing signs of buds turning into blossom. She took a deep breath in, already feeling more relaxed.

She had to slow for strategically placed speed bumps, all accompanied by a cute sign stating the speed limit as 6¾ mph. As she drove over the third one, the façade of the fourteenth-century manor house came into view. It was amazing. The two-storey stone building with its higgledy-piggledy roof stretched out into an L shape, fronted by beautifully appointed gardens and a line of branded deckchairs that were placed to maximise the sunshine and the amazing views across the surrounding Cotswold countryside. It was a quintessential scene, very much the essence of what foreign tourists were looking for when it came to finding the true heart of a classic English experience, constantly re-enforced by TV programmes like *Downton Abbey*.

The driveway bent round to the left, and they passed a tennis court on the right and helipad on the left. She raised her eyebrows. "Should have brought the helicopter."

Her passenger smiled. "Maybe next year."

The final stretch of the driveway narrowed between two raised beds, resplendent with tall trees and well-tended shrubs. It finally opened out to the front entrance to the hotel. An amazing arched doorway, straddled on either side by a pair of stone lions, greeted them. They parked their car in one of the spaces outside the entrance and got out. They both stretched out their aching bones, which had not been helped by the 2½-hour drive from West London.

The door was huge, like some entrance to a medieval castle. They grabbed the large, circular iron handle and pushed. The door opened out to a small reception area, with beautiful flagstones on the floor immediately re-enforcing the classic English country house feel.

They were greeted by a happy, professional receptionist who asked their name.

"Mr and Mrs Walker," she said. "We have a two-night reservation."

The receptionist checked them in with a minimum of fuss, confirming their dinner reservation for 6.45pm and giving them a fob to the leisure facilities in case they wanted to use the gym or swimming pool. It was a level of exceptional customer service that they would get used to on their visit.

They were helped with their bags up to their first-floor room, which was immaculate. A large double bed dominated the space. This was complemented by a small, circular table containing a bowl of fruit and some local water. Two occasional chairs were placed next to the table, with a further dressing table and free-standing mirror on the other side of the room. A large TV was on an extendable arm, attached to the wall, allowing flexible watching positions from the bed or chairs.

She stood in the centre of the room, looking out of the small, rectangular windows at the view of the garden. "Wow," she said, "this place is amazing."

"Yes, well picked," he replied.

As they began to unpack, she heard a phone beep. "What is it?" she said.

"I don't know. I need to make a phone call. Something's going down at work."

"No!" she exclaimed. "Not again."

He grimaced and walked out of the room. Ten minutes later, he walked back in, a look of dread on his face. "I'm sorry, but I'm going to have to go and get something sorted. I'll leave after dinner."

2

THE DINING ROOM
FRIDAY EVENING

They sat at a small, cosy round table for two in the centre of the long dining room. The decor was perfect, with all the restaurant tables bedecked with tablecloths, candles and a small posy of flowers in a bud vase, all complemented by beautiful glasses and cutlery. The maître d' and his staff created an ambience of sophisticated elegance with more of the effortless, exceptional customer service they had experienced at reception.

The friendly and efficient front-of-house team were delivering starters of soup or pâté, main courses of pork loin or sea bass, all of which were accompanied by satisfied noises from the people consuming them.

The restaurant was busy with an eclectic mix of people, which was lucky because Angela Walker was still fuming and wasn't in the mood for idle chit-chat. It meant she could indulge in one of her favourite pastimes of people-watching.

She sipped at a lovely glass of merlot as they waited for their starters. He had his head down, trying not to catch her eye, worried that it would start another argument. She looked across from where they were sat at an older couple. The man was smart in blazer and tie, waxing lyrical about his time in the Royal Navy. His accent was what some would call *plummy*, very much the quintessential mark of an upper-class English gent. Next to them were a younger couple with strong American accents, whose every other word seemed to be *awesome*, which she felt was very much playing up to how the English stereotyped your average American. To her left were another older couple celebrating some anniversary or other, evidenced by the complimentary glasses of champagne that had been brought to them by the maître d'. Whilst everything about the hotel was focused on everyone feeling relaxed, she couldn't shake the feeling that they seemed uncomfortable in this environment. Maybe they just weren't used to such luxury. She thought that was a shame and very much reflective of some people of her generation who had struggled for every penny but, now that they had some money behind them, found it hard to spend it on themselves.

The starters arrived, and they ate in silence. The pâté was exquisite and, now sensitive to every little annoying thing he did, she winced as he slurped his soup. He tried to make some small talk about how good it was, but she did no more than give him a reluctant grunt.

As the starters were cleared, she noticed a man had walked in and sat on his own on a table to their right. He was dressed in a smart shirt, no tie, with a pair of light-coloured chino trousers. She guessed he must be in his fifties as his short-cropped hair and goatee beard were showing signs of greying as the advent of old age crept up on him. He was quietly spoken, as she struggled to hear what he was saying to the maître d'. She attempted to catch his eye to smile at him, but he just looked off into the distance. She was always fascinated by people on their own. Sitting down to dine alone. What was his story? It always intrigued her what had led to people being on their own. This wasn't a business hotel, so she doubted he was stopping over for work. She continued to speculate. The man continued to stare into space.

The entrées arrived and, just as she was about to fork the first piece of sea bass into her mouth, she was distracted by a woman flouncing into the dining room, loudly announcing her arrival and demanding that she be shown to the corner table that she had reserved. The maître d' was the epitome of calm professionalism as he navigated her to said table. She began to eat but couldn't take her eyes off this fascinating creature. Apart from being loud and brash, she wore dark glasses and a wide-brimmed straw hat, bedecked with fake flowers. Considering the time of the evening and the fading light outside, this ensemble seemed so out of place. She speculated that this woman was someone famous and the dark glasses were just one of the many pretensions that these types of people indulged in. The problem was that she was so loud, you couldn't help but be drawn to everything she was doing and saying. The woman had immediately reeled off her order to the maître d', not waiting to see if maybe other people needed attention before her. Champagne, pâté and pork were demanded before she dismissed the maître d' with a wave of her hand and pulled out her mobile phone.

Angela Walker tried not to look at her as she continued to eat the incredible plate of food but, as her attention flicked between her plate and this fascinating woman, she noticed most of the restaurant were staring at her.

"What a strange creature," he said.

"For God's sake, stop staring," she retorted. "She obviously wants to be the centre of attention, and you're not helping by gawping at her."

They ate the rest of the meal in silence.

3

THE HOTEL ROOM
BEDTIME

Angela Walker hung her dress in the wardrobe and put on the complimentary dressing gown, in readiness for her pre-bed bath. She peered out of the window. The garden was lit up by subtle lighting, the only thing that was piercing the total blackness of the surrounding countryside. The night was clear, and she smiled briefly at the twinkling of the stars, a scene that would have been more romantic had she anyone to share it with. She decided to stop stewing and ran her bath.

As she lay still in the tub, the bubbles tickling her nose, she began to notice the noises in the hotel. It was an old manor house, which meant that every floorboard creak, every squeaky door, seemed to resonate through the hotel. She realised her bathroom must be above the downstairs drawing room, as she could hear the faint voices and laughter of other residents, probably enjoying a pre-bed drink. Not that she was jealous. She didn't feel she needed any more alcohol to get to sleep. The brief walk around the lanes of the hotel before they'd had dinner was enough to fill her lungs with beautiful country air, a sure-fire remedy to any sleep problems people may have.

She got out of the bath and put on her nightdress. She made a cup of cocoa and got into bed, grabbing the book she was reading. She was halfway through it and was finding it hard to put down.

The cocoa was finished and, despite the gripping storyline, her head was beginning to nod. She shut the book and took off her glasses, rubbing her tired eyes. Just as she was considering whether she needed to go to the toilet again before bed, she heard faint voices coming from the room next door. The voices were mostly inaudible, but the volume of their conversation seemed to be rising, like they were arguing. She craned her neck to see if she could make out what they were saying.

Intrigued, she got out of bed and opened her door. There was a fire door in the corridor between their rooms, which meant the noise was less obvious than being in her room. She closed the hotel room door and moved towards the adjoining wall. The conversation was still going on and, whilst she could barely make out the words, the pitch of the voices suggested that the conversation was heated.

She chuckled to herself at her nosiness but couldn't help it. Especially when she was on her own, she always got more fascinated by what everyone else was up to. Curiosity got the better of her. She grabbed her dressing gown and key, creeping out of her room and navigating as quietly as she could through the fire door.

The door to the room, that she surmised was adjoined to hers, was on the left. As she got closer, she could indeed hear raised voices. She got snippets of the conversation.

"…you betrayed me…" A woman's voice.

"…you'll never get your hands on…" A man's voice.

"…you'll pay…" The woman again.

Just as she felt a sudden pang of embarrassment at eavesdropping on their conversation, she gasped as there was a loud grunt, followed by a heavy thud. The room fell silent.

She put her hand over her mouth. She didn't know what to do. Her survival instinct kicked in and she quickly turned around, back through the fire door, fumbling with her key when she got back to the door of her room. She kept looking over her shoulder, hoping that whoever was in that room had not heard her.

She got through her bedroom door and leant against it, trying to calm her heart rate. What the hell had she just heard? What was the sudden thud? She knew it sounded like someone falling on the floor, but she didn't want to believe that something bad had just happened in that room.

She moved and sat down on the bed. She shook her head. What the hell was going on?

4

HOUSEKEEPING
SATURDAY MORNING

Evangeline had been a reliable member of the housekeeping team for two years now. The money had allowed her to move away from her toxic home life and rent with friends in a small three-bedroom flat in Shipston-on-Stour. She struggled to make ends meet but saved money by using a bike to get to work, and the staff were given free meals, which helped with the monthly food budget.

She loved working at the hotel. The guests were always so nice and were often generous with their gratuities. The standards that the hotel set for room cleaning were high, and she worked hard to make sure that everything was perfect for every guest.

Some of the guests were down at breakfast, which had allowed her to get three of the ten rooms she had on her rota to clean done by 10.30am. She moved her cleaning stuff through to the next landing. The *do not disturb* sign was hung on the door of the next room. She had a brief listen at the door but could hear nothing. It was always a difficult call as to how long to leave it before potentially disturbing the guests. The absolute worst thing you could do was wake someone up who was having a lie-in. On the other hand, guests sometimes forgot to turn their signs round and they ran the risk of not getting their rooms cleaned if the housekeeping team didn't at least make an attempt to see if the room was indeed empty.

Evangeline left it for now and moved on to the next room that was up a couple of steps at the end of the landing. She was done by 11am. Whilst she still had several rooms to do at the other end of the hotel floor, she wanted to get this end finished, to save her having to lug all her cleaning stuff backwards and forwards. She listened at the door of the *do not disturb* room. There was no sound. She risked it. "Housekeeping," she shouted as she tapped on the door. There was no response. She tried again. Still nothing.

She got out her master key and turned it in the lock. As the door creaked inwards, she was relieved that the bed was empty. The light in the en-suite bathroom, that led off the far corner of the room, was off. She smiled at her luck. The room was definitely empty.

She moved her cleaning stuff into the room. She stopped for a second, curious that the bed didn't appear to have been slept in, yet there were two half-filled wine glasses on the small, round table. She grabbed the glasses and went into the bathroom area to clean them out. As she rinsed the wine away and dried up the glasses with a towel, she realised something else. There were a couple of towels in the bath, an indication that the guest wanted them replaced, but there were no toiletries in the bathroom.

She frowned and went back into the main room. There weren't any guest bits in the room either. She went back to her printed schedule. The room was booked for two nights by a Mrs Deveraux. Single occupancy on Friday and Saturday night. It was clear that someone had been in the room the previous evening, obviously drinking with someone from another room, but now there was no sign of them.

Suddenly, Evangeline realised the other obvious place to check. The wardrobes. She moved to the right-hand side of the imposing four-poster bed, where two ornate free-standing wardrobes were placed. She opened the one nearest to the door. It was empty.

As she shut the door to that wardrobe and went to open the door to the other one, she stopped in her tracks. There was a large stain on the carpet next to the bed. She instinctively looked over to where the wine glasses had stood. What type of wine had they been drinking? The stain was red, but she couldn't remember whether the dregs of the wine were white or red. She pulled a confused expression. Something else had struck her. Where was the wine bottle?

Evangeline didn't move. The whole situation was so weird. The guest had clearly been in the room at some point during the evening, but it looked like they had cleared out all their belongings before it was time to go to bed, which left the key question: where were they?

She continued to stare at the stain. Whatever it was it would need to be cleaned. She eyed it curiously. For some reason, she began to doubt that it was a wine stain. A flutter of fear gripped her chest.

She knelt down to examine it closer, holding her breath as she did. The stain was a deep red and there was no hint of an alcohol smell. She let out a piercing scream.

It wasn't wine. It was blood.

5

THE CRIME SCENE
SATURDAY MORNING

Mr Moretti, the general manager, heard the scream from his office and rushed to see what was up. His housekeeper was in the room just across from his office, kneeling on the floor. She was crying and shaking. He knelt down. "What's up, Miss Stimic?"

She had her hand over her eyes and was sobbing convulsively. He put his arm around her. "Come on. What's the matter?"

He was relieved as she slowly began to calm down, taking in a deep breath to ease the sobbing. She took her hand from her eyes and looked briefly at him. He gave her a wide-eyed expression, encouraging her to speak. She said nothing, just extended her arm and pointed at something ahead of her.

Moretti moved his focus towards what she was pointing at. His heart skipped a beat. Was that…? He looked back at his housekeeper, and she nodded her head up and down in acknowledgement of what he was thinking. He put his hand over his mouth. It was blood.

He encouraged the housekeeper to stand up. "Come on, Miss Stimic, let's get you out of here. If that's blood, I need to call the police."

She looked at him, fear etched across her face. He gave her a reassuring smile, but in truth, his stomach was doing somersaults. He radioed for help from the reception team, and they were there in seconds, taking the sobbing housekeeper away. He locked the room and went back into his office to call the police.

It only took the police half an hour to get to the hotel. It seemed that his description of a bloody crime scene had been enough for them to treat his call as a priority. He bound down the stairs to reception when the team called him to say the police had arrived. He was expecting an officer in uniform so was surprised to be met by a young lady in a smart business suit, flanked by a very tall young man, who was equally suited and booted.

"Good morning, sir," she said, "my name is Detective Chief Inspector Chloe Taylor and this is Detective Sergeant Michael Spence."

"Welcome, I am the general manager of the hotel. Mr Roberto Moretti."

The DCI didn't stand on ceremony. "Can you show me the potential crime scene?"

Moretti led them up the stairs, looking back at the DS. "You'll need to watch your head. These types of buildings weren't designed for people so tall."

The DS smiled. "I get used to it, sir."

Moretti unlocked the door to the room, stepping in and inviting them across the threshold. "There is a blood stain to the right of the bed," he said, quite matter-of-factly, now the stress of coming across the scene had dissipated somewhat.

He watched with curiosity as the DCI took one step towards the blood stain, shining her torch on the area. The DS looked over her shoulder. She gestured for him to give her something. A few seconds later, she was holding up a swab.

"Well, it's definitely blood." She stood up and placed the swab in a forensic bag. Moretti already felt like he was under scrutiny as she scanned the rest of the room, catching his eye briefly. Eventually, she spoke. "Whilst I accept that is a blood stain, what makes you think a crime has been committed?"

Moretti frowned. "I don't know. I guess the blood stain seemed like enough to call you."

The DCI nodded. "Okay, we always encourage the public to call us in these circumstances, but beyond this stain, I can't see anything else in this room that suggests a crime has been committed. I mean, where are all the items belonging to the guest who's staying in this room and indeed, where is the guest?"

Moretti grimaced. "My housekeeper was the one who came across the scene. She noticed the stain after she'd starting cleaning the room. From the little I've been able to glean from her, it seems as though the guest who was staying in this room has cleared all her belongings out, even though she was booked in for two nights."

While he was speaking, he noticed a subtle eye roll from the DCI towards her sergeant. She didn't take long to explain the gesture. "Hold on. Are you saying that your housekeeper was cleaning in here before she saw this blood stain?"

"Er, yes."

The DCI sighed. "I'm sorry, sir, but her actions have almost certainly compromised any forensics that we might have been able to get from this scene."

"Oh, so what does that mean?"

"Well," she frowned to add to her serious tone, "we have an unexplained blood stain in a room that has been forensically compromised, coupled with a missing guest. Not a great start, is it, sir?"

Just as Moretti was considering his response, a voice came from the corridor.

"Something bad happened in this room. Last night. I heard it."

Moretti watched as the DCI took a step back towards the entrance to the room. "I'm sorry," she said, "what did you say?"

They all stared at an older woman, stood in the corridor outside the room.

"My name is Angela Walker and I'm staying in the room next door. Something bad happened in this room last night."

6

MRS WALKER'S ROOM
SATURDAY MORNING

Angela Walker invited the detectives back to her room and
sat on the edge of her bed, nervously rubbing her hands
together. DCI Taylor and DS Spence sat on the two chairs
by the round table, as Moretti stood by the door.

Taylor wasted no time in launching into her inquiries.
"Mrs Walker. Can you explain what you mean about
something bad happening in that room?"

Walker took a moment to compose herself. "Oh gosh. I
feel so stupid. I should have raised the alarm last night, but
I was so frightened that I just hid back in here."

"Hid? Was someone following you?"

"No. No. I heard the noise. I think I screamed or gasped,
or something. I was so worried that someone would come
out of the room to confront me that I turned and bolted
back to my room."

"So, no one came out after you?"

"No. Thank God."

"Okay. Tell us what happened from the start."

"Well, my husband left me alone after dinner because he's had to go back to work to sort out a crisis."

"On a Friday night?"

Walker sighed. "Yes, an all-too-frequent occurrence I'm afraid."

Taylor raised her eyebrows, glancing briefly at Spence.

Walker continued. "I was just getting ready for bed around 11pm, when I could hear faint voices coming from the adjoining room. I must admit that I was curious because, although I couldn't hear what they were saying, the pitch of their voices sounded like they were arguing."

"What did you do?"

"I listened for a bit and then my curiosity got the better of me, so I put on my dressing gown, grabbed my door key and went out into the corridor. The fire door was closed, so I couldn't really hear any better. I decided to go through the fire door and listen outside that room."

"What did you hear?"

"Well, they were definitely arguing."

"They?"

"Yes, a man and a woman. Now, even though I was outside the door, I still couldn't make out everything they were saying, but I remember she said something about being betrayed; he said something about her never getting her hands on it; and she replied saying that he would pay. And then…" There was a brief pause as Walker tried to calm herself.

"It's okay," Taylor said, "take your time."

"I'm sorry. It was all so horrible, but straight after the woman said *he'd pay*, there was a loud thud, and everything went quiet."

"What do you think happened?"

"The thud sounded like someone had fallen to the floor."

"And this was the point that you came back to your room?"

"Yes, I was petrified."

"Did you hear anything else after that?"

"No, it took me a while to calm down, but the whole time I was sat in bed, I didn't hear another sound."

Taylor rubbed her eyes. "Well, thank you, Mrs Walker. It does sound as though something happened in that room last night, but it begs the obvious question, where are the two people that you heard?"

"I... I don't know."

"Are you sure you didn't hear anything else, after the apparent incident?"

"No. Nothing. I think I lay there for quite a while, but I heard nothing else while I was awake."

Taylor looked at Spence and then to Moretti. "I'm going to call my guvnor for authorisation, but this does seem at least worthy of a bit of our time, even though we don't appear to have a victim of any apparent crime. Is there somewhere we can set up an incident room?"

Moretti stood up straight. "Oh yes, of course. You can use the conference room. It's not being used this weekend. I'll get the team to sort that straight away."

Taylor stood up. "Okay. I'd like to speak to the housekeeper first, and then it would be helpful if we could speak to some of the guests that are in the other rooms on this corridor."

Moretti frowned. "Er, I guess, though I can't guarantee that the guests will still be in the hotel. I imagine many of them will have gone out for the day."

Taylor looked back to Walker. "Thank you again, and I'm sure we can get to the bottom of what happened here. Try not to worry, and enjoy the rest of your day."

For a second, it didn't seem like Walker had heard what Taylor had said. She was staring out of the window. "Mrs Walker," probed Taylor, "are you okay?"

Walker jumped. "Oh sorry, miles away. It's just…"

Taylor impatiently filled the void. "It's just what, Mrs Walker?"

Walker looked at her, tears beginning to form in her eyes. "There's something else. After I came back into my room, I tried to phone my husband. I needed to speak to someone, but he didn't answer his phone. Just went to voicemail like it always does."

"What does that have to do with what happened here?"

Walker bowed her head. "Oh Lord, this is going to sound so ridiculous, but the male voice I heard in that room sounded just like my husband's."

7

THE INCIDENT ROOM
SATURDAY, 1PM

Taylor plugged her laptop in and checked her email. The chief super had responded straight away and given them authorisation to complete the initial investigations.

The conference room had a large whiteboard on one side and the staff had quickly got them some coffee and sandwiches, which was a welcome energy boost, since breakfast was a distant memory for both of them.

She stood up and grabbed one of the whiteboard markers. "Right, Sergeant, what have we got?"

He pulled a pinched expression. "Not much. Have we? I guess we have a potential crime scene with one small patch of blood, plus a man and a woman heard arguing who have apparently disappeared."

She wrote this on the whiteboard, the start of an incident board that she hoped would grow as they spoke to more people. She wrote the name of the room in the middle of the board, with the words *unidentified blood stain by bed* written underneath it. On the left of the board, she drew an arrow from the room name, recording Angela Walker's details, with a narrative underneath that said, *heard male and female voices… thought the male voice could be her husband. Heard a thud which she thinks was someone falling to the floor.* She drew two more arrows on the right side of the board, with large question marks and a moniker that said *missing woman* and *missing man.*

She stood back from the board. "Hmm, you're right. Not much to go on. Have you got SOCO organised to scour that room?"

"Yes, ma'am," he replied. "They promised they would be here within the hour."

She sat down, devouring a couple of sandwiches and cherishing the caffeine hit from the excellent coffee, all the while staring at the incident board. "Do you think this is a murder scene?"

He pulled a quizzical expression. "I guess it's possible, but that does mean that one of these missing two must have somehow moved the body out of that room."

"I know. That's what's bothering me. Mrs Walker said she heard no more sounds after the thud. You can't tell me that a body was moved out of the room and down the stairs without anyone hearing anything."

"I guess we can get SOCO to scan the area outside the room and down the stairs, but with so many people moving around the hotel, I guess that might prove fruitless."

She shook her head. "Shit. I hate cases like this when we don't even know what we're dealing with. Why can't we just have a nice body to examine and get on with it?"

He gave a quiet chortle. "Sorry, ma'am, doesn't look like it's gonna be that easy."

She took another gulp of coffee. "What do you make of this husband thing? Do you really think that Mrs Walker's husband would have lied to his wife so he could meet up with some random woman in the adjoining room? It seems so improbable."

"Who knows? Do you want me to investigate her husband? See if I can find him and suss out whether he has an alibi for that time."

"Yeah, that's a good idea. If we can't find him, it might add credibility to Mrs Walker's theory."

"Okay, ma'am. What about the motivation behind this alleged crime. Any thoughts?"

"Well, murder 101 will tell you it's always about sex or money."

He screwed his face up. "Eww! Sex?"

"Come now, Sergeant. Old people do still have sex you know."

He frowned. "Hmm, I think I'll stick to the money angle."

She stood up and started to examine the board, searching for inspiration. "Let's do some background checks on both the Walkers. See if we can find any skeletons in their closet. We also need to get the details of the woman that was supposed to be in that room and do the same checks. There'll be something there for us to investigate. I'm sure of it."

"Do you want me to cover all that?" he replied.

"Well, at the moment, the chief super has only authorised you and me to work on this job so, yes, if you can do the leg work on that side, I'm going to start interviewing the staff and guests. Unless we find a body, I can't see him letting us have any more resources, so we are just going to have to get on with it."

They both sat back down and got consumed in their laptops. A few minutes later there was a knock at the door of the conference room. She bellowed for the person to come in and a sheepish-looking young girl came through the door.

"Ahh," said Taylor, "you must be the maid. We have a lot to talk about."

8

INTERVIEW WITH EVANGELINE STIMIC, HOUSEKEEPER
SATURDAY, 1.30PM

The maid walked in, head bowed, not wanting to make eye contact with Taylor. She still had her uniform on but had a light cream cardigan draped around her shoulders. She sat down on one of the chairs opposite Taylor, looking up briefly to acknowledge she was ready to talk.

Taylor eyed her with curiosity. The girl looked petrified. In these scenarios, Taylor knew there were two ways to go. The classic good cop, bad cop scenario. She could handle her with kid gloves and coax the information out of her slowly but surely, or she could go heavy-handed and frighten the poor girl into blurting out all she knew. The maid looked up again briefly, unsettled by the silence. Taylor went for good cop.

"Miss Stimic—"

"Oh please, call me Eva. Everyone does. Except the boss. He calls everyone by their surnames, and of course my mum, who always calls me Evangeline because she refuses to shorten my name, but then again, I do like the long name, it's just a bit of a mouthful and…"

Taylor couldn't help but smirk at the sudden outburst, which made Eva stop for a second. "Oh, sorry. It's a bad habit of mine. When I get nervous, I just start talking and, oh shit, I'm doing it again, aren't I."

Taylor smiled. "It's fine, Miss... sorry, Eva. There's nothing to be nervous about. We just need to know what happened in that room this morning."

Eva took in a deep breath. "I guess it was about 11am when I knocked on the door. They had their 'do not disturb' sign on the door, and most of the time we aren't supposed to disturb the guests, but sometimes they forget and get annoyed if we haven't cleaned the room when they come back from being out all day. I didn't hear a response when I shouted *housekeeping*, so I took a chance and, thankfully, the room was empty."

"Okay. So, what were your first impressions when you walked in the room?" probed Taylor.

"At first, not much. I plonked my cleaning stuff in the middle of the room. I saw the two glasses on the table and decided to sort them out first, but I must admit, as I went to do that, I realised that the bed had not been slept in."

"Anything else?"

"I think I washed the glasses first, in the bathroom sink, and it was then that I realised that there were no toiletries. I walked back into the main room and could see that there were no personal belongings anywhere in the room. I went to the wardrobe to check on her clothes, but there was nothing there either. It was then that I spotted the stain by the bed."

"That's great, Eva. Now let's go back to the two glasses..."

Eva put her hands on her cheeks. "Oh God, I messed up, didn't I? I've compromised the forensics by washing those glasses up."

Taylor pulled a sympathetic expression. "Well, yes, that is true, though it's unusual for people to be that forensically aware. Have you got some background in our line of work?"

Eva let out a nervous laugh. "God, no! I'm just a bit of a crime buff. I can't get enough of those TV shows like *CSI*, *NCIS* and all that. I also love Agatha Christie. I guess you're more Miss Marple than Hercule Poirot."

Taylor smiled. "Well, I guess I'm not a short, portly Belgian detective, if that's what you mean, although I hope you don't think I'm as old as Miss Marple either."

Eva flushed with embarrassment. "Sorry, I just meant, it must be amazing to be a detective. Solving the puzzles and apprehending the baddies. I'd love to do what you do."

"Look, Eva. You can be really useful to this investigation if you can just tell us everything you remember. You can be my trainee detective for the next few days."

Eva beamed from ear to ear. "Wow. God, yes. That would be amazing."

"Okay then. Back to the glasses. Tell me everything you remember."

Eva sat up straight, a determined look on her face. "Right. There were two wine glasses on the table. There was a bit of wine, red I think, in the bottom of both glasses, but no bottle, so I assume they got them from the bar and brought them up to the room. There was a lipstick mark on one of the glasses, which I assume belonged to Mrs Deveraux."

"Ah, yes," said Taylor, "the lady who was booked into that room."

Taylor looked over to Spence, who nodded an acknowledgement, writing it down on his list of people to look into.

"Carry on," Taylor said.

"Erm, that's about it. As I said, I took them into the bathroom and washed them up. Do you think you still might be able to get anything off them?"

"We'll see. The SOCOs are on their way. Now, what about this blood stain?"

Eva stopped for a second to compose herself. "I'm sorry, but that was horrible. When I first saw it, I thought it was a wine stain, but as I knelt down, I could see it wasn't."

"So, you knew it was blood. When you got closer to it."

"Er, well, yeah. I mean, what else could it be?"

"What did you do when you realised it was blood?"

"I screamed. I just couldn't help myself. I closed my eyes and screamed."

"What happened next?"

"The boss came in and took over. I guess he phoned you."

Taylor typed a few notes on her laptop before looking back at Eva. "Thank you. That has been really helpful. I assume you never saw this Mrs Deveraux?"

Eva sat up straighter. "Actually, I did. After she checked in, she asked for some more coat hangers. I took them to her room just as my shift was ending."

"What can you remember about her? You know, what did she look like? Was there anything about the room that you noticed?"

Eva looked to her left, her brain trying to recall what she'd seen. "Hmm, she was a very strange woman. She had massive hair, you know, like they used to have back in the '80s, and was wearing dark glasses, which was weird because that room is quite dark at the best of times."

"Anything else?"

"Oh shit… oh God, sorry for my language, but there was something. The wig. She had one of those head stands that you drape wigs over when you're not wearing them. She had one with a wig on it, on the round table."

"This is great, Eva. Is that it?"

"Well, this place is expensive, so it obviously attracts people who have a bit of money, but I reckon this woman was loaded."

"Why?"

"There were clothes strewn across the bed, that all looked good quality, and she had an expensive top and jeans on. Also, the jewellery she had on. That weren't cheap. I'd put money on it."

Taylor smiled. "Eva, you've been amazing. I think you've qualified as a trainee detective!"

"Really?" She beamed.

"Well, unofficially at least, and given that we are going to need to speak to other guests on that floor, your insights into what you've seen and heard will be invaluable. Can we talk again?"

"Oh yes. Amazing."

Taylor let Eva go and turned to her sergeant. "Well, she's a little firecracker. I reckon she might just help us to solve this riddle."

He grimaced. "I'm not sure. Can't stand these *CSI* wannabees, always thinking they know it all just because they've watched a couple of episodes of a TV show. And anyway, with the greatest of respect, ma'am, should you really be involving a civilian in our work and treating her like she's one of the team?"

"Look, Sergeant, first and foremost she's a key witness and could be really useful to us. She's clearly a very observant girl and she gets access to all the rooms without question, something that may prove problematical for us if this thing turns into something more serious. I think she can be our eyes and ears."

"Do you really think the whole 'trainee detective' thing is necessary?"

"Oh, I'm just playing up to her ego. It's not like I'm going to give her access to any of our work."

Spence pulled a disapproving expression. "Well, you know best, ma'am, but I don't think we should be doing that, and I assume by bringing her into the fold, you are ruling her out as a suspect."

"I didn't say that. Everyone is under suspicion while our investigations continue. I just want to exploit every opportunity that presents itself, and Miss Stimic seems like someone who can help us at the moment. You have to realise, Sergeant, that the chief is on our back about our reducing clear-up rates, and I'm going to do anything I can to make sure we solve this case."

Spence shook his head and went back to tapping away at his laptop.

Taylor brushed off Spence's disapproval. He had no idea what it was like having the responsibilities and stresses that she faced every day. She stood up and updated the incident board, absentmindedly chewing the end of the pen as she viewed the content. As her mind tried to process the possibilities, there was a sudden commotion at the door. An elderly man and woman stood in the doorway.

"I need to speak to you," the woman said. "I heard it all."

9

INTERVIEW WITH MR AND MRS KENDAL
SATURDAY, 2PM

Taylor beckoned the couple into the room. "Please sit down. I'm DCI Chloe Taylor and this is DS Michael Spence. Can I ask who you are?"

The woman took the lead. "Yes, dearie, I'm Mavis Kendal and this is my husband, Alan. We're celebrating our golden wedding anniversary. This place is all a bit posh for us, but we thought we'd treat ourselves."

"Okay, so what did you mean when you said you *heard it all*?"

"Well, I did," Mrs Kendal replied, a deep frown appearing on her face. "There was a right to-do in that room."

"Oh, Mavis, stop exaggerating," her husband interjected, "the police are not interested in your idle gossip."

Mrs Kendal turned to look at her husband, the frown deepening. "It's not gossip. If something bad happened in that room, I need to tell these nice police officers what I heard."

Her husband rolled his eyes but chose not to respond.

Taylor tried to stifle a smirk as she watched the interaction between Mr and Mrs Kendal, wondering for a moment if this was what fifty years of marriage did to you. She soon shook it off and cut across the minor spat. "Let me decide what is relevant. Please, Mrs Kendal, do tell me what you heard."

Mrs Kendal gave her husband a side look that told him she thought she'd won this one. Her brow furrowed in concentration, and she launched in. "Now, dearie, I first heard something around 10.50pm. We'd just finished watching an episode of that *Vera* programme, and when we turned the television off to get ready for bed, I could hear raised voices. Now, we are in the room just up the steps from where all the commotion was, and I opened our door a crack to see if I could hear what was going on."

Taylor gave a nod of encouragement for Mrs Kendal to carry on.

"Well, they were having a right barney. A woman was saying something about him needing to know his place, and he was saying that she would never get her hands on the merchandise. I thought that was a funny word to use. Merchandise!"

Taylor looked over to Spence and raised her eyebrows. "Hmm, yes, I guess so. What else did you hear?"

"Oh gosh, I'm trying to remember now, but I think she said that he was playing a dangerous game and people would be after him. I mean, it frightened me to death."

"Anything else?"

"Oh my, yes there was. A second later, the door in the corridor opened, and I saw this older woman go and stand outside the door of that room. I'd pulled my door to, so she couldn't see me, but I could just see enough through the crack in the door. I reckon she must have heard them arguing too, because she listened at the door for about a minute before there was that awful thud. She scuttled off like some naughty child, and I didn't see her again."

"A thud?" enquired Taylor.

"Yes, like something had fallen down."

"What happened next?"

"Well, that was the odd thing. After the thud, everything went quiet."

"What did you think had happened?"

"I didn't like to think. I shut the door and Alan here told me to stop being a busybody and get into bed."

"Why didn't you report what you'd heard?"

"I… I… don't know. I guess I didn't know what to do, and Alan was getting annoyed with me."

Taylor gave a sympathetic smile but continued to probe. "Do you know who the woman was who was stood outside the door?"

"No, but we'd seen her at dinner with her husband."

"Did you see him at all after dinner?"

"No, dearie, Alan and I came straight back to our rooms and didn't leave."

"Thank you, Mrs Kendal. One final question. Did you hear anything during the night?"

Mrs Kendal gave Taylor a wide-eyed expression. "Yes, I did. I must admit that right frightened me and I didn't sleep that well, tossing and turning all night. At one point, I did hear a bit of noise out in the corridor."

"Do you know what time it was?"

"I don't know. It was pitch black and I couldn't see my watch, so I rolled over and tried to get back to sleep."

Taylor sensed that Mrs Kendal had run out of steam

and changed her focus to Mr Kendal. "Sir, do you have anything to add?"

Mr Kendal gave a *hurumph* sound and shook his head. "No, my love. I think my wife has given you enough gossip without me adding my two penn'orth in."

Taylor let them go, amused at the non-verbal signals that Mrs Kendal was giving to her husband, clearly unhappy with his apparent disapproval of her actions.

She turned to her sergeant. "What do you make of that?"

"I guess if we ignore the fact that she's a bit of an old gossip, she does at least corroborate some of what Mrs Walker told us and, if what she heard was right, I reckon that was a conversation between a couple of criminal lowlifes."

Taylor nodded. "Yes, I was thinking the same thing."

10

THE INCIDENT ROOM
SATURDAY, 2.30PM

Taylor wrote up the key points from her conversation with Mr and Mrs Kendal on the growing incident board. Spence confirmed that the SOCOs had arrived and were processing the crime scene. She tapped the whiteboard marker repeatedly in her hand, impatience coursing through her.

"What have we got here? I mean, it does sound like we've had an incident in that room, but with nothing more than a blood stain and witnesses confirming an argument, I'm not sure what else we can do here. The chief super is not going to let us work on this indefinitely if we don't start finding something more tangible to work on."

For a second, he didn't answer, and Taylor was about to give him a narky nudge when he suddenly looked up. "Sorry, ma'am, I've just completed the preliminary analysis on our..." he did the double-fingered gesture in the air, "... suspects. Something interesting has come up."

"Oh, what?"

"Well, Mrs Walker is squeaky clean, but her husband is known to the police, although I can't access his record on the crime system."

Taylor moved to look over Spence's shoulder. "What the…" she exclaimed. "Why can't we see his record?"

"It looks like it has a restricted marker."

Taylor's heckles rose. "What are we supposed to do with that? You need to try and find out why his record isn't available to us. I mean, for God's sake, how are we supposed to do our jobs when we can't even get basic intel on our suspects?"

"I'll get onto the crime bureau and see if they can help."

Taylor walked towards the window at the far end of the room, which looked out onto the back car park. She watched as a couple of guests got out of their car and walked back towards the entrance to the hotel. Her mind was spinning. She turned back to look at Spence.

"I wonder whether Mrs Walker knows about her husband's criminal leanings?"

"I don't know. Do you think we should ask her?"

Taylor frowned. "Hmm, maybe, though let's see how things develop. There might be a time and a place to throw that potential curveball into the mix, especially as we don't know what he's been up to."

"Okay, schtum for now."

Taylor sensed Spence had more to say. "Is there something else?"

"Yes, there's something equally perplexing. Mrs Deveraux is apparently in a nursing home in Bagshot, Surrey, because of an aggressive form of dementia."

"Eh?"

"Exactly, so it seems improbable that she has come to this hotel for the weekend."

Taylor screwed her face up. Something about what Spence said immediately set her brain racing. The realisation came to her in a flash.

"The wig!" she exclaimed. "Remember what our Miss Stimic said. Our apparently fake Mrs Deveraux had a wig on a head stand. If that isn't evidence of someone trying to disguise their identity, then I'm the Queen of Sheba."

"Okay, sounds feasible."

"Yeah, so. Working strategy. We have a man and a woman arguing in that room, who have both since disappeared. If we assume that the man is in fact Mr Walker and the woman is pretending to be Mrs Deveraux, we have the foundations of some potential criminality. My guess is that the argument ended in one of them being assaulted, which explains the thud. Based on what Mrs Kendal heard, whichever one of them was still standing did something in the wee hours of the morning, making sure that they fled our crime scene."

"I agree, ma'am. That sounds like a decent assumption."

Taylor wasn't sure whether it was her growing stress levels, but she bristled at Spence's apparent endorsement of her strategy. For some reason, his tone had triggered her. She wasn't looking for his approval and had a flashback to the numerous times that she had been patronised by male colleagues, as she battled her way up the ranks. She tried to shake it off and cracked on.

"Thank you, Sergeant, I'm glad you approve. So, to test this strategy, have you been able to find Mr Walker?"

"Hmm, not really. He told his wife that he was going back to work on Friday night to deal with a crisis, but I can't find any evidence to suggest he was there. I spoke to the receptionist at his office this morning and she said he hadn't signed in either last night or today."

"Okay, but he may not have been going into the office. I'm not sure that's conclusive evidence of his whereabouts. What about credit card transactions?"

"No. He hasn't used his credit card since he paid for the hotel on Friday afternoon."

Taylor stood up and resumed her focus on the incident board, hoping for some inspiration from what was written up. Spence had gone back to his laptop, but she cut across his aggressive tapping. "Didn't we ask that general manager for a full list of the guests staying here last night?"

"We did, ma'am."

She sighed. "Where the hell is it then? I don't have the patience to be waiting around for him to pull his finger out. We need to get through preliminary interviews with all the guests before there's any chance of us going home today."

Taylor watched as Spence stood up, with an "I'll go and find him" comment trailing in the air as he moved quickly out of the room. She sighed and tapped on her phone.

Sorry, darling, I've got a live one here. Not sure when I'm going to get home. Give Emma a kiss for me and I'll be back as soon as I can.

She hit send and waited a second to see if her husband responded. A heart emoji pinged back immediately which just made her feel worse. She was thirty-four and had been married to her husband Trent for five years. Emma was two, and although she meant everything in the world to her, she was not going to let a child get in the way of her career. She'd been promoted to DCI a year ago and was determined to make it work. It didn't mean it was easy though. Guilt, an ever-present bedfellow.

A few minutes later, Spence returned closely followed by Moretti. She could tell by the look on Moretti's face that something was wrong. He was white as a sheet.

"What's up? You look like you've seen a ghost."

Moretti leant against a chair, shaking his head. "This… this can't be happening. One of the guests has found a body. It's floating in the lake."

11

THE LAKE IN THE HOTEL GROUNDS
SATURDAY, 2.40PM

Taylor and Spence rushed out of the room. Taylor followed Moretti while she dispatched Spence to go and get the SOCOs from the hotel room they were processing.

Moretti led her along the main corridor on the ground floor of the hotel, her urgent pacing echoing on the flagstone flooring. They rushed past reception, through the lounge and out into the garden. They walked along the path that led through the formal gardens and down some steps that led to a grassy area. The lake was a further fifty yards away, and Taylor could see several people gathered at the water's edge.

She quickened her pace, passing Moretti. She immediately went into command mode. "Ladies and gentlemen, can I please ask you to move away from the crime scene. My sergeant will be here shortly to take your initial statements."

The two men and three women did as they were told and Taylor was vaguely aware that two of them had uniforms on, suggesting they were staff, and the other three were clothed as though they had been out for a walk. She moved past them and stopped. There was a body floating face down in the water. It looked like a man.

She looked around for something that could hook the body and drag it to the bank, but there was nothing. As she considered her options, she spotted Spence running down the hill, closely followed by who she assumed were the two SOCOs.

Spence breathlessly introduced the two SOCOs as Keith Brennan and Angela Whiting. Taylor gave them appropriate courtesies and then directed them to the crime scene. "We need something to hook that body and drag it to the bank, or one of you is going in," she said, using her rank to ensure she was not the one that was going to get wet.

The three officers looked at each other, before Spence turned to Moretti and asked if the gardeners had a long rake they could use. Moretti radioed and, within a couple of minutes, an old guy came down the hill with a large leaf rake.

Taylor watched as the two SOCOs grabbed the rake and attempted to hook something on the body so they could drag it to the bank. After a couple of failed attempts, they snagged a spine of the rake on the back of the man's trousers and slowly managed to navigate it towards them. As the body reached the bank, they all knelt down and hauled it out of the water. The body was now face up. It was indeed a man. Taylor flashed a look at Spence. They were both thinking the same thing. Was this Mr Walker?

As the body was hauled out, Taylor was aware that there had been a gasp from one of the group that had found the body. She quickly barked out some orders, firstly focusing on the SOCOs. "One of you go and get the canopy urgently so this doesn't turn into some freak show." Brennan nodded and ran back towards the hotel car park where their van was parked. Whiting began a preliminary examination of the body.

Taylor turned to Spence. "Move these people away from the scene but get their preliminary statements. I want to know who was where and how they came to find the body."

She watched as Spence engaged the crowd, his annoying ability to charm anyone immediately evident. She turned back to Whiting. "What are your first impressions?"

Whiting screwed her face up. "Purely based on the skin condition and colour, I would say the body has been in the water for some time, maybe between eight to twelve hours. There are no obvious injuries on his body, but I noticed when we dragged him out of the water that he has a blunt force trauma on the back of his head."

Taylor examined it. Her stomach began to flip. This had all the signs of being the male figure that had been arguing in the hotel room.

"Does he have anything on his body that could identify who he is?"

Whiting checked his pockets and frowned. "How odd. He doesn't have anything on him. Not even a wallet."

Taylor looked around. "Hmm, I guess it could be in the water or someone has deliberately removed it so we can't identify him."

Brennan returned quickly and they began to erect the canopy to shield the body from prying eyes. Whiting continued to examine the body, but after a few minutes, she stood up and sighed. "Not much more to say, ma'am. My best guess is that the blow to the head killed him, and he was thrown in the lake post-mortem, but we really need a medical examiner to confirm that."

Taylor frowned. "We need to get organised. Phone the on-call ME and get them to pick up the body. Tell them I need a post-mortem straight away. If you two can split yourselves between this crime scene and finishing off processing the room, I will see if I can get some more support here ASAP. I think we can safely assume we have a full-blown murder inquiry on our hands."

Brennan and Whiting nodded. He went back to the hotel room, while Whiting went to retrieve her bag so she could process the lakeside crime scene.

Taylor walked out of the canopy to see Spence still in deep conversation with the people who had found the body. She got out her phone and called the chief super. He didn't need much convincing that they had a suspected murder on their hands and agreed to immediately dispatch an additional SOCO, another detective sergeant and two detective constables. He promised they would be there within the hour.

She waited for Whiting to return before pulling Moretti aside, who had been patiently waiting with the guests while they spoke to Spence.

"Mr Moretti, I think you can see that we have a very serious situation here. Based on the guests' statements about what went on in that room and the injuries that this man has sustained, we are working on the assumption that we have a suspected murder case."

Moretti still looked a bit pale but muttered his understanding.

"I have additional officers turning up to assist the investigation and it now becomes imperative that my team talk to all the guests about last night and today. I'm happy to do a short briefing to all your residents if you think that will help."

"Yes, yes, of course. I will get my team straight onto it. What time do you want to do it?"

Taylor looked at her watch. It was nearly 3pm and she was conscious that time was against them. "Can you get it organised for 5pm? That will give me a chance to brief my team."

"No problem."

Moretti began to walk away, but Taylor remembered the one thing she still hadn't got from him. "Oh sorry, Mr Moretti, but you were going to give me the guest list from last night and who stayed in what room."

He tutted to himself. "I'm sorry, I was on my way to give that to you when this all happened. I have it in my office and will bring it to you as soon as I can get my team to organise the guests for your briefing."

Despite his obvious impatience to move on, Taylor still needed more to settle her increasingly addled brain. "Look, sorry, but just before you get on with that, I really need a profile of how many guests we are dealing with here and when they are all due to leave the hotel."

Moretti frowned. "You need to check the list I will bring you, but from memory, we have twenty-three rooms and fifteen of them were occupied last night. The rooms were mostly couples, but I think we do have a few single-occupancy rooms. I know that two couples checked out this morning, and I think most of the remaining guests are checking out tomorrow or Monday."

The time pressure hit Taylor once more. Unless she arrested everyone in the hotel, she couldn't insist that they stayed around. Another thought struck her. "Do you have guests checking in tomorrow?"

Moretti took in a deep breath. "Oh dear. Yes, we do. I need to check with the reception team exactly how many."

"You may want to get your team to contact them to explain the situation. I appreciate you still have a hotel to run, but I have a potential murder to solve. I could do without any more variables to this situation."

Moretti nodded and took off. Taylor turned back towards where Spence had been talking to the guests. He was just finishing up and the group began walking back towards the hotel.

"What did you find out?" she asked Spence.

"It seems that the American couple had been on a walk and were just coming back up the drive when they saw a load of bird life around the lake. They came over here to have a look and saw the body floating. She said she screamed and another resident, American as well, weirdly enough, was walking down the drive and came over to see what was up. They went to find someone, and they were the two other women at the scene when we arrived. They both work on reception. I think they are all a bit shook up."

Taylor sighed. "No shit."

"So, what next, ma'am?"

"Well, I spoke to the chief super and he's dispatched a load more resources. I'm doing a briefing to the guests at 5pm and, ideally, we need a team briefing at around 4.15pm when hopefully everyone is here. We are going to have to split up the interviews between us and get as good a picture as we can of what the hell happened here. Whiting is examining the body but has called the ME for an urgent post-mortem. The biggest head-fuck of all is that we are likely to lose most of our suspects when they check out tomorrow morning."

"Oh shit. That is a problem."

"Yeah, so I hope you didn't have any plans tonight, because we are going to pull an all-nighter."

"Nah nothing planned, ma'am."

"Good, meet and greet the officers that are arriving and assemble them in the conference room. Talk to the SOCOs and tell them I want their preliminary reports. For my part, I need to see this list that the GM has produced. I need to work out how the hell we are going to get to interview everyone with the clock ticking."

"Okay, ma'am. I'll get straight onto it."

"Actually, Sergeant. One more thing. Ask if that lovely housekeeper is still here. I think I may have a job for her."

With that, Taylor stood and gazed across the beautiful countryside, allowing herself a minute to calm down her growing stress. She shook her head at how such a beautiful place could be tainted with the spectre of murder.

She pulled out a phone and crafted another message to her husband. She wouldn't be tucking her daughter into bed tonight.

12

THE INCIDENT ROOM
SATURDAY, 3.30PM

Taylor sat in the incident room, taking a moment to revel in the peace of being on her own, while she waited for the investigation team to arrive and assemble. She had the guest and room list in front of her and was just about to start reviewing it when there was a gentle knock at the door.

She shouted for whoever it was to come in and was pleased to see it was the housekeeper, Eva Stimic. "Ahh, Miss Stimic… sorry, Eva, thank you for coming to see me. I wasn't sure whether you had left for the day."

"Well, er, I was about to go when your sergeant said you wanted to speak to me."

"That's right. Now look, I don't want to delay you, but if you don't mind staying around for a couple of hours, there's something really important I want you to do for me."

Eva went wide-eyed with excitement. "God, yes, anything."

Taylor took in a deep breath. "What I'm about to ask you to do is probably on the cusp of being acceptable practice, but now that we've found a body…"

Eva gasped. "Really. Where?"

"Oh, sorry, I assumed that Mr Moretti had told everyone what has just happened. A guest found a body in the lake within the last hour."

Taylor could see that Eva was fighting back tears, but after a moment, it seemed she righted herself and a determined look came over her face. "No, I haven't seen him, but holy shit, this is getting scary. I want to help."

"Okay. So, I'm doing a briefing to all the guests at 5pm, which means all their rooms will be empty. You are clearly a very observant young lady, and I wondered whether you could do a quick scan in each of the rooms that will still be occupied this evening."

"Oh. Why?"

"I don't want to guide you to a conclusion. I just want you to look in each room and tell me if there is anything that strikes you as unusual."

"Um, I guess, but I need a reason to be going in there."

"Look, as I said, I know this is unorthodox, but I'll be absolutely honest. The police do not have the remit, without probable cause, to search any guest's room. Now, whilst my team may find something in the coming hours that will allow us to get a warrant, it would be so helpful if I could get an initial scan of the rooms. You know, just in case you see something that gives us a head start."

Eva shifted uncomfortably in her seat, but a second later, a beaming smile spread across her face. "Chocolates!"

Taylor gave her a quizzical look.

"If anyone asks why I'm still here and what I'm doing, I can say I'm doing the chocolates. We regularly put them in guests' rooms as a little thank you, so it won't seem odd.

If he sees me, I'll just tell Mr Moretti that I stayed behind to help out."

"Okay, if you are comfortable doing that."

Eva grimaced. "I can't deny this is really scary, but if I can do just one thing that helps you catch a murderer, then I'm in."

Taylor smiled. "Thank you, and if there is any fallout from this, I will take the heat and smooth it over with Mr Moretti."

Eva said no more but began to chew her nails.

"Look," said Taylor, "you don't have to do this."

"No, no. I'm fine. I'm going to make myself scarce for a bit and then I'll be ready at 5pm to do what you ask."

With that, Eva left and Taylor put her head in her hands. She knew she would be hauled over the coals if this went south. Whilst what she was asking Eva to do was not breaking any laws, she knew that any defence brief would have a field day if they ended up relying on what she saw as evidence for a conviction. Taylor shook it off. It was done and she trusted Eva to be discreet.

She glanced at her watch. There was still half an hour until the team was due to assemble. She had to review the guest list so she was ready to split out the interviews. Time was still against her. She smoothed out the report that Moretti gave her and groaned at the enormity of the task. Fifteen rooms and nearly thirty potential suspects. She focused on the piece of paper in front of her.

Main House

Room 100 – Mr and Mrs Jenkins

Room 101 – Miss Sanchez-Vicario

Room 102 – Mr and Mrs Johnson

Room 103 – unoccupied

Room 104 – Mr and Mrs Walker

Room 105 – Mrs Deveraux

Room 106 – Mr and Mrs Kendal

Room 107 – Mr Bush

Annexe

Room 108 – Miss Ella Jones and Miss Jemma Grounds

Room 109 – Mr and Mrs Webster

Room 110 – Mr and Mrs Smith

Room 111 – Mrs Jennings

Room 112 – Mr and Mrs Morgan

Room 113 – Mr and Mrs Li

Room 114 – Mr and Mrs Cole

Room 115 – Mr Young

Room 116 – unoccupied

Moretti had annotated the list. Room 100 and 109 had checked out that morning. All but rooms 101, 112 and 115 were due to check out in the morning.

Taylor cursed. Her head began to pound as the mental clock ticked away in her head. She circled a few rooms on the list: the murder scene, room 105; rooms 104 and 106 where the Walkers and Kendals had heard the commotion; and room 110. Mr and Mrs Smith. She huffed incredulously. "What a cliché," she muttered to herself. She'd put money on that being a couple who were having an illicit liaison.

As she sat back scanning the list, the door opened, and her new team bundled through it. She scanned their faces. They at least looked alert for what was going to be a long night.

13

THE TEAM GATHERS IN THE INCIDENT ROOM
SATURDAY, 4.15PM

Taylor tried to show a calmness and authority as the team assembled. Not wanting to frighten them off but also sufficiently distant that they understood she was in command. She introduced herself and then got Spence, Whiting and Brennan to do the same. She then turned to the bright-eyed newbies.

The additional SOCO introduced herself as Lixuan Chang. She seemed immediately at ease having worked with Whiting and Brennan on many occasions. Taylor was comfortable she would hit the ground running.

The new detective sergeant was Thomas Ablett, whom Taylor had worked with before. She recalled him being a solid detective but, a bit like Spence, tended to rely on his boyish charm and good looks to get by. She was a bit unnerved at the immediate laddish banter that was going on as soon as Ablett saw Spence.

The two detective constables were new to her, as they were normally attached to her colleague on the West

County team. The first one introduced herself as Durga Joshi and the second as Brian Chesters. They both seemed alert and respectful, which was enough for Taylor at that precise moment. She encouraged them to quickly grab a coffee and biscuit, which had been supplied by the hotel. Within a few minutes, they were gathered around the table, ready for Taylor's direction.

The DCI took in a deep breath. "Right, we have a serious developing situation here, which we are assuming is a murder case. DS Spence and I were called to the hotel this morning when a maid found a blood stain on the floor in room 105. She unfortunately compromised forensics by starting to clean the room before she spotted it. The scene was at least secured before any more damage could be done. The woman staying in that room has disappeared and, at some point, cleared all her belongings out. A male voice was also heard in the room by two separate witnesses but initially there was no sign of him. However, since then, a male body has been found in the lake at the bottom of the hotel gardens. He has a blunt force trauma to the head which is consistent with a potential assault that was heard by our witnesses."

Spence raised his hand. Taylor nodded for him to speak. "Ma'am, I'm guessing that we think the body is Mr Walker. Are we going to get Mrs Walker to identify the body?"

Taylor frowned. "Yes, a good point, Sergeant. To bring the rest of you up to speed with DS Spence's point, Mrs Walker, who was in the room next to the one where we think the murder may have been committed, had been left on her own last evening because her husband told her he had to get back to work to deal with an urgent problem. She heard the argument in room 105 and listened at the door. She was very frightened when she thought she heard the assault so ran back to her room. She said it was only afterwards when she realised the male voice sounded like her husband."

Ablett interjected. "Why didn't she go to the room and confront him, if she thought he had lied to her?"

Taylor shrugged. "She just seemed really scared and probably thought her mind was playing tricks on her."

Ablett pulled a face like he didn't see that as a credible explanation but said no more.

"Anyhow," said Taylor, "it's a good point that we have not asked anyone to identify the body. Although three guests and a couple of staff were at the lake when we arrived, the body was face down and we moved them away as we hauled it out of the water."

"Do you want me to ask Mrs Walker if she'd be willing to do that?" said Spence.

Taylor pondered for a moment and looked at her watch. She looked at Whiting. "When is the ME taking the body away?"

Whiting sat up straight like a meerkat. "He's doing his preliminary examination of the body on scene, right now. I said I would go and see him after this briefing to give him your authority to release the body."

Taylor glanced at her watch again. It was nearly 4.30pm. She swore under her breath. "Okay, as you can tell, time is against us, and we have most of our suspect pool about to leave the hotel in the morning. I was hoping to get initial briefings from DS Spence and the SOCO team in this session, but given this body identification issue and the fact I'm due to do a briefing to all the residents at 5pm, we need a new plan."

The team continued to hang on her every word. A blessing, at least, Taylor thought.

"Right, DS Spence, get one of the reception team to escort me, you and Mrs Walker to the body. DS Ablett, you and the two DCs take this list and work out a split of interviews between the five of us, which I want to do straight after the briefing."

She turned to the SOCOs. "Bring Miss Chang up to speed with both crime scenes and work out what your next steps are. Also, I want one of you to go with the ME and get live updates from the post-mortem, which must be done this evening."

The team murmured their understanding and dispersed. Taylor glanced at her watch. She had twenty-eight minutes until the briefing. She necked the rest of her coffee and walked back to reception.

*

Angela Walker had seemed reluctant at first to do what Taylor needed her to do, now less convinced that she had really heard her husband and that he could be the one who had been fished out of the lake. Eventually, a bucketload of reassurances from Taylor, Spence and the receptionist who was escorting them had convinced her.

That said, Taylor noticed her progress towards the crime scene was slow, each step edgy and reluctant. In the end, they were stood outside the canopy within five minutes.

Taylor looked at Walker and the receptionist. "Okay, the body is covered at the moment. The medical examiner will remove the cover from his face when you are ready."

They both nodded and followed Taylor to the entrance of the canopy that was shielding the body from public gaze.

Taylor looked at Walker. "Are you ready?"

She could see Walker was fighting back tears but was relieved when she nodded her agreement. The ME pulled back the sheet and both Walker and the receptionist gasped in unison.

Taylor looked at Walker's face, etched with shock. Before Taylor could say anything, Walker shrieked out the words.

"My God. That's… that's not my husband."

With that, she turned and walked out of the canopy.

Taylor looked at Spence, who was looking straight at the receptionist, fear across her face. Taylor took the initiative. "Do you know who this is?"

The receptionist turned to look at Taylor and Spence, all the colour drained from her face.

"Yes. That's Mr Bush."

14

BRIEFING TO GUESTS IN THE ORANGERY
SATURDAY, 5PM

A sea of concerned faces greeted Taylor as she entered the room. The low murmuring tailed off and she stood in front of them, ready to ruin their evening. Moretti did a brief introduction before Taylor began. Her team of detectives assembled around her.

"Ladies and gentlemen, my name is Detective Chief Inspector Chloe Taylor and my team are Detective Sergeants Spence and Ablett and Detective Constables Joshi and Chesters. I am afraid to inform you that we have a serious developing incident within the hotel. A body of a man was found floating in the lake at the bottom of the gardens this afternoon, which has subsequently been identified as a guest who was staying in this hotel last night. His injuries are consistent with the outcome of an argument in room 105, that was overheard by two independent witnesses last night. We are treating this as a murder case."

She paused to allow the information to sink in, giving her a brief moment to scan the faces. She recognised the

American couple who had found the body and the man who had come to their assistance. They sat together, their faces serious but otherwise inexpressive despite the shock of finding the body. Taylor spotted Mrs Kendal with her husband. There was a hint of a smile on her face, apparently revelling in the mileage she was going to get out of this situation as she gossiped with anyone who would listen. Mrs Walker had joined them after the identification debacle, but her head was bowed, and Taylor couldn't judge how she was. The remainder of the faces were new to her, and she quickly tried to do a mental recollection of the rooms and names but soon got lost in the sea of faces, which were mostly etched with concern. The only other thing she noticed before responding to a hand that was raised, was a woman on her own, sitting near the back. Something about her immediately set her detective instincts racing, but she had no time to think as the guy with his hand up spoke before she had a chance to process it.

"Are we all suspects?" he said, a well-spoken plummy English accent framed with a hint of aggression.

"At the moment we are investigating all possibilities and one of the purposes of this briefing is to seek your assistance."

"So, yes, we are all suspects," he retorted.

"We would just appreciate your help, sir."

He stood up, ignoring his wife's attempts to grab his arm and force him to sit back down. "I'm a retired admiral from the Royal Navy. I served my Queen and country for forty years and should be beyond reproach. This is most irregular."

Taylor said no more, just stared him down until he relented and resumed his seating position, muttering under his breath to his wife.

"Look, I am sorry for the disruption to your evening and for the terrible circumstances that we are all facing, but it is imperative that we investigate this quickly and thoroughly."

Another male voice piped up. "Are you going to stop us leaving in the morning?"

Taylor tried not to show her annoyance at the question, not pleased to be reminded of the ticking clock that was threatening to hamper their investigation. She steeled herself and responded, "We can't stop you from leaving unless we have reason to believe you were somehow involved in this situation."

The comment was met with a few frowns and further murmuring, but she cracked on. "I know this is inconvenient and unsettling for you, but we want to get through interviews with each of you as quickly as possible so you can carry on with your evenings. There are five of us, and we will split up the interviews to get this done by 6.30pm, at the latest, so as not to disrupt your dinner plans. My sergeants will hand round a schedule and the locations where we will be holding the interviews. Finally, please be aware that I have three scenes of crime officers on site processing the crime scenes in room 105, 107 and around the lake. Please can I ask that you avoid those areas, within reason."

The crowd seemed restless and not enamoured by her request, so she nodded to Spence and Ablett to quickly hand the schedules round so as not to let the mob mentality get any worse.

Taylor gestured for her team to move on and get in their respective rooms as quickly as they could. She had decided to speak to Mrs Walker first and was staying in the orangery. As people filed out, she touched Mrs Walker gently on the arm, which drew a gasp.

"I'm sorry, Mrs Walker. Are you okay?"

Walker looked at Taylor, shaking her head. "I… I don't know what to do. I was convinced you were going to show me my husband's body, but seeing that other man… gosh, I've never seen anything like that. Poor man."

Taylor sat down on the chair beside Walker. "Have you tried to contact your husband?"

Walker pulled out her phone from her purse and glanced accusingly at the screen. "Yes, and nothing. Absolutely nothing. I've left messages on his voicemail, sent him a couple of texts, but the bastard is ignoring me. When I heard you'd found a body, I almost forgave him in a weird sort of way, but now, I don't know what to think."

"Is this normal for your husband? You know, to ignore your messages."

Walker let out a mocking laugh. "I'll say. I don't know why I'm surprised. When he's away with work we can go days on end without speaking. I'm very low down his priority list."

Taylor tried to speak as softly as possible but knew the conversation was heading in a direction that Walker wouldn't want to go. "Er, I wonder, Mrs Walker, whether you have something we could potentially get a DNA sample from. In respect of your husband, I mean."

Walker looked a bit taken aback but, after the initial shock, she responded, "Uh, why?"

"As much as it seems that your husband wasn't in that room, as you thought, it would be good to have a DNA sample from him so we can compare it with any samples we collect. The fact that you can't locate him does make me a bit concerned as to what he's doing and where he is."

Walker's facial expressions deepened with every sentence. "I think his toothbrush is probably still in the bathroom. Would that do?"

"Yes, that would be amazing. Can you bring that back here as soon as possible?" Taylor gave her a forensic bag to put it in and then moved on to the next line of questioning. "Can you tell me what you did after we spoke this morning?"

Walker gave an ironic smile. "I guess we are all suspects. I mean, I probably would kill my bastard of a husband if I thought I could get away with it, but I don't have any reason to kill random strangers."

Taylor frowned. "Just your movements please, Mrs Walker."

Walker sighed. "After we spoke, I nipped to that little farm shop just down the road and had some lunch. I got back here about 2pm and went into the drawing room with my book. I reckon it was a little after 3pm when one of the receptionists told me what happened, so I went back to my room to see if I could contact my husband. Your sergeant came and saw me around 4.30pm and now we are here."

Taylor watched Walker's face intently as she spoke. There were no hesitations, no facial ticks or eye movements that would suggest she was lying. She was as straight as a die. A good upstanding citizen, which just made Taylor more concerned about asking the nagging question. Did she know about her husband's criminal involvements? She knew she had no choice.

"Mrs Walker, I have a difficult question for you. Were you aware that your husband has come to the attention of the police?"

The frown that had seemed ever present since Walker had been asked to look at the body, deepened further. "You what!"

"I guess from your reaction the answer's no, but our crime system has him flagged as a person of interest. Do you know why that might be?"

Walker couldn't answer. She just burst into tears.

15

THE ORANGERY
SATURDAY, 5.30PM

Taylor had no time to comfort Mrs Walker. She stormed out of the room muttering expletives under her breath. If Mr Walker was still in the land of the living, Taylor surmised that he was in a whole heap of trouble. But, now the cat was out of the bag with Mrs Walker, Taylor really needed Spence to find out why Mr Walker's police record was restricted. She knew that it probably meant he had a national intelligence or terrorism marker, which made his apparent disappearance all the more concerning.

The reason that Taylor's attention had to move on was the figure of Eva Stimic stood in the doorway as Walker stormed out. Eva had that determined look on her face that Taylor had noticed when she'd convinced her to do a scan of the rooms. Taylor gestured her in.

"So, what happened, Eva? Everything okay?"

"Yes, yes. God, my heart was pounding, but I managed to get in every room before anyone came back."

Taylor knew she had blurred the lines of proper police

procedure, but she kept her tone light-hearted so as not to concern Eva any further than she needed to. "So, tell me what you observed."

Eva gave an embarrassed smile but then her expression grew more serious as she went through the mental recall of what she'd seen. "Right, rooms 100 and 109 checked out this morning. Nothing left behind. All in order. I couldn't look in room 105 for obvious reasons and your team have now cordoned off room 107 as I guess that was Mr Bush's room. I didn't feel anything was wrong or out of place in most of the rooms, but there were three things that struck me as odd."

Taylor smiled and encouraged her to carry on.

"Well," said Eva, "firstly, room 101, Miss Sanchez-Vicario's room. She had a whole load of make-up products in her room, but they weren't like normal."

"How do you mean?" said Taylor, her curiosity immediately peaked.

"They weren't normal pots of concealer or foundation that you'd buy in Boots. I don't know how to explain it, but they just didn't look like the type of thing you get in a shop."

Taylor frowned. "Okay, anything else?"

"Not in that room."

"Fine. What are the other two things you thought were odd?"

"Room 103. That is supposed to be empty. I cleaned that room on Friday morning after the guest checked out, and there wasn't supposed to be anyone in there on Friday night, but when I went in there, the bathroom had been used. There were water stains in the sink and one of the hand towels was wet. There was also an indentation on the bed, like someone had been laid on it."

"Could one of the staff have used it?"

"We're not supposed to, but I guess it's possible."

"And the final thing?"

"Room 115, Mr Young's room. Now he's been here since Wednesday, so I've done his room for a few days. He's a real tidy freak but tonight there was something else in his room that I'm convinced wasn't there before. I noticed it because it was just lying on the floor, you know, kinda untidy like."

"Oh, what was it?"

"A walking stick."

Taylor's head was spinning but Eva had done exactly what she'd hoped she would do. Look at the guest rooms with her unique perspective. "Eva, that is brilliant. Thank you so much for doing that. Now get yourself home before anyone starts asking questions as to why you're still here."

"Did I do good?" she said, an almost childlike reverence in her tone, like she was seeking her mother's approval.

Taylor stood up and rubbed Eva's shoulder. "Oh yes, you did good."

Eva bounced out of the room, an obvious spring in her step. Taylor went back to the incident room and stared at the board, trying to process what Eva had told her. A few minutes passed and she grabbed the pen, scrawling her immediate thoughts on the board.

Room 101 – Miss Sanchez-Vicario – odd make-up
Room 103 – who was in that room?
Room 115 – walking stick. Who was using one?

She glanced at her watch. She'd asked the team to get their interviews done by 6.30pm and Moretti was due any minute with some of his team. There was something about the investigation that was nagging at her. None of the staff had come forward with any information. Why was that? Spence and Ablett had managed to split the remaining interviews up between them, leaving her a gap, which she'd decided to fill with the interrogation of the staff.

A minute later there was a knock at the door and Moretti and four of his team filtered into the room. They all looked nervous.

16

THE INCIDENT ROOM
SATURDAY, 5.50PM

They all sat down across from Taylor on the other side of the conference table. The DCI noticed a few furtive glances at the incident board and made a mental note to cover it up when people came in. The last thing she needed was people gossiping about what was on there.

Moretti invited his team to introduce themselves. First was Don Thompson, the front of house manager who had been the maître d' in the restaurant the previous night. The two women she recognised from the lakeside crime scene. They were both members of the reception team and introduced themselves as Luna Bartok and Brianna Svetlana. The last one was a guy who seemed younger than the rest of the team. He introduced himself as Jamie Mellon. Taylor was immediately intrigued to discover that he was the night porter throughout the previous night, being on from 10pm to 7am, when he was relieved by the reception team that came on shift. He also doubled as one of the gardeners.

Taylor took the floor. "Thank you for coming in, and I will try not to keep you too long as I know you are all busy. Now, we obviously have a serious situation here, and my team are currently in the process of interviewing all the guests. There is a lot for us to get through, so we will be working through the night, as I am conscious that most of the guests are checking out in the morning."

Moretti piped up. "You obviously think one of the guests is responsible for the death of Mr Bush."

"We are investigating all possibilities at the moment, Mr Moretti, but I can't deny it is a bit problematical that so many of our suspect pool are leaving the hotel in the morning."

Taylor let that settle and turned to Don Thompson. "Mr Thompson, can we start with you, as I'm sure you need to be focusing on the dinner service presently?"

He gave a charming smile which Taylor guessed had been honed over years of high-end hospitality experience. He seemed like the oldest in the group, a well-worn face struggling to hide his advancing years, although the deep copper tan and distinguished greying of the hair made Taylor think that he would be very attractive to a certain kind of woman.

"Can you confirm who was in for dinner last night?"

Thompson glanced at the folder he'd brought in with him. "All the guests came in for dinner except for Miss Sanchez-Vicario in room 101, Mr and Mrs Johnson in room 102 and Mr Bush in room 107."

"Oh, so our victim wasn't down for dinner. Did anyone see him last evening?"

Bartok responded, "I checked him in around 3.30pm on Friday afternoon. I saw him go out of the hotel about an hour later but didn't see him after that."

The others confirmed they hadn't seen him.

"Was he due to have breakfast, Mr Thompson?"

Thompson scanned the folder. "Yes, he was, but it doesn't look like he was present."

Taylor nodded. That immediately supported the notion that Mr Bush was assaulted and potentially killed in room 105, which piqued her interest in the night porter.

"Mr Mellon, given what Mr Thompson has just said and the evidence that we have been able to collect so far, it seems extremely likely that Mr Bush was present in room 105 last night. Two independent witnesses heard a male arguing with a female, followed by a thud, which we are assuming was an assault that could have killed him. There is a suggestion that there was noise outside that room in the early hours of the morning, which we believe may have been someone moving the body from that room to the lake. Can you explain why you didn't report seeing anything untoward last night?"

Mellon started fiddling with his perfectly manicured hair. "Are you accusing me of something?"

His reaction intrigued Taylor but she remained courteous. "Not at all. I'm just curious as to how someone could potentially move a body down the stairs and out through the garden in the dead of night, without you seeing anything."

Mellon's face was tinged with anger. "Well, I guess that's why you're the detectives."

Taylor noticed a glance from Moretti to Mellon, that suggested he needed to rein his attitude in, but pushed on. "Have I done something to offend you?"

Mellon huffed. "No, sweetheart. Just not a great fan of the police."

Taylor made a mental note to check him out, as it sounded like he was known to them. She tried to remain calm and not get riled by his attitude. "Okay, I guess we are not everyone's cup of tea, but I would appreciate an understanding of how you operate your shift so I can work out how someone could have moved a body without being seen."

She noticed Mellon's glance at Moretti, who was still staring him down with a disapproving glare. It seemed to work. He sighed. "I spend most of my shift sat in the reception area, manning the phone in case any guests have problems in the night. I walk around the interior of the hotel two to three times during my shift to do a visual check that everything is okay. I do a complete tour of the hotel each time."

"And you didn't see or hear anything that was odd?"

"No."

Taylor's detective experience was kicking in. She didn't believe him. She decided to take a step back so as not to expose her suspicions. She reverted her attention back to Don Thompson.

"Mr Thompson, can you describe what happened in the restaurant area last night?"

"How do you mean?" he replied.

"Well, was there anything unusual? Where were people sitting?"

Thompson pulled a thoughtful expression. "The seating arrangements generally follow the room numbers. We tend to have rooms in the main house down one end of the restaurant and the annexe rooms at the other end, although I think there were a few tables moved about to accommodate people's specific requests last night."

"Anything unusual?"

"I don't think it's my place to comment on the guests."

Taylor stifled a laugh, before realising he was deadly serious. "Oh, well, I'm not looking for you to destroy their characters or anything. I just wondered whether there was anything odd in anyone's manner."

Taylor noticed a furtive glance from Thompson to Moretti, which she clocked was met with a subtle nod by the GM. It seemed to loosen Thompson's tongue.

"I guess there was one thing that caused a bit of a stir. Mrs Deveraux, who was in room 105, made a loud and dramatic entrance into the restaurant, immediately demanding my attention and reeling off her order to me before we could even give her a menu. Her whole performance was complemented by a strange ensemble of a long, flowing dress, dark glasses and a straw hat. I know it garnered several surprised looks from the other guests in that area."

"Performance? Why do you use that word?"

"That's what it seemed like to me. Like she was playing the room, wanting to make sure that everyone was looking at her."

Taylor cocked her head to one side. "That's interesting seeing as she has disappeared. If she had planned to meet someone secretly in her room, I would have thought she would have tried to keep a low profile."

Thompson shrugged but made no response.

"So, who was sat in her area? Who would have seen the 'performance'?"

Thompson grabbed his folder. "Mr Young, room 115, was sat on a table right next to her. Mr and Mrs Kendal, room 106, were across from her in the other corner of that part of the room. Mr and Mrs Walker were sat on the next table as you go back towards the entrance. Beyond them were Mr and Mrs Morgan from room 112 and Mr and Mrs Cole in room 114. I think all those tables could see Mrs Deveraux from where they were sitting."

"You mentioned it garnered some reaction from this group. Anything specific?"

"Not really. I could just see most of them looked up while she was loudly announcing her needs to me, and I sensed a bit of general amusement at her antics."

"Anything else, Mr Thompson?"

"Well, I don't really feel comfortable saying this, but it did seem like Mrs Walker was very unhappy with her husband. There was definitely some tension there, throughout the meal."

Taylor leant forward. "Interesting. Especially considering that we also can't locate Mr Walker at the moment."

Taylor looked across the group. "Okay, beyond the evening meal, did anyone see Mr Walker or Mrs Deveraux after, say, 9pm?"

She was met with five shaking heads.

Just as Taylor thought she was running out of steam with the group, she glanced up at the incident board, spotting the notes she had just written up.

"Oh," she said, "did any of the staff use room 103 last night?"

The group looked at each other, confusion on their faces. Moretti took the lead. "Absolutely not. The staff are not allowed to use empty rooms for any reason."

Taylor nodded, satisfied that Eva's observations now

gave her another clear line of inquiry. "Finally, can any of you recall if one of the guests was using a walking stick?"

Bartok gasped. "Gosh, yes. He was using it when he checked in. Seemed to be leaning on it quite heavily."

"Who are you talking about?"

"Well, the victim. Mr Bush."

17

TEAM BRIEFING IN THE INCIDENT ROOM
SATURDAY, 6.30PM

Taylor let the staff get back to their guests. Their feedback had been interesting and set another load of theories swimming around her head. Both receptionists seemed pretty solid. Kind and professional; happy to answer her questions. Don Thompson had been thorough in his feedback, once he realised it was okay to speak about the guests. Moretti had been quiet but had at least subtly encouraged his staff to speak with a variety of non-verbal indicators. The person that most interested her was Jamie Mellon, the night porter/gardener. He seemed flighty, nervous and inherently dishonest. She made a mental note to task one of them to do a deeper dive into his background.

As she surveyed the board, the last things the team had confirmed interested her most. Someone had been in room 103 and their victim was the one with the walking stick, so why had Eva found it in Mr Young's room?

Her mental deliberations were interrupted by Mrs Walker who had returned with her husband's toothbrush.

Her face was like thunder and glassy eyes showed she'd been crying. She offered nothing more to Taylor, getting in and out of the room as quickly as she could. Taylor couldn't help but feel sorry for her. It now seemed extremely likely that Mr Walker was somehow involved in this and had been deceiving his wife about his potential criminal behaviour for years and years. She made a note to check in with her again. Mrs Walker was alone with her world crumbling around her.

Taylor watched as the team filed in and sat down, all seemingly alert and ready for a long night. "Right, team," she said, "we've got a lot to get through, and I'm afraid to say that we might be working through the night on this one. The hotel is going to bring us some food in a bit, and they have given us the use of room 116 if anyone needs to freshen up or take a power nap. Coffee will be available in the jugs over there, and they will bring us more if needed."

The promise of food and unlimited coffee was met with a few smiles. Taylor knew a well-fed, caffeine-powered team were always more effective. She stood up and looked at the incident board.

"Okay, before I get your individual feedback, let me summarise my working strategy on this case. We know that there was an argument in room 105 somewhere between 10.30 and 11pm on Friday night. Two independent witnesses heard an argument between a man and a woman. We are assuming the woman was Mrs Deveraux who booked the room, although we now know that name is a cover, as the real Mrs Deveraux is in a nursing home in Surrey with severe dementia. Our impostor has disappeared and none of the staff I spoke to said they saw her after dinner. We originally assumed that the man could be Mr Walker as his wife was one of our witnesses and said she realised after she'd gone back to her room that the voice sounded like her husband's. Now that we have the body of Mr Bush from room 107, we are assuming he was in fact the man she was arguing with as his head trauma seems consistent with the blood spatter in room 105 and the thud that was heard by our witnesses. Mrs Kendal in room 106 said she heard noises in the corridor in the middle of the night, but when I spoke to a Jamie Mellon, who was the night porter on all last night, he claimed not to have seen or heard anything. My instincts are that he is lying, and I want a deeper look into his background, because I'm doubtful that a body could be moved out of that room and into the lake in the pitch dark by one person. Finally, despite not appearing to be the man that was in room 105, Mr Walker remains a person of interest in this case as we can't track him down and he is known to the police. Mrs Walker has given us his toothbrush for DNA sampling."

Her summary was met with nods of agreement.

"Right, as I said, we have a tonne of information to discuss, so let's get on with it." She turned to the three SOCOs. "Can we have your update first?"

Whiting took the lead. "Ma'am, I focused on the body in the lake and have been liaising with the ME. He has taken the body back to Cheltenham General Hospital for an urgent post-mortem. I'm driving over there to get the results once we've finished here. There was limited forensic evidence due to the body having been in the water for some time. However, I agree with your summary in that Mr Bush's head wound is consistent with an assault with a blunt instrument, matching what the witnesses heard and the blood pool in the room. Brennan is going to take all the samples back to the lab tonight to get them checked and processed."

Taylor turned to Brennan. "So, you've managed to get some decent forensics despite the maid starting to clean the room."

"Yes," Brennan replied. "We've obviously got the blood stain, but I've also managed to get hair fibres and some possible DNA from one of the wine glasses even though the maid had rinsed them under the tap."

"That's good. Get that done as soon as you can and report back here."

"There is one other interesting point, ma'am," said Brennan. "We found a round imprint in the blood stain. It was a circular indentation in the blood-stained carpet about 19mm in diameter. At this stage we don't know what it is, but I have a picture of it which I will add to the incident board."

"Okay, good." She turned to Chang. "How about you? Are you up to speed with what is going on?"

"Yes, ma'am. I've been briefed and done a preliminary processing of Mr Bush's room. Brennan has some initial samples that he is going to process to check they all belong to Mr Bush."

"That's great. Now, I really need you guys to get on with those tasks. Whiting and Brennan. You can leave and get back here with those results. Chang can stay here and liaise with the detective team."

Just as the two SOCOs got up to walk out, Taylor suddenly remembered something. "Oh, actually, can one of you also process room 103? The maid said that the room should have been empty last night but there was evidence that someone had used it. The general manager insisted that none of the staff would have used it, so I would be really interested to see if we can pick up any DNA samples."

Chang immediately offered to cover that off. Taylor turned her attention to Spence. "Can we have your update next? You've obviously been here since the start so it would be useful if you could give your perspective from the start of the investigation, what you gleaned from the witnesses at the lakeside crime scene and anything from your interviews."

Spence sat up straighter and took the lead. "Thank you, ma'am. As DCI Taylor said, I've been present since the call came in. I think everyone is up to speed with the crime scenes and the fact we have now cordoned off room 107, having had the lake victim identified as Mr Bush by one of the reception team. I interviewed the two receptionists and three guests that were at the lakeside crime scene. It seems that Mr and Mrs Cole from room 114, the American couple, were out for a walk this afternoon. They were attracted to the lake when they were walking back up the hill by some bird life. As they got close to the lake, they saw the body floating. Mrs Cole said she screamed, which attracted the attention of Mr Young, who's staying in room 115. He was coming down the hill from the hotel and ran over to see what was up. It appears he then ran back to reception to raise the alarm, which resulted in DCI Taylor and I being at the crime scene. I've spoken to all three of them again about their movements on Friday night and they say they had dinner and stayed in the hotel."

Taylor spoke. "Do they seem credible witnesses?"

"Hmm… sort of," replied Spence. "Whilst Mr and Mrs Cole check out in respect of the fact that I can find the flight details they gave me into the UK from Texas, I can't find the same details for Mr Young."

"Oh, what did he say about that?"

"That's the thing. He also has a strong American accent. When I began to probe deeper about his movements and why he was in the UK, he became very evasive. Made some vague comment about how he was over here on business but didn't want to expand. He said he'd been in the UK for a while and couldn't remember the exact date he flew in."

"Okay, have you had a chance to look any further into him?"

"Well, yes," said Spence. "The problem is that UK passport control don't have any record of him coming into the country."

18

TEAM BRIEFING IN THE INCIDENT ROOM
SATURDAY, 6.50PM

Taylor annotated the incident board as the team updates continued. Every bit of information was just making the case more complex. Two missing people, one dead body and a man who by all accounts was a 'ghost' in the UK. She knew she had to get through all the feedback before she could reasonably update her theories and lead the team towards a conclusion to this intriguing case.

She turned to Ablett. "Sergeant, can you tell me about your interviews?"

"Yes, ma'am. I interviewed Mr and Mrs Kendal from room 106. She repeated much of what she already told you about Friday evening, and they were out for most of the day. Whilst she seemed to be revelling in the gossip potential of this situation, I don't think she can add much more to our evidence, and I can't see either her or Mr Kendal being involved in this."

Taylor nodded. "Yes, she likes the sound of her own voice that one."

Ablett smirked. "I also spoke to Mrs Jennings from room 111. She is here for the weekend visiting her daughter who lives in Chipping Campden. She had dinner in the hotel last night and was at her daughter's most of today. Again, I can't see she has anything to do with this."

"Anyone else?"

"Yes, and I thought I would leave the most intriguing one to last. Miss Sanchez-Vicario from room 101. A very strange woman. She kept making out that her English was poor and didn't understand my questions. When she did speak, I reckon she had a Spanish or Portuguese accent."

"So, what's the problem?"

"I dunno. To me, she seemed like she was putting it on. Like she was acting. In the end, I gave up because I just couldn't get any sense out of her."

Taylor grunted. "Interesting. Tell me, Sergeant, what did you make of her appearance?"

"In what way?"

"Just your impressions."

"Er, well, she was wearing a blue top and light-coloured trousers. Nothing that unusual but she had loads of jewellery on and it didn't look like the cheap stuff. She was also caked in make-up—"

"Bingo," interrupted Taylor.

"Ma'am?"

"The maid said that she had loads of unusual make-up in her room, but not the type of stuff you buy from Boots."

"I'm not following, ma'am."

"Theatrical make-up. She's trying to disguise who she is, and the make-up is all part of the deception. I'm sure of it."

"To what end, ma'am?"

"I don't know yet, but it seems like half the people in this bloody hotel aren't who they say they are, which begs the question. Was she wearing a wig?"

"Definitely not. She had a short-cut hairstyle."

Taylor frantically updated the board. The thing that had niggled her in the guest briefing, when she first saw Sanchez-Vicario, was now front and centre in her mind. The suspect pool was growing.

19

TEAM BRIEFING IN THE INCIDENT ROOM
SATURDAY, 7PM

Taylor changed her focus to the two DCs. Her head was spinning with all the possibilities, but she needed to get this last batch of feedback before she could take a step back and process all the evidence.

"DC Joshi. Tell me about your interviews."

"Thank you, ma'am. I interviewed Mr and Mrs Johnson from room 102. They are down for a wedding celebration and were at the reception in another hotel on Friday evening. They had a heavy night so had a late breakfast this morning and chilled out around the hotel for the rest of the day. They came back in around 1am last night but said the hotel was quiet. They did see the night porter on the front desk."

"Interesting, so our Mr Mellon was on reception for part of the night."

"Indeed. I also interviewed Mr and Mrs Li from room 113. A lovely couple who are here on holiday. Nothing suspicious about their movements as far as I can see, which just leaves your shouty man from the briefing. The retired admiral and his wife: Mr and Mrs Morgan from room 112. He continued to be very vocal about our methods and seemed more interested in complaining than telling me anything useful. I did manage to confirm that he saw our fake Mrs Deveraux, and Mrs Morgan commented on what a *strange creature* she was. They apparently stayed in the hotel lounge after dinner and had a few drinks. They went to bed around 10.30pm but said they didn't hear or see anything else. They've been out of the hotel most of today."

Taylor pondered what Joshi had said. "We need to be careful with our admiral. Whilst he's a typical bully, he may be well connected, so we'd better play it straight with him. That said, I am always suspicious about people who protest too much. Makes me think they are hiding something."

She turned to DC Chesters. "Right, last but not least. Tell me about your interviews."

"No problem, ma'am. Firstly, I called Mr and Mrs Jenkins and Mr and Mrs Webster, who both checked out this morning. They were at dinner last night but were all down the other end of the restaurant so didn't see anything around Mrs Deveraux. Both couples went to bed early as they checked out by 9am to get on the road. I can't see they are in the frame for this. I also interviewed Miss Ella Jones and Miss Jemma Grounds from room 108 and Mr and Mrs Smith from room 110. I got a similar vibe from them also and both of these couples have been out of the hotel all day. All pretty normal and not at all suspicious."

Taylor grunted. "Mr and Mrs Smith. Did she look like his PA?"

"Ma'am?"

"Sorry, just a bit of a cliché. They always used to say that people checking into hotels as Mr and Mrs Smith were having an affair."

"I don't think so, ma'am," replied Chesters. "I reckon they were both in their eighties."

As Taylor took a moment to take it all in, her concentration was broken by Spence letting out a loud *ooh*. She looked at him expectantly.

"Well, well," he exclaimed. "The crime desk has just come back to us. The marker on Mr Walker's crime record is counter terrorism. They have it locked down, but the desk has managed to find a detective superintendent contact."

Taylor rubbed her face. This was getting serious.

20

THE CALL TO ACTION
SATURDAY, 7.10PM

Taylor's heartbeat was beginning to pound that little bit faster. This was it. This was the feeling she always had as the chase began. Like a leopard ready to kill. Dozing up a tree but with one eye open, ready to pounce on the antelope that was oblivious of its presence. The team had done well. They'd used their well-honed detective instincts to filter out the good from the bad. There was no guarantee that they'd got it right first time, but with such a large suspect pool, they had to start somewhere. The characters that were on their radar had all done something to make the team suspicious. She blew out her cheeks and engaged the team.

"Right, thank you for all that. A great start, and we have the foundations of an investigation. Whilst I trust your instincts about the people we should focus on, I still want a general check on all our guests. So, taskings as follows. Spence, get Mr Young back in here for a follow-up interview with you and me. He has some explaining to do. Also, get me that CTU contact. I want a call with that superintendent as soon as possible. Chang, finish off processing rooms 103 and 107. Ablett, Chesters and Joshi, I want background checks on all our guests but with a deep dive into Jamie Mellon, Miss Sanchez-Vicario and our victim, Mr Bush. I also want one of you to see if you can find where Mr Walker has been since he left here. Spence drew a blank when he first tried but keep on it. I'll ask Brennan and Whiting to get back here for a 9.30pm debrief. Hopefully by then we will have the outcomes of the PM and the initial forensic report. I don't need to remind you that we are against the clock, so contact any family you need to, as we're going to pull an all-nighter on this one."

As the team got up from the meeting table, there was a knock at the door. The hotel team brought in a load of food. Taylor knew she had to feed them but didn't want to slow things down. "Okay, eat and work, please."

As she opened her laptop, her email pinged. "The contact, ma'am," said Spence. "At CTU."

Taylor rapidly opened the email and grabbed her phone. She dialled the number. For a moment, she thought no one was going to answer, but after several rings, a male voice answered. "Sharpe," the voice said.

"Oh, hello, sir, this is Detective Chief Inspector Chloe Taylor from Gloucestershire CID. I'm the SIO on a murder case in a hotel in the Cotswolds and we have a suspect that has come up with a CTU marker. A Mr Walker. I need to know why you've secured his record."

There was an uncomfortable silence which Taylor felt she had to fill. "Sir?"

"What is your security clearance?" he said.

"I have the highest level."

"Okay, but I need to check you out and our chief supers will need to talk. Give me an hour."

"I don't have an hour."

"Well, that's how it is. For me to even begin to talk to you, I need some protocols to be followed. I'll contact you when and if I am able to."

With that, he disconnected the call and Taylor felt like a rejected girlfriend. "What happened?" said Spence.

Taylor shook her head. "Oh, just those CTU boys being their normal precious selves. I have to wait to see if he will grant me an audience."

"So, you think he has something to say about our Mr Walker?"

"Oh yeah. As soon as I mentioned his name there was a long silence. I've got a feeling we've landed ourselves in a middle of a CTU shitstorm."

21

THE INCIDENT ROOM
SATURDAY, 7.35PM

Taylor stewed on the phone call and her mood wasn't helped by having to wait for Young to finish his dinner. She'd had a five-minute video call with her husband and daughter, as he tucked her in bed, scant consolation for the guilt she was feeling about not being there for bedtime. She'd wolfed down some of the lovely food the hotel had provided and drunk two cups of coffee in quick succession, which just made her more wired. When Young eventually came through the door, she was ready for him.

Taylor eyed him curiously as he walked in, a confident, assured manner as he sat down opposite her and Spence. He had short-cropped hair and a vague goatee. She reckoned he was pushing fifty. His clothes were smart but unassuming. A nice shirt, corduroy trousers and a good pair of shoes, which she'd clocked as soon as he walked in. It was one of the things Taylor always looked at. You could tell a lot about people by their shoes.

"Mr Young. Thank you for coming to see us, and apologies for further disturbing your evening."

"No problem," he said in a thick New York accent.

"The thing is," Taylor probed, "my sergeant here didn't feel he really got much out of you when you spoke earlier."

"Oh," he said, pulling a confused expression. "What did you want to know?"

"For my benefit, could you confirm what you do and explain why you are in the UK?"

"Er, yeah, I guess. I'm a software engineer, and I work in the field diagnosing client problems. I'm based in New York, covering jobs on the eastern side of the US and Europe."

"How long have you been in the UK?"

"Gosh, a while. This has been a long stint. I reckon this my sixth week in the UK. At the moment, I'm supporting a client in Chipping Norton, but I should be going home at the end of this week."

"Where are you flying from?"

"Gatwick."

Taylor briefly glanced at Spence. He picked up on the non-verbals. They had no record of him entering the country, so it would be interesting to see if his story checked out. She watched Young's facial expressions and body language intently as he answered her questions. She was convinced he was lying about his identity, but his responses were calm and without any of the usual indicators that they had been trained to pick up on. She ploughed on.

"We understand you were sat next to a Mrs Deveraux at dinner last night."

Suddenly, there was a twitch, which Taylor tried not to react to. It lasted a second, but it was there, before he righted himself and responded. "Gee, she was a character alright."

"How so?"

"She waltzed in like some film star, loudly announcing what she wanted, without any consideration that there may have been other tables that should have been served first. The waiter guy handled it real well though."

"Had you seen her before?"

Young frowned. "Er, no. Why would I?"

"Just wondered," said Taylor, a conspiratorial edge to her voice.

She left a brief pause before she asked the next question. Criminals generally hated silence in interviews and, more often than not, would reveal something of themselves as they filled the silent void. Young didn't do this. He was as cool as a cucumber.

"Do you have mobility problems, Mr Young?"

Taylor clocked the confused expression from Spence, which gave her a brief sense of satisfaction. She liked to pull these rabbits out of the hat sometimes.

Young frowned. "What a strange question. Why would you ask that?"

"Just a question, Mr Young."

"Well, no, I consider myself to be a very fit individual. The benefit of getting some downtime in lovely places like this is the great walks you can do."

Taylor smiled. "Thank you, Mr Young, you have been very helpful. We'll contact you again if we need to."

Young seemed shocked by the sudden cessation of the interview but got up and began to walk out. As he neared the door, he turned and looked at Taylor. "There is one thing I reckon I can help with. Try looking at what's hiding in plain sight."

22

THE PLOT THICKENS
SATURDAY, 7.55PM

Taylor flashed a look of confusion at Spence. "What the fuck was that?"

"I dunno," Spence replied.

"What does he mean *look for what's hiding in plain sight*?"

"Do you think he saw something and is refusing to tell us?"

Taylor grunted. "If he is, I'll have him for obstructing a police inquiry faster than he can say, New York, New York."

Spence huffed. "He was very calm, but I thought you had him on the rocks a bit when you asked him about his mobility. What was that all about?"

Taylor allowed herself a brief smile, softening the frown lines that had been a permanent fixture on her face for the last few hours.

"Well, regardless of what you think of me using her, that is down to our observant maid."

"Oh," replied Spence, a slight edge of annoyance in his voice.

"Yes, he's been here a few nights and Eva said that he was a real tidy freak, but when she went into his room earlier to replenish the chocolates, she said there was a walking stick just strewn on the floor."

"Ah," said Spence, catching up with Taylor's interrogation tactics, "so you think it's not his?"

"I know it's not his. The receptionist said that the only person using a walking stick was our victim, Mr Bush."

"Holy shit! So, you know he's lying."

"A hundred per cent. He's no more a software engineer than I'm Steve Jobs. If I was to hazard a guess, he's been trained in counter interrogation techniques. He was too cold and calculating. The only time he gave anything away was when I mentioned Mrs Deveraux. Most normal people would have been naturally more nervous at being questioned by two police officers. He hardly flinched."

"Why didn't you ask him directly about the walking stick?"

"I want to see what he does. If he somehow obtained it from our victim, he may panic and try to get rid of it. We need to keep an eye on him. In the meantime, look into him again and see if you can find his flight booking out of Gatwick this week."

Spence broke off and started tapping away at his laptop. Taylor checked in with Ablett and the DCs. They were beavering away at the background checks but hadn't found anything significant, so she left them to it.

Just as impatience was about to get the better of her, the ping of a text message refocused her mind. It was from her chief super. He'd had a call from some high-up in CTU. She was going to get a call back from Detective Superintendent Sharpe.

She stared at her phone willing it to ring but, as so often in her life, her professional career was interrupted by a reminder of the real reason she did this job. Her husband had sent her a picture of their sleeping daughter with the caption, *Night Night, Mummy.* She choked back a sob, grateful that her team all had their heads in their laptops and hadn't seen her distress.

The call came and she shook off the ever-present feelings of sadness and guilt. "DCI Taylor," she said, picking up the call before the second ring.

"Chief Inspector," said the voice on the other end. "Detective Superintendent Sharpe from CTU. It seems like I am permitted to talk to you. What do you need to know?"

His tone wasn't unfriendly, but Taylor couldn't help but feel that his businesslike manner suggested he wanted to get this call over with as quickly as possible. She ploughed on, hoping that he would be forthcoming.

"I am at the scene of a suspected murder in a hotel in the Cotswolds. We are investigating several leads and a number of suspicious individuals, which include a Martin Walker, who is flagged on the crime system as having a restricted record due to a CTU marker."

"Yes, that's correct."

Taylor waited for more, but it was obvious she was going to have to drag every piece of information out of him.

"The thing is, we are currently processing some DNA samples to see if we can place him at the scene of the crime but, since last night, no one has seen him. He told his wife he had to go back to work to deal with an urgent problem, but then she thinks she heard his voice in the room next door."

"Didn't she check?"

"Er, no. She heard what we think was an assault and ran back to her room. She was really frightened. It was only when she calmed down that she realised it sounded like her husband."

"Sounds very mysterious, Detective."

Taylor frowned. She knew when she was being patronised, and he was doing a very good job of sidelining her. She wasn't going to have it. "What can you tell me about Walker?"

"He is a significant person of interest to us, but unless I can see some link to our ongoing investigations, I am not at liberty to divulge details of what we are working on."

"Is he a suspected murderer?"

"No."

"Violence?"

"No."

"So, what is he?"

"He's a thief. A good one. Connected to some nasty people."

Taylor sighed. "This isn't giving me much to go on. At the moment we seem to have an argument in one of the hotel rooms which was overheard by two guests. It sounded like a disagreement over some sort of criminality, but all we have is one dead body."

"The group we are monitoring deal in major heists. Cash, jewellery, bonds, whatever they can get their hands on. Martin Walker has been placed at the scene of several unsolved crimes, but we've never had enough to arrest him or his associates. He's a nasty conman but he's no murderer."

"What about a Geoffrey Bush. He's our victim."

"No, that's not a name we know, but if you send me a picture of him, we can process it through our facial rec to see if he's known to us under another name."

"Great. Finally, do you have a Mrs Deveraux on your radar?" Taylor waited. No response. "Sir?" she probed.

"Um, maybe. Can I check something out and come back to you about that?"

"Oh, yeah, I guess," said Taylor, pleased that she finally seemed to be getting some engagement with Sharpe. She wasn't sure how much longer he was going to give her, so she went for broke.

"Do you know where Mr Walker is?"

"Yes, we do."

Taylor's heart skipped a beat. "Really? Do you have him under surveillance?"

"Yes, we have been tracking him and his gang twenty-four seven."

"Where is he?"

"As far as we know, he's still at the hotel."

"What!"

Taylor's head was spinning but then the realisation hit her. "You've got someone here watching him."

"I'm afraid I'm not able to confirm or deny that."

Taylor ended the call. She couldn't believe it. CTU had an insider on the premises.

Which begged the obvious question: who was it?

23

THE INCIDENT ROOM
SATURDAY, 8.20PM

Taylor stood stock-still for a second, barely able to process what Sharpe had just said. How could Martin Walker still be in the hotel, and who the hell was the CTU mole keeping him under surveillance?

"Sergeants. Here."

Spence and Ablett walked over to the corner of the room where Taylor was now chewing her nails, a bundle of stress. "We have a significant development. I've just spoken to CTU, and they have confirmed that Martin Walker is a significant person of interest in high-end robberies. He is a thief, but Detective Superintendent Sharpe said he is not prone to violence. However, the real left-fielder is that they have him under surveillance."

"What!" blurted out Spence.

"Yes," replied Taylor, "that was my reaction too, but that's not the best of it. I asked him if he knew where Mr Walker was, and he claims that he's still here. In the hotel."

Taylor could almost see the cogs whirring in her sergeants'

heads. Ablett got there first. "Oh, so if Walker is still here, that means whoever has him under surveillance is also here."

"Exactly!"

"It's got to be that Mr Young," said Spence. "You said you thought he had some sort of intelligence background."

Taylor nodded. "Yes, I can see he is the obvious candidate. On his own. A ropey cover story and no evidence of entering the country. If he's deep undercover, it would at least explain why we can't find anything about him."

"Definitely," replied Spence, "and I can't find him booked on any flights out of Gatwick in the next week."

Ablett piped up. "What about Sanchez-Vicario? We haven't been able to find any records for her either. The address details she gave the hotel are fake and we can't track anyone with her name coming into the country. She's another ghost."

Taylor shook her head. "What the hell is going on here? Is there anyone in this hotel who is actually who they say they are?"

As they all pondered the implications of these latest developments, Joshi walked towards them. "Ma'am, sirs. We've found a couple of things you might be interested in. Our admiral is lying. He was in the Royal Navy for nearly forty years but only made the rank of captain. We can't find any evidence that he was ever at any of the admiral ranks. Also, our Mr Mellon came to the hotel under a young offenders' rehabilitation scheme. The hotel gets his wages subsidised as a result."

Just as Taylor was about to respond, Chesters joined them. "Something else, ma'am. Mr Johnson from room 102 has a record as long as your arm. GBH, drunk and disorderly, disturbing the peace, drink driving. Seems he can't handle his alcohol and has a very short fuse."

Taylor gestured for them to gather around the table. She glanced at her watch. "Okay, good work. The SOCO team are due back at 9.30pm, which gives us about an hour to do some more work on our mystery people."

The team sat opposite her. Perky and attentive. The antithesis of what she was feeling. She shook off her malaise.

"Right, does anyone speak Spanish?"

The quizzical looks from the guys were juxtaposed by a broad smile from Joshi. "I can get by, ma'am."

"Good. Get Sanchez-Vicario in here for an interview with you and me."

Joshi's smile broadened. An expression that Taylor recognised. The satisfaction of standing out amongst your male colleagues.

Taylor turned her attention to the others. "Ablett and Chesters, I want you to do a search of the hotel. Be subtle and obviously do not go into any guests' rooms without their permission. If our Mr Walker is still here, work out where he could be hiding. There are lots of nooks and crannies in this place. See if you can find any evidence of him still being around, and check in with Chang in room 103. I want to know if that's where he hid last night."

She turned to Spence. "I want you to have a wander around the hotel. Make sure people see you. I want them to know we are still around. Whilst doing that, keep an eye on Mr Young. See what he does. Also, check in with Mrs Walker. Make sure she is okay and see if she has anything more to tell us about her errant husband. But, before you do that, can you sit in the background of this interview? I want your opinion on Miss Sanchez-Vicario."

The team stood up, ready for action. "Back here at 9.30pm," she shouted as they noisily exited the room.

Five minutes later, Joshi came back in with Sanchez-Vicario. Taylor eyed her curiously. She was wearing a long, flowing dress, complemented by what looked like an expensive wool cardigan. Her fingers had several different rings on them, and she wore a large pearl necklace, all of which looked like high-quality jewellery. Her face was once again heavily made up, with substantial foundation, bright-red lipstick and thick, dark eye make-up. Her hair was a neat, short-cropped style that looked perfectly coiffured. Everything about her said *money*.

Taylor didn't waste any time. "Miss Sanchez-Vicario. Thank you for coming to talk to us again. There have been some developments in our investigations which we think you can help with."

Sanchez-Vicario just stared back.

"Do you understand what I'm saying?" probed Taylor.

"I… um… I… no speak good English."

Taylor frowned and looked at Joshi. "Ask her what her real name is."

"*¿Cual es tu nombre real?*" Joshi said in her best attempt at a Spanish accent.

Sanchez-Vicario's expression barely changed.

Taylor frowned. "Did you not understand that either?"

No response.

Taylor sighed. The volume of her voice rose. "Look. We know you are a fake. We don't believe that Sanchez-Vicario is your real name as we can't find any record of anyone entering the country with those credentials. Your address in Spain is fake, and there is no record of you living in this country.

I don't buy this nonsense that you can't speak English, and don't pretend that you didn't understand my DC's question."

Sanchez-Vicario fixed Taylor with an unsettling icy stare. No one spoke. Taylor tried to hold her nerve in the battle of wills.

Joshi repeated her question in Spanish.

Nothing.

"I can arrest you," said Taylor, slightly annoyed at herself for breaking the silence.

Suddenly, there was a crack in the ice queen's expression. She spoke. "Really. And exactly what do you think I've done, Inspector?"

Taylor tried not to get riled up. Her English was perfect. There was a slight Spanish twang mixed with a curious bit of East End London.

"How about we start with using a false identity?"

Sanchez-Vicario smirked and reached into her bag, pulling out a passport and throwing it in Taylor's direction. Taylor opened it. It had her picture and her name.

"How do I know this isn't a fake?" said Taylor, realising she was on the back foot.

Sanchez-Vicario stood up and retrieved her passport. "I don't give a fuck what you think. Unless you are going to arrest me for something, then I'm going back to enjoying my holiday."

Taylor and Joshi watched her walk out. She was right. They had nothing. She looked at Spence, who just raised his eyebrows.

Taylor turned to them both. "I'll give her round one, but that passport is a fake and she's now top of my suspect list."

24

TOUR OF THE HOTEL
SATURDAY, 8.30PM

Ablett and Chesters went straight to room 103. Chang was still processing the scene.

"Anything interesting?" said Ablett.

"Yes," said Chang, "I've got a hair sample from the towel in the bathroom. When Brennan comes back, we should be able to compare it with what he's been able to process from the other crime scenes."

"Could it be the maid's DNA?"

"Er, I hope we took a verification sample from her so we can rule her out."

Ablett shrugged. "I dunno if anyone did that."

"Don't worry, I'll check."

"So, any theories?" probed Ablett.

"Well, the maid said this room was supposed to be empty, but the bathroom has been used and someone has been lying in the bed. I'm just seeing if I can get anything else from here."

Ablett let her get on with it and left the room, Chesters in tow. "Right," he said, "let's take a walk around the main house first and see if there is anywhere else that Walker might have hidden." As they did that, all they saw were the closed doors of each room. There were a couple of store cupboards but nothing that leapt out.

"Do you think he's in cahoots with someone else in the hotel? You know, could he have stayed with them overnight? Could he still be in one of these rooms?" Chesters said.

Ablett considered the point. "That would explain why no one has seen him, and at the moment, we have no probable cause to search the rooms."

They both walked down the stairs and began to explore the ground floor. The restaurant had the last few diners finishing up their meals, and there were a few people in the bar, lounge and drawing room. They went outside the main door and explored the parking area that was lit by outside lighting. They walked around the perimeter of the hotel but beyond the immediate grounds, the area was pitch black. They walked back into the hotel from the side door. "Hold on," said Ablett, "I've just realised something."

He began to stride purposefully back towards the incident room but, instead of going back in, turned left down the stairs towards the leisure centre and rooms in the annexe of the hotel. After exploring the corridors around the other rooms that had been occupied, they walked towards the far end of the annexe. There was a barrier and some dust sheets protecting the corridors where the refurbishment was happening.

"Be careful," said Ablett to Chesters as they tiptoed past building materials and various bits of machinery. The doors to the six rooms were all open.

"What are you thinking, Sarge?" said Chesters.

"I dunno. I was just wondering whether someone could have stayed here overnight without being seen?"

They searched each room, being careful not to disturb the builder's materials. Of the six rooms, five were in no state that anyone could have camped down in them. The last one was different. Although there were dust sheets over the chairs and small table, protecting the furniture from the last bits of painting that was being done around the window, the rest of the room was pristine. It looked like it was ready to be used any time soon. Most significantly, in the bin was an empty packet of sandwiches, a screwed-up crisp packet and an empty bottle of water.

"Hmm," said Ablett. "Do you think these belong to the decorators or could they be evidence of our Mr Walker being in this room?"

Chesters pulled on his gloves and an evidence bag, depositing the three items inside. "Only one way to find out," he said.

25

SPENCE
SATURDAY, 8.45PM

Spence began to walk along the main hotel corridor on the ground floor, his boots squeaking on the polished flagstone flooring. As he rounded the corner to go towards reception, he spotted Young through the window that allowed a view into the restaurant from the corridor. He quickly stepped back out of view, hoping that he hadn't seen him. Spence risked a peek. Young was looking at his phone while he drank his coffee, oblivious of Spence's scrutiny.

Spence stood still, trying to keep a discreet eye on Young. A couple of guests walked past him, and he smiled, trying not to look too conspicuous. A few minutes passed. Young didn't move.

Just as Spence was about to give up the surveillance, Young suddenly pushed his chair out, exchanged a few pleasantries with the waiting staff and walked out of the restaurant. Spence watched as he walked along the corridor towards reception, keeping a discreet distance. As Young reached the reception area, he stopped. A few seconds later he turned and walked into the lounge. Spence quickened his step so he could reach the reception area and see what Young was up to.

As Spence got to a point where he could see into the room, he was surprised to see Young speaking to Mrs Walker, who had a book in her hand and a pot of tea on the table to her right. Spence couldn't make out what they were saying but Walker looked concerned and not enamoured by his questions. Spence moved a bit closer but still couldn't make out what they were saying. He contemplated intervening, given that Taylor had asked him to make sure Walker was okay. As he watched some more, Walker's growing distress was obvious but just as Spence decided to intervene, Young got up and strode purposefully out of the room and straight up the stairs, not noticing Spence's presence.

Spence walked into the drawing room and sat in the chair that Young had just vacated. "Are you okay, Mrs Walker? Was that man upsetting you?"

Walker eyed her book, rolling it over in her hands. As she looked up, Spence could see she was fighting back tears.

"He asked where my husband was."

Spence frowned. "Why did he want to know that?"

"I don't know. It was the first thing he asked when he sat down, uninvited I might add."

"What did you say?"

"I said I didn't know and asked what business it was of his."

"What did he say to that?"

"He said my husband is in trouble and he needed to find him. I told him I had no idea where he was. I said that he left on Friday to sort out a problem at work and I've not heard from him since."

"Was his manner threatening?"

"Agitated, I would say, more than threatening, but I didn't like it either way."

"Did he say anything else?"

"No, he just shook his head and walked out."

Spence was torn between going to confront Young and looking after Walker. He chose the latter. "Is there anything I can do for you, Mrs Walker?"

She sipped the last of her tea. "To be honest, Sergeant, I don't know what to do. My husband has always been absent in our marriage, but I just put it down to him prioritising work over me. I got used to it. I never credited him with the energy to have an affair, so I just assumed he was a workaholic. We never wanted for anything. We have a lovely house and always had nice holidays when he could be bothered to take time off. I just assumed he was earning good money, but now your inspector tells me that he's a bloody criminal. I guess it all makes sense now."

Spence decided not to distress Walker any more by telling her the depth of his criminal activity but did probe a bit deeper.

"When he was at home, did he used to receive phone calls or messages on his phone at odd times of the day?"

"Yes, all the time. He was forever up and down from the dinner table or when we were sitting trying to watch some telly. Always going out of the room to take the calls."

Spence tried to look sympathetic, but Walker picked up on his failed attempts at trying to not show concern. "You think he was getting calls about…" she hesitated, caught in a sob, "…whatever it is he's been up to."

Spence grimaced. "I think that is quite likely."

Walker shook her head in resignation.

"Can I get you another pot of tea… or something stronger?"

Walker smiled. "No thank you, Sergeant. That is very sweet of you to offer. I'm going to finish this chapter and then go up to my room."

Spence made his excuses and left, going straight up the stairs to the first floor. Room 105 was still cordoned off. He turned left and went through the fire door. As he did, he was alerted to the creaking of the door to the next room. He took a step forward to see the door slowly closing shut. As his brain tried to catch up, he realised it was Mrs Walker's room. She was downstairs and… a noise. He could hear footsteps. He ran towards the next door, opening it quickly. He cursed the hotel layout. There was a short corridor to the left, steps right in front of him leading down to the ground floor and a staircase behind him leading to two of the rooms. He stopped and listened. Nothing. He hadn't been quick enough to catch which direction the footsteps had gone.

Suddenly, Chang peered out of room 103. "Are you okay, sir?"

"Oh, Chang, did you see someone come past here a second ago?"

"Er, no sorry."

"Shit!"

Spence thanked Chang and sped back to Walker's room. Just as he walked through the door, she was putting her key in the lock.

"Oh, Sergeant, are you stalking me?"

"Um, Mrs Walker, can I look in your room?"

"Why?" she said, concern suddenly etched on her face.

"I was walking along the corridor when I saw your door shutting. I realised it couldn't have been you. I heard footsteps beyond the next door but couldn't see who it was. I think someone was in your room."

Walker frantically opened the door. As the room was revealed, they both gasped. It had been ransacked.

26

MRS WALKER'S ROOM
SATURDAY, 9PM

Spence stepped past Walker and instinctively put his arm out to stop her moving any further into the room.

She was close to tears, but Spence knew he needed to get her focused on what was in front of them. "Mrs Walker, first impressions. Can you see if anything has been taken?"

She sucked in a breath and scanned the room. "I... I don't know. There's nothing obvious."

Spence gently put his hands on her upper arms. "Look, I'm so sorry this has happened, but can I ask that you give us a few minutes to process the room, to see if we can get any forensic samples. If someone's been in here, I don't want to miss the opportunity to catch whoever did this."

She couldn't stop the tears, moving away from Spence's grasp and covering her face with her hands. Spence let her get it out before gently coaxing her out of the room and asking for her key. She reluctantly followed Spence down the corridor. As he passed room 103, he called for Chang, explaining what had happened. She was just finishing up so immediately grabbed her stuff and walked back towards Walker's room.

Spence navigated down the stairs and went back to the incident room. As soon as Taylor saw Walker's face, she leapt up. "What's happened?" she said.

"Her room's been ransacked. I was just walking along the corridor when I saw her door closing shut. I heard footsteps but couldn't catch whoever it was. I've asked Chang to go in there to see if we can get anything."

Taylor shook her head, coaxing Walker to sit down. "I'm so sorry, Mrs Walker, but my sergeant is right. If that's just happened, we can go in there and see if the perpetrator has left any evidence."

Walker was still fighting back tears. "What is happening here? I mean, what the hell have I done to deserve this?"

Spence sat opposite Walker. "You don't deserve this, so we are going to do our best to find out what is going on here."

Spence noticed a glance from Taylor, which he assumed was a look of disapproval due to him cutting across her. He ignored it and carried on, feeling like he'd made a connection with Walker.

"Do you have any idea what they might have been looking for?" he said.

"No! I thought I was going to have a nice weekend in the Cotswolds and then this horror show started. I can't even begin to process it."

"It's fine," interjected Taylor, clearly determined to grab back the lead from Spence. "Do you want us to talk to reception, to see if we can get you another room?"

Walker shrugged. "I don't know. I guess, but what about my stuff?"

"We'll let you get your stuff once we've finished in there."

Spence noticed Taylor's expectant look. "Sergeant. Go and sort that out for Mrs Walker?"

Spence was a bit taken aback but righted himself and got up. "Of course, ma'am. I'll be right back, Mrs Walker."

As Spence began to walk to reception, he reflected on what had just happened with Taylor. Why was she subtly busting his balls? He thought he was trying to help Walker, but Taylor seemed to resent his attempts at taking the lead. "Bloody women," he muttered under his breath.

He reached reception, and one of the receptionists from earlier was just handing over to Jamie Mellon. Once Spence explained what had happened, she was immediately on it, while Mellon seemed to brood in the background. Spence remembered what Joshi had said. He was an ex-con, so Spence guessed why he was a bit antsy when it came to the police. She quickly got a new key organised. Room 109.

Just as Spence was about to scuttle back to Walker, he had a thought. "Room 104. I presume you have a spare key for each room?"

Mellon ignored the question while the receptionist continued to help Spence. "Oh," she said, "it's not here. How odd."

Spence looked at Mellon. "Have you given the spare key to room 104 to anyone?"

Mellon screwed his face up. "Why would I?"

"Just a question, sir. Someone has been in Mrs Walker's room, and it now seems likely they got the spare key from reception."

Mellon shrugged. "I've no idea."

Spence looked back at the receptionist. "No, sorry, but I will contact Mr Moretti about what has happened."

Spence thanked the receptionist whilst giving Mellon a lingering look, which was met with a fierce stare. As he walked back to the incident room, Spence resolved to look even deeper into Jamie Mellon. He couldn't help but feel that he was somehow part of what had happened the previous night. It just wasn't probable that he didn't see or hear a dead body being moved from the upstairs room. And now, they had a missing key.

As Spence walked back to the incident room, he was still brooding at the way Taylor had treated him. He'd worked with her on and off for about a year and was getting tired of her attitude, always using her gender as a reason to throw her weight around with the subordinate men in her team. He sighed. He didn't give a shit what Taylor thought of him. He was ambitious and wasn't going to let anyone stand in his way. He was determined to solve this case and get the credit he deserved.

He was going to come out of this smelling of roses, even if he had to trample over his colleagues to do it.

27

PHONE CALL
SATURDAY, 9.20PM

Taylor left Spence to sort out Mrs Walker, as she frantically updated the incident board in preparation for the major briefing that was due in ten minutes. The volume of information they now had was beginning to get a bit overwhelming and she was sure the team were about to bring her a load more.

She felt a flutter in her stomach. They were onto something. This had all the markings of a major crime incident, and she was determined to solve whatever was going on here.

As she took a step back to review the board, her phone rang. It was Sharpe. "Chief Inspector," he said, "it seems like we might have some crossover in our investigations."

"Oh," she said, mixed emotions suddenly flooding through her mind. She really didn't want CTU all over her case as she knew it may be taken out of her hands. "How so?"

"Your Mr Bush. We know him as Charlie Stonor. He's connected to the same gang we have been tracking for the last ten months. He's a grunt. Seems to be the one doing the risky stuff."

"Okay, so he connects with Martin Walker?"

"Yes, we have Walker and Stonor meeting in a coffee shop in London a few months ago. Walker passed him an envelope which we now believe contained a key to a safety deposit box. Stonor was seen going into a bank, although the CCTV we have from there is inconclusive, as he was wearing a hat and seemed to be aware of the surveillance. Anyhow, Stonor accessed a safety deposit box and, although the bank has no idea what it contained, they believe that Stonor may have removed the contents."

"Do you know who it belonged to?"

"Yes, and here's where it gets interesting. The box belonged to the real Mrs Deveraux."

Taylor's mind was suddenly racing. "Holy shit. So, we may have three members of your gang meeting up at this hotel and Bush, aka Stonor, had a falling-out with our fake Mrs Deveraux."

"That now seems likely."

"What is this about?"

"We are trying to clarify with Mrs Deveraux's family what was in the safety deposit box, but what we do know is that she is incredibly wealthy and the type of mark our team target. My guess is there are large amounts of cash connected to whatever they are doing."

"How do you want me to keep you up to date with what's going on?"

"I'm sending one of my DCIs straight over to you. He should be with you within the hour."

Taylor's heart sank but she knew she had no choice.

She would have to phone her chief super. This thing was now getting serious. As she tried to hold it together, a final question came to mind. "Is Walker his real name?"

"Funnily enough, yes it is. He seems to think that his best cover is to hide in plain sight."

The call was ended, but all Taylor could focus on was the last words that Sharpe had just uttered. *Hide in plain sight.* Exactly what Mr Young had said to her. Was Young Sharpe's man on the inside? They had already been running with this theory, but was this Sharpe's attempt to open his hand? Give her some subtle clues as to what was going on.

She closed her eyes for a second. So much to process and now a DCI turning up to interfere in her case. She refocused, picking up her phone to speak to her chief super.

Things were escalating fast, and she didn't like it.

28

MAJOR BRIEFING IN THE INCIDENT ROOM
SATURDAY, 9.30PM

By the time Taylor had finished her call with the chief super, the whole team had gathered back in the incident room. She was pleased with their enthusiasm and time discipline.

She blew out her cheeks. "Right, we have a lot to get through, but let me first update you with the things that have happened since our earlier briefing. Firstly, and most significantly, we appear to have landed ourselves in the middle of a counter terrorism case. I've been speaking to a detective superintendent at CTU, and it appears that three members of a gang who have been executing high-end robberies over the last two years have been in this hotel. Our victim, Mr Bush, is in fact a guy called Charlie Stonor, seemingly a foot soldier for the gang. Martin Walker, which is his real name, has been linked with this gang on several unsolved cases. Stonor and Walker have been under CTU surveillance and were spotted meeting in a London café before a potential safety deposit box robbery at a bank in London, executed by Stonor. The third member of the gang

118

is the woman that was posing as Mrs Deveraux. As we don't have anything to go on from the hotel, in respect of our mystery woman, he hasn't yet offered any idea who she could be. However, the key connection is that the safety deposit box that they targeted belongs to the real Mrs Deveraux, who is an incredibly wealthy woman. He is sending one of his DCIs to come and assist us. He should be here within the hour."

Taylor paused for a second to let the information sink in. There were no questions, which she took as a sign to carry on. "Okay, other things. The CTU guy said that Martin Walker is still in the hotel. He wouldn't confirm whether he had someone here who was keeping an eye on him, but it begs the question, how would he know this otherwise? Spence and I think that Mr Young is the CTU mole based on our interactions with him, as he made some strange comment about looking for things hiding in plain sight, a phrase repeated by CTU."

Taylor noticed a sudden flinch from Joshi but ignored it and ploughed on. "Also, our Miss Sanchez-Vicario is a significant person of interest. She is now speaking excellent English and every part of her seems fake, despite her having a passport. Our night porter Jamie Mellon is also on our radar. An ex-con with a bad attitude and no real explanation as to how he didn't see a dead body being moved in the night. We've also just had an incident where Mrs Walker's room has been ransacked. Someone seemed keen to find something in her room, which we assume is linked to her husband. Finally, a couple of minor things. Our admiral is apparently lying about his rank – he only made captain – and Mr Johnson from room 102 has a record as long as his arm."

She paused again. The faces remained alert and expectant.

"Right, time for your updates. Let's get our ducks in a row before the bloody CTU come in to interfere."

Taylor invited the SOCO team to go first. Brennan took the lead.

"Okay, ma'am. Chang and Ablett have given me a few more samples for processing, which I can do now I've got the mobile lab with me. However, what we do know is as follows. The blood in room 105 matches our victim. From Whiting's liaison with the ME on the PM, we know he was killed by a single blow to the head, meaning he was dead when he was thrown into the lake. We have also been able to cross-reference the DNA from our victim to samples collected from his room. There were no other DNA samples in that room other than the maid's, which we have been able to identify from a reference sample she gave us. We have a female DNA sample from room 105, which must belong to our fake Mrs Deveraux. Unfortunately, she is not known to us, so we have been unable to identify her."

Taylor was taking it all in but was distracted by Brennan's excitable manner. She could tell he was leading up to something big.

He smiled before he carried on speaking. "But the big news is that we can place Martin Walker in room 105. The DNA sample I managed to get from one of the glasses matches DNA from his toothbrush."

There was a deathly hush in the room as everyone tried to take in the implications of what Brennan had just said.

Taylor got there first. "Hold on, so there were three people in that room, not two." She looked at Spence and Ablett. "Did

Mrs Walker or the Kendals make any comment about the male voice they heard in terms of accents or tone?"

Spence and Ablett both shook their heads.

Taylor rubbed her chin. "Well, this puts a different complexion on what happened last night. If Bush/Stonor was double-crossing both of them, it follows that they worked together to move the body in the night, which makes a lot more sense."

Brennan interjected. "Sorry, ma'am, but just because we found Martin Walker's DNA in room 105, it doesn't necessarily mean he was there when the murder took place."

Taylor frowned. "Oh shit, good point, but if CTU are right, Walker is hiding somewhere in the hotel, which gives us a decent probability that he was somehow involved."

She turned to Ablett. "Any progress on finding our Mr Walker?"

"Not really," he replied, "but Chesters and I searched the hotel and found that one of the rooms under refurbishment was almost finished and could feasibly have been used as an overnight hidey-hole. There was empty food and drink packaging in the bin, which we've given to Brennan to see if the DNA matches."

Taylor looked at Brennan. "Yes, ma'am, I'll do those checks as soon as this briefing is done."

She turned back to Ablett. "Anything else?"

"Yes, ma'am. Chesters and I didn't really find any other obvious places he could be hiding, so we are running with the theory that he may be with another guest."

Taylor turned to Chang. "Unless he was in room 103."

"Yes, ma'am," said Chang, "there is definite evidence that someone was in that room last night, and Brennan has samples that he needs to process to confirm whether it was Mr Walker."

Taylor was getting frustrated at not having all the answers, but her annoyance was deflected by Ablett speaking. "One more thing, ma'am, which supports the theory that Walker didn't leave the hotel. We checked with all the local taxi firms and none of them had a booking from this hotel last night."

Taylor shook her head. Where the hell was Martin Walker?

29

THE BRIEFING CONTINUES IN THE INCIDENT ROOM
SATURDAY, 9.40PM

Taylor invited updates from the others. Mr Johnson was discussed but, despite his eclectic record, the fact he had an alibi for the time of the murder meant he was dismissed as a suspect. There was a similar discussion about Mr Morgan, the fake admiral, his dishonesty dismissed as an ego that wouldn't let go, now he wasn't the *dog's bollocks* in the Navy. The team surmised that his stories probably got more elaborate as time went on, his blustering, bullying manner putting people off engaging with his fantasies.

Joshi and Chesters summarised the work they had done on all the other guests. The team agreed that there wasn't anyone else who should really be on their radar.

The ransacking of Angela Walker's room cemented the theory that Martin Walker was squarely in the middle of this thing. It led to a long discussion about the fake Mrs Deveraux and where she could be. They had focused so much on the possibility that Martin Walker was hiding in the hotel that no one had considered the possibility that their mystery woman had done the same and was the perpetrator of the room trashing. Taylor made a mental note to get one of them to look more into that theory.

Jamie Mellon was the next subject of discussion. The views were mixed. His attitude to the police meant some of the team had him banged to rights but some of the others thought the fact he had come to the hotel on a rehabilitation programme should be seen as a good sign. Taylor was in the first group and had his name loud and prominent on the incident board. Whatever people's opinions, the question as to how he missed a dead body being moved from room 105 to the lake in the middle of the night remained unanswered.

Taylor next introduced the development around the walking stick. "Now, we've already discussed our theories about Young being the CTU mole, a question I will be asking their DCI about when he arrives. However, the maid who has been assisting us with our inquiries claims Young had a walking stick in his room that had not previously been there. We have since confirmed that the walking stick belongs to our victim, Mr Bush, which poses the inevitable question as to why Young has it in his possession."

"Have we asked him?" enquired Ablett.

"No. Spence and I want to see if he does anything with it. I did make a comment about his mobility in our last interview to see if this would flush him out, but he was as cool as a cucumber and didn't seem to make any connection to what I was getting at."

Just as Taylor's sentence was trailing off, Brennan got up and attached a picture of the blood stain in room 105 to the incident board. As all the faces turned to watch what he was doing, he tapped the picture. "There. Look. That circular mark in the blood stain is an indentation from the knob on the end of a walking stick. I'm sure of it."

Taylor and a couple of the others took a closer look at the picture. "Yes," said Taylor, "I think that is a decent assumption, which means Bush, sorry Stonor, had it with him when he was assaulted."

"We need to go and get it then," said Spence, "it's evidence."

"I agree," said Taylor. "As soon as we've finished this briefing, we are going to have another chat with our Mr Young."

Taylor was pleased that leads continued to develop and was now itching to go and confront Young, but she knew they had to discuss the complete picture before she could reasonably task out the next jobs.

As she scanned the incident board, she realised there was one more person they hadn't discussed. Miss Sanchez-Vicario. Joshi confirmed that they had been unable to validate her identity. The address in Spain was a fake; there was no record of her entering the country; and, despite her producing a passport, there was no evidence of her existing. The performance she had put on at her first interview, claiming not to speak English, added to the suspicions that she was somehow involved, but without anything more than suspicions, they had limited options to investigate her further or have justification to gain a warrant to search her room.

Just as Taylor was bringing the briefing to a natural conclusion, she noticed the deep frown on Joshi's face. "DC Joshi. You seem troubled. Tell me what you are thinking."

Joshi grimaced but focused on Taylor. "I don't know, ma'am, but there's something about that comment made by Young and CTU. You know, the *hiding in plain sight* comment."

"Go on."

"Well, so far, we seem to be assuming it's all connected to whatever Young is up to, but I have another theory."

The whole team looked at Joshi, expectantly.

Joshi drew in a deep breath. "Have we ever considered the possibility that Miss Sanchez-Vicario is also our fake Mrs Deveraux?"

30

WHO IS MRS DEVERAUX?
SATURDAY, 9.50PM

It started as a low murmur, which turned into several people talking at the same time, the volume rising as everyone tried to speak. Joshi's theory had livened up the room.

"Quiet," shouted Taylor. They all complied. "Well, DC Joshi, it seems you've put the cat amongst the pigeons with that theory, based on the noise levels in the room."

Spence spoke first. "It's got to be right. Why didn't we see that before?"

Taylor noticed a satisfied smile on Joshi's face.

"Now, hold on," she said, "I agree that Joshi's theory has some legs, but let's examine the evidence. Firstly, did we get a description of Mrs Deveraux in terms of height, weight, build?"

The team looked at each other. Their blank faces confirmed Taylor's immediate concerns. "Okay, that's a problem, but on the positive side, we did have a description of what Mrs Deveraux was wearing. The hat, glasses and wig are a sure-fire sign that she was trying to disguise herself despite the *performance* that the maître d' described in the restaurant. If we consider this alongside what we know about Sanchez-Vicario, then the theory does work. The maid said she had odd make-up in her room, which I am guessing is the type of stuff they use in the theatre. When we interviewed her, we all saw how heavily made up she was. It follows that this was further evidence of her trying to disguise her identify."

Taylor noticed Joshi leaning forward, almost like she was waiting for further validation of her theory. She saw her face drop as soon as she started the next sentence.

"But… am I correct in recalling that we do not have a DNA sample for Sanchez-Vicario?"

The team instinctively looked at the members of the SOCO team. Whiting took the lead. "That's right, ma'am. We have a female DNA sample from room 105, which must belong to our fake Mrs Deveraux, but we have been unable to match this to anyone known to the police, including Sanchez-Vicario."

"We could try and get a sample off Sanchez-Vicario without her realising," said Ablett.

Taylor frowned. "I do hope you are not suggesting that we compromise the chain of custody by obtaining a sample by false pretences."

Ablett did the cheeky smile that he and Spence always used when they thought they could use their boyish charms to get away with not doing a proper job. "Of course not, ma'am, but you know, if the opportunity presented itself…"

Taylor fixed Ablett with a firm expression. "I don't cut corners, Sergeant. We do things by the book round here."

There was a sudden hush in the room. Taylor could immediately sense the room dividing. The DCs and the SOCO team all seem to nod in unison, respectful of Taylor's statement. Ablett and Spence did not. A collective look of annoyance on their faces that pissed Taylor off.

She decided not to respond and addressed the wider group. "Look, I think DC Joshi has a credible theory here, but we must stick to the evidence. I am happy for us to request a DNA sample from Sanchez-Vicario, but if she refuses, there is nothing we can do. Spence, please go and find Sanchez-Vicario and make that request. Explain that we are asking for voluntary samples to exclude people from our inquiries. Take Joshi with you."

Spence nodded and looked at Ablett. His face was still pinched with disapproval. Taylor ignored it and carried on.

"There is one person who could give us a good description of our Mrs Deveraux. The maid. She told me that she took up some coat hangers to her room when she first arrived. I will give Miss Stimic a call to see if her description could feasibly match the physical make-up of Sanchez-Vicario."

The sea of faces stared back at her.

"So, here's what I want in the next half an hour, before the CTU turn up. Spence and Joshi. Talk to Sanchez-Vicario. Brennan. Process those additional samples ASAP. I want to know who was where. Chang. Process Mrs Walker's room quickly and then help her move her stuff. Whiting. I want Bush's room searched from top to bottom. I'm running with the theory that he had something that Walker and Deveraux were expecting him to deliver from that safety deposit box. The fact that the Walkers' room was trashed suggests that someone thinks Bush gave them the *merchandise*. Let's see if we can find anything in Bush's room to support that theory. Finally, Ablett and Chesters. Go and get Mr Young and bring him back here. I want another word with him."

31

MISS SANCHEZ-VICARIO
SATURDAY, 10.05PM

Spence and Joshi walked up to room 101 and tapped on the door. The wind outside was making the old house creak and groan, but they couldn't hear anything from inside the room. They banged on the door a bit harder and called out her name. No response.

Spence looked at Joshi. "Do you think she's in there?"

Joshi frowned. "I'm not sure, sir. Why don't we see if she's downstairs."

They walked down the stairs and back towards reception. As Spence emerged into the entrance hallway he stopped, instinctively putting an arm out to stop Joshi's progress. She shot him a look of confusion. He responded with an eye movement that suggested she looked towards the lounge.

As they both looked into the room, Joshi immediately knew what Spence was up to. Sanchez-Vicario was drinking a glass of wine.

He manhandled Joshi back towards the bar area and

proceeded to grab his gloves and an evidence bag. "Sir," said Joshi, "the boss won't be happy if you do that."

Spence shook his head. "Don't worry about it. If the DNA off that glass proves that Sanchez-Vicario is in fact Deveraux, it will blow this case wide open."

"But—"

"But nothing, Joshi. The boss had to say that. She's the one in charge and has her arse on the line. If we can help her crack this case, she won't worry about how we got a conviction. And anyway, she's been blurring the lines of proper investigative procedure by using that maid to search guests' rooms. No, I'm sorry, this don't seem like some run-of-the-mill murder case. If CTU are involved, this is big-time-Charlie stuff and we need every edge we can get."

Spence gave Joshi no opportunity to protest further and proceeded to walk back towards the lounge. Joshi followed reluctantly and her heart sank further when Spence quickened his pace. She realised why. Sanchez-Vicario had just walked out of the lounge and up the stairs, oblivious of their presence.

She caught him up just as he was depositing the glass in the forensic evidence bag, a big grin on his face. Joshi said no more. She had made her feelings clear, but he was her superior and she would make sure that if the shit hit the fan, he would be squarely in the firing line. She sensed that Taylor was intolerant of this macho bravado and was confident she would have her back when this all went south.

She followed Spence outside, in search of Brennan and the mobile lab. It was parked in the first bit of car park on the road that led away from the hotel entrance. Spence didn't stand on ceremony and went straight in, garnering a disapproving look from Brennan, who was in the middle of processing the new samples. "Something I can do for you, Sergeant?" he said.

Joshi stifled a laugh as Spence's enthusiasm was cut down with Brennan's spiky attitude. She shook her head in resignation as Spence brushed it off and demanded attention. "Yes, process this."

Brennan glanced at the evidence bag. "What is it?"

Spence shot him a confused look. "It's a glass."

Brennan sighed. "I can see that, but what relevance does it have to this case?"

"It has Sanchez-Vicario's DNA on it."

Brennan stopped what he was doing and took the bag off Spence. "Oh, she gave you this voluntarily?"

Spence didn't respond. Brennan looked at Joshi, who gave an almost imperceptible shake of the head.

"I can't process this," Brennan said.

"You what," exclaimed Spence.

"The boss was clear about your instructions. A voluntary sample or nothing."

"What the fuck difference does it make to you?"

Brennan stood up, changing the dynamic where Spence's height had put him in the dominant position. "The fuck difference it makes to me, Sergeant, is that you will compromise the chain of custody if we process this sample. We only have a theory that she's Deveraux, and without better probable cause, this evidence will be blown out of court."

Joshi realised she was holding her breath. A classic *Mexican stand-off*. Brennan didn't flinch, staring Spence down. He won. Spence shook his head and stormed out.

Joshi looked at Brennan. "Thank you. I did warn him, but he didn't listen."

Brennan smiled. "An arrogant prick that one. Probably be an ACC before he's thirty-five. Exactly the type the suits like."

Joshi grimaced. "Yeah, you're probably right, but I'm not having him put the boss in the shit."

Brennan nodded. "You did the right thing, and I'll back you all the way. Don't you worry about that."

32

MR YOUNG IN THE INCIDENT ROOM
SATURDAY, 10.10PM

It didn't take long for Ablett and Chesters to return with Young. As he walked into the room, Taylor could tell he wasn't pleased.

"This is getting real tiresome, Chief Inspector," he said, a distinct hint of anger in his tone.

"Well, Mr Young, or whatever your real name is, maybe if you started to tell us the truth, this wouldn't be necessary."

Taylor was surprised to see his anger quickly turn to amusement. "What an interesting opening. What makes you think that I'm not who I say I am?"

"How about no evidence of you entering the country anytime in the last six months. How about no evidence of the flight you claim you've booked from Gatwick in the next few days. How about you having a critical piece of evidence in your room, which you have failed to tell us about. Do you want me to go on?"

The steely coldness in Young's manner that Taylor had seen the first time she interviewed him was still there. He rubbed his chin. "Hmm, interesting. You've clearly... now what's that phrase you English use... got your knickers in a twist."

Taylor was steaming. Everywhere she turned there were arrogant male arseholes trying to belittle her. She wasn't having it. "I can arrest you for perverting the course of justice."

"Good luck with that," he said, his response laden with the arrogance that was annoying Taylor.

Taylor tried to read what he was playing at. Why was he so confident that she couldn't arrest him? She ignored the growing niggle in her brain and cracked on.

"Your real name please."

"It's Mr Chesney Young, aged fifty-four from Augusta, Georgia." He smiled, goading Taylor.

"Really, so can you explain why the UK passport authority does not have you entering the country?"

He pulled a wide-eyed expression. "IT, huh. You can never rely on it. I should know."

"That's not an answer."

"It's the only one you are going to get."

"Okay, *Mr Young*, explain to me why you have a critical piece of evidence in your possession."

Young didn't answer for a second, leaning forward with a deep frown across his face. "I really don't know what you mean, Chief Inspector. Can you be more specific?"

Taylor glanced at Ablett. He was staring out of the window, still pissed at her. Chesters was at least watching the interaction, but she knew she was basically on her own with this one.

"The walking stick."

Young made an attempt to look nonplussed, but for the first time in this interaction, Taylor noticed a slight twitch in his facial features.

"It was seen. In your room."

"I don't own a walking stick."

Taylor was just about holding her patience. She would have to go with his pathetic attempts to annoy her.

"I know, Mr Young. It belongs to our murder victim, which begs the question why you have it."

Young sighed and threw his key across the table. "If it makes you feel any better, go and search my room. You won't find any walking stick."

Taylor shot a look at Ablett and Chesters. Ablett at least had re-engaged and stood up, grabbing the key. "I'll be a minute," he said, walking quickly out of the room, followed by Chesters.

Taylor eyed him curiously. "You're a real piece of work. You've obviously ditched it, otherwise why would you be so brazen?"

Young smirked. "It's a right old mystery, ain't it, Detective."

Taylor was ready to lose it but decided to calm herself by standing up and refilling her coffee cup. She didn't speak, hoping that the silence might unnerve him. It didn't work.

She was annoyed at herself for breaking the silence first, but there was one more thing that was bugging her. "Okay, Mr Young, while we are waiting, can you explain to me what you meant when you said to look for what's *hiding in plain sight*?"

He pulled a disinterested expression. "Just something to say."

"I don't think so. I don't believe for a minute that you're an IT guy. I think you're here watching someone, and you thought it would be funny to throw me a bone. Am I right?"

"You're the detective. You tell me."

Taylor shook her head. Whatever he was, she wasn't going to get anything out of him. She turned away from him and stared out of the window, curious to see a fox sniffing around the cars in the dimly lit car park. A weird metaphor for her current situation, though she wasn't sure whether she was the fox or the prey.

Five minutes later, Ablett and Chesters were back. Taylor's heart sank as Ablett re-entered the room, shaking his head. Young smirked. "Can I go now?"

Taylor snapped. "Mr Young, I'm arresting you—"

Her sentence was immediately cut off. "Ah, ah, ah," he said, wagging his finger annoyingly in her direction, "I don't think so."

Just as Taylor was about to protest, he pulled a passport-style document out of his pocket and lobbed it across the table. Taylor's heart sank at the words emblazoned on the document: US DIPLOMATIC IMMUNITY.

33

Taylor had been stewing for nearly fifteen minutes. Young had played her for a fool, ceremoniously grabbing his documents and walking out, once he allowed his big reveal to land. She tried to take some solace in the fact that she had been right about him. He wasn't an IT guy. He was a spook. CIA she guessed, which just added to the sense that this thing was so much bigger than she thought. She glanced at her watch, wondering when the CTU guy was going to turn up. There were so many questions that he had to answer, not least why she was seemingly being played like a fiddle by everyone around her.

She was dog-tired, but she had to carry on. As she rubbed her eyes, there was a commotion at the incident room door as the team filed back in. All, that was, except Spence. As they settled around the table, she looked at Joshi.

Joshi picked up on the vibe. "He's... um, having a break."

Taylor glanced at the other faces, trying to work out what was going on. Nothing was forthcoming. She cracked on. She didn't have time for Spence to have a hissy fit.

"Right, SOCO team. I hope you have something for me."

Chang went first. "I processed Mrs Walker's room and the only significant thing we found was an artificial strand of hair."

Taylor caught on straight away. "What? From a wig?"

"Yes, ma'am."

"Well, well. So that rather places our fake Mrs Deveraux in Mrs Walker's room."

Chang grimaced. "Well, possibly, but as we don't have any samples from the wig that was observed by the maid in room 105, it's impossible to prove."

Taylor looked at Brennan and Whiting. "That's a good point. Did we not find any evidence of a wig in that room?"

"No, ma'am," they chorused.

Taylor refocused on Whiting. "What about our victim's room?"

"I haven't quite finished in there, but I can't find anything suspicious. There are no secret compartments in his luggage, no hidey-holes in the room where he might have stashed something. At the moment, it's clean."

Taylor frowned and turned to Brennan. "Come on then. Give me some good news."

Brennan smiled. "Well, there are some things that will help. Firstly, I can confirm that the DNA samples from the food and water packets, which the team found in the room under refurbishment, do not belong to Martin Walker. In fact, we couldn't match them with anyone on this case or known to the police. This means that the only evidence we have of Walker being somewhere he shouldn't be is in room 105."

Taylor turned to the wider team. "Hmm, if we believe the CTU assertions that Walker has not left the hotel, I think we need to run with your theory, DC Chesters. Someone is hiding him in their room."

There was a brief smile from Chesters, seemingly happy to get some credit. Taylor refocused on Brennan. "Anything else?"

"Oh yes," he said. "We know who was in room 103 last night."

34

CTU ARRIVAL
SATURDAY, 10.37PM

The team hardly had time to process what Brennan had said when the door to the incident room opened, and a tall, smartly dressed man entered the room. He strode up to the team, scanning the faces, eventually landing on Taylor.

"Can we clear the room, Chief Inspector?"

Taylor was immediately annoyed with his arrogance and superiority, not helped by the fact that he looked like a clone of Spence and Ablett. Another alpha male, groomed to within an inch of his life, a face that had probably broken a hundred hearts and a body that had been sculpted in the gym. She stood up, offering her hand. "I'm Detective Chief Inspector Chloe Taylor; I'm the SIO on this case."

He reciprocated the handshake. "I'm Detective Chief Inspector Simon Banbury from CTU. I need to speak to you alone."

Taylor resisted the urge to fight this battle. "Okay, team, give us a few minutes to catch up and I will call you back in when I can. If you have tasks to be getting on with then please do them, otherwise go and sit in the lounge and have a quick break. I won't be long. Oh, and someone find our errant DS."

Once the team filed out, Banbury launched in. "I'm sorry about that, but we need to debrief before I can decide what can be released to your wider team."

Taylor decided to let him have the floor for now. She nodded her agreement.

"Okay, so I think my super has given you the basics, but I'll take you through where we are with the case. Basically, we have been tracking a UK cell who have been linked to several high-end robberies. They've knocked off numerous jewellers, done a couple of security vans that were transporting decent amounts of cash, and their most recent MO is to target the safety deposit boxes of wealthy people. The police always seem to be one step behind them, but by using a decent amount of surveillance, we have been able to identify a number of individuals involved in this group."

"I assume this includes Walker and Bush, aka Stonor."

"Yes."

"Why haven't you bought them in for questioning?"

"They are pretty small fish in what we believe is a significant cyber terrorism ring, based out of New York. The real money behind these crimes comes from extortion. They hack into the networks of major companies and hold their data to ransom, only releasing it when they've been paid a big wodge of cash. You never hear about these incidents because the companies don't want the bad PR. We've been hoping that the UK team would eventually lead us to the bigger fish, as we think they are generating cash to fund the team that run the cyber terrorism. I can imagine that the skills needed to pull this off are significant, and a hacker of that standing is going to demand a lot of money to do what they do. They also need significant computer technology to work their scams."

Taylor nodded. "Okay, figures, so where does my little situation fit in?"

"I think the super confirmed that your victim, who you know as Bush, is in fact Charlie Stonor. He's definitely a grunt in this operation. Seems to do all the risky stuff. We have his face on CCTV at several of the jobs. Walker is a go-between. Seems to be Stonor's handler, probably briefing him on each job. We've had them meeting together on a regular basis before jobs are pulled off."

"What about our fake Mrs Deveraux?"

"We think that is Maria Gonzalez. She's the fence. We have her meeting with Walker on several occasions, receiving packets or briefcases from him. The big problem is that she has an incredible knack of avoiding detection. We've lost her trail every time, although we are fairly sure she meets her contact at the major UK dockyards, the ones that move huge numbers of shipping containers from the UK across the world. It's a perfect cover for small packages of cash or jewellery to be smuggled out of the country."

"Do you have a picture of Gonzalez?"

Banbury opened his laptop and punched away on the keyboard, turning the screen towards Taylor when the photo was on the screen. Taylor stared at the image. "Hmm, maybe," she said.

Banbury looked at her expectantly. "We have a single woman staying here, called Maria Sanchez-Vicario. We are running with the theory that she is our fake Mrs

Deveraux and booked two rooms in the hotel, playing the part of Deveraux first and then turning into Sanchez-Vicario. She pretended not to speak English to start with, but when I threatened to arrest her, she suddenly found her voice, speaking perfect English with a Spanish twang. The maid said she had loads of odd make-up in her room, which I think is theatrical, adding to the theory that she is disguising her identity. There are some elements of that picture that could be her, such as face and eye shape, but the make-up she was wearing here definitely makes it hard to be conclusive."

"I'd say that is a good call," replied Banbury. "One of the reasons Gonzalez is so hard to track is she is a master of disguise."

Taylor remembered that she was going to call the maid to get a better description of the fake Mrs Deveraux, but she was now feeling certain that they had their woman. The guilt of using Eva Stimic in the way she had still troubled her, but now things were hotting up, she didn't have time to worry about what had been done over the last few crazy hours. She refocused on the conversation with Banbury.

"So, do you have any theories as to what happened here?" Taylor said.

"Isn't it obvious?" retorted Banbury. "Our Mr Stonor has broken rank. I reckon he got fed up with taking all the risks and decided to keep the latest booty for himself. Based on what you told the super, I reckon the incident in that hotel room was supposed to be the exchange, and when he refused to give them the merchandise, they killed him."

"Yeah, I get that, but surely doesn't it leave them with some missing merchandise?"

"Yes, by the sounds of it."

Taylor nodded. "Which explains why Mrs Walker's room was ransacked."

"Oh, really."

"Yeah, we're processing the scene and found a strand from a wig, which is consistent with what the maid said she saw in Mrs Deveraux's room and this whole disguise theory. Based on what you've said, I'm now more convinced than ever that Sanchez-Vicario is both our Mrs Deveraux and this Gonzalez creature."

They both paused for a moment to process their exchange of information, but it didn't take long for one of Taylor's major niggles to surface. "Oh, your super was being cagey about it, but you have someone here, doing surveillance."

Taylor noticed the briefest of smiles crack across Banbury's face. "We do," he said. "We managed to get ears on a meeting in a café between Stonor and Walker, and they mentioned this hotel as being the drop point for whatever was going down."

"So, I was right. We have a guy called Young, who is claiming to be an IT guy, who has been very evasive, but I could tell he had been intelligence trained." Taylor's self-congratulatory mood was short-lived as she noticed the deep frown on Banbury's face. "Oh, that face suggests I'm wrong."

"Er, well yes. The guy we have on the ground is not called Young and his cover is not as an IT guy."

"He showed me US diplomatic papers when I tried to arrest him. I assumed he was CIA and that it naturally followed that he was your man on the inside."

Banbury immediately bolted up from his seat, muttering expletives under his breath. He went to the far end of the room and made a phone call, which Taylor could not hear. After a few minutes, he returned to the table, his face like thunder.

"Something up?" she probed, mischievously.

"I'll say, if he is fucking CIA they have no jurisdiction here. I've just escalated it to the super. Someone needs to come down on our US friends like a tonne of bricks. If they are interfering in our investigation that is totally fucking out of order."

Taylor let the rant subside and asked the obvious question. "So, who is your man?"

Banbury calmed himself and crafted a text message. A few minutes later, the door to the incident room opened.

Taylor could not believe who was standing there.

35

THE HOTEL LOUNGE
SATURDAY, 10.40PM

Most of the team gathered in the lounge. The SOCO team had gone back to processing their respective rooms and evidence, leaving Ablett, Joshi and Chesters to sit and wait.

"Where's Spence?" said Ablett.

Joshi realised he'd aimed the question at her. "Oh, um, he's taking a break."

"Bullshit," replied Ablett. "What happened?"

Joshi tried to resist the urge to be bullied by Ablett but eventually decided that life was too short to get in the way of an ambitious sergeant looking out for his mate. "He did something he shouldn't have done."

Ablett laughed. "I doubt that."

Joshi shrugged. "Well, he got a DNA sample from Sanchez-Vicario without her consent."

Ablett leant forward. "Oh, how?"

"We went to her room to ask for a sample, but she wasn't there. Spence and I went downstairs, and she was sat in here drinking a glass of wine."

Ablett picked up on what happened straight away and clapped his hands. "Result!" he shouted.

"No, sir, I'm sorry. When Spence took the glass without consent and gave it to Brennan for processing, he rightly refused to handle it."

Ablett snorted in derision. "Oh, fuck off. Do you have any idea how important that evidence could be to this case? If that glass places Sanchez-Vicario in room 105, we have probable cause to search her room and bring her in for questioning."

Joshi just sat there, not knowing how to respond. Ablett and Spence were clearly cut from the same cloth, but she didn't have the rank to pull them into line. She was glad of Brennan's support, but she knew ultimately it would be up to the boss to decide what to do with the glass. She did the only thing she could and removed herself from the situation. "I'm going outside for a ciggie," she said, not waiting for any more of Ablett's bad attitude to bring her evening down.

Ablett watched Joshi walk out and looked at Chesters. "Fuck me, must be the wrong time of the month."

Chesters didn't seek to validate Ablett's misogyny but tried to act as peacemaker. "Do you think we'd get away with processing that glass then?"

"Course we would, especially if it confirms she was at the scene of a murder."

"Why did Brennan refuse to process it?"

"Ah, he's just a bloody jobsworth. Probably still needs his mum to wipe his arse."

"What about the boss? Do you think she will allow it?"

Ablett screwed up his face. "Bloody women. Why can't they just leave the important work to the men? We aren't

149

scared to take risks. To get results. I don't credit her with the balls to make the tough decisions."

"Too bloody right."

Ablett and Chesters turned to see where the new voice had come from. Spence was standing in the doorway.

"I assume we are talking about our chief inspector," Spence said.

"Too right, mate," replied Ablett. "She's gonna fuck this case right up."

Chesters couldn't stand it anymore and made an excuse to leave.

Spence looked at Ablett. "What's up with him?"

"Oh, I dunno. Let them go down with that stupid cow. We need to stick together, mate, if we are going to come out of this with any credibility."

Spence sat down. "What's going on? Why are you all down here?"

Ablett smirked. "CTU are here. Their DCI started throwing his weight around the minute he arrived and told us all to bugger off."

Spence's eyes widened. "Really. This might just be the break we need. Let's hope he takes over the investigation."

36

CTU IN THE INCIDENT ROOM
SATURDAY, 10.55PM

Taylor was gobsmacked. Standing in the door to the incident room was Jamie Mellon.

"I... I don't understand," she spluttered.

She tried to ignore the smug look on Mellon's face as she focused her question to Banbury, who wasted no time in resolving her confusion. "Can I introduce Detective Sergeant Jamie Wellington. He has been working undercover on this case for several months. Mellon is his cover identity, and the stuff you will have found about him being an ex-con on a rehabilitation programme is all part of the fake cover story. We placed him in the hotel about six weeks ago as a porter-cum-gardener so he could keep tabs on when our little gang arrived."

Taylor looked back at Mellon/Wellington, trying not to hold a grudge at the way he'd interacted with her team, but his next comment suggested she hadn't hidden her feelings well enough.

"I'm really sorry, ma'am, you know for the anti-police stuff. All part of the persona."

Taylor did an involuntary *huh*. Banbury cut across the awkward introductions. "Sergeant. Can you tell our DCI what you've observed over the last few days?"

"Yes, sir. We had intel that Walker, Stonor and Gonzalez may be using this hotel as a meet. I was able to verify Walker and Stonor's arrival pretty easily, but Gonzalez uses multiple identities and disguises, making her difficult to track. We had three single female bookings for the weekend, and I've been trying to establish whether any of them could be her."

Taylor's annoyance with Mellon/Wellington mellowed, and she engaged in the debrief. "My DC has a theory that the fake Mrs Deveraux and Miss Sanchez-Vicario are one of the same. Deveraux was down at dinner on Friday evening, but Sanchez-Vicario wasn't. We haven't been able to place Sanchez-Vicario in room 105, where the murder took place, as we don't have any DNA samples. I sent my team to see if they could get a voluntary sample from her but, with all this drama, I don't know what's happened there."

"I think that's a good call," he replied. "Based on what we know about Gonzalez, I would say that Deveraux and Sanchez-Vicario could be her playing both roles."

The niggle that had been preying on Taylor's mind about involving Eva Stimic once again came to the surface, but she trusted her and desperately wanted to validate what the CTU team were saying. She stood up and asked them to wait for a second, dialling the number that Eva had given her. She was relieved when the call was answered. Taylor gave her apologies for ringing so late, but Eva was delighted to be relied upon once again. Taylor posed the question and listened intently to what Eva was saying about Mrs Deveraux.

As Taylor disconnected the call, she flashed a brief smile, glad that she had her own sources of intel to feel like she was still in control of the case. "Sorry about that. I've been meaning to make that call. The maid who cleaned the rooms has been helping me, and she was one of the few people to get a really good look at Mrs Deveraux. She has confirmed our theory that the height and build of Mrs Deveraux is consistent with what we know about Sanchez-Vicario."

As her sentence trailed off, further discussion was interrupted by the incident room door opening. Banbury flashed a look of annoyance at Taylor, but she ignored it as she saw the concerned face of Brennan staring back at her. She apologised and went to see Brennan. As he spoke, her stress levels started to grow. She dismissed him and went back to the discussion.

"Something up?" said Banbury.

Taylor frowned. "Yeah, a few team issues that I need to sort out. Seems we've obtained a DNA sample for Sanchez-Vicario under false pretences."

"Oh," said Banbury, "what are you doing with it?"

"I've told my SOCO to process it against the female sample we have from room 105. I've made it clear that it can't be used in the chain of custody, but if it confirms Sanchez-Vicario was at the murder scene, we may have probable cause to search her room."

Banbury nodded. "I don't think we're far off that now, but I guess that would strengthen any application for a warrant. I can probably get one now based on an anti-terrorist angle, but maybe we should wait and see."

As the three officers took a moment to reflect, Taylor knew she had to deal with the elephant in the room.

"Um, Sergeant, I'm sorry to be so blunt, but while I wait for that sample to be processed, I wonder if you could explain something for me."

Her question was met with confused faces from both the CTU colleagues.

She went for it. "Could you explain to me why we found your DNA in room 103?"

37

A MYSTERY GETS SOLVED
SATURDAY, 11.05PM

The accusation hung in the air. Banbury sat open-mouthed looking at Mellon. "Sergeant, would you like to explain yourself?" he said, his tone laced with anger.

Mellon's chirpy attitude was gone in an instant. "Er, sir, ma'am, I'm sorry. I took a nap halfway through my shift. The hotel was quiet, and I was so tired. I know I shouldn't have done it."

Silence fell on proceedings, as both DCIs tried to reconcile what they'd just heard.

Taylor spoke first. "What time was this?"

"Um, I don't know exactly, maybe between 3 and 4am."

Taylor rubbed her eyes. "You know what this means, Sergeant?"

"Yes, ma'am."

Banbury look confused, not following the implications of the interaction.

Taylor picked up on his uncertainty. "The thing is, one of the major questions we had not been able to answer about this case, was how one or more of our perps had managed to move a dead body from room 105 to the lake in the middle of the night."

Taylor watched as Banbury's emerging understanding began to show in his facial expressions. She carried on. "We have a witness from the room next door who said she heard noises outside the room in, as she put it, *the middle of the night.* Now, she was unable to verify the exact timings, but I'm guessing it would have been around the time you were having your impromptu nap."

Mellon bowed his head. "I'm sorry. I think that is most likely as there had not been any movement around the hotel from about midnight. I was on reception the whole rest of the time and would definitely have seen or heard something happening around room 105."

Banbury stood up, muttering expletives under his breath. "Right, DS Wellington, I suggest you get back to your role as Jamie Mellon before we blow your cover and make any more mistakes in this case."

Taylor and Banbury watched as Mellon scuttled off. "Holy shit," said Banbury, "I'm so sorry about that. I'll deal with him at another time but for now, I still need him in place."

"I understand," replied Taylor. "I've got a couple of misbehaving sergeants myself that I need to deal with."

They both took a moment to refill their coffee cups as Taylor asked the inevitable question. "Are you taking over this investigation? Do I need to stand all my people down?"

"No, we must keep everyone thinking that we are focused on the murder case as the police priority. You and I need to discuss the strategy moving forward, especially as it's getting late and we can't reasonably expect to speak to any guests unless we are going to place them under arrest."

Taylor nodded. "I'm inclined to pare my team back to a few individuals. We've got through the grunt work and my SOCO team is almost done. Once we know about Sanchez-Vicario, we are going to have to make some decisions about search warrants. The real buggeration factor is that the majority of guests are checking out in the morning."

Banbury's stress lines formed on his forehead once again. "The problem is, if Walker and Gonzalez are still in the hotel, we need them to lead us to the big fish. I'm guessing that the fact you've been questioning all the guests will have got them nervous."

Taylor immediately understood the implications of what Banbury was saying. "Oh, so you think they will bolt in the night?"

"I'm not sure but, regardless, we need to be vigilant. As well as my sergeant, I reckon we could do with a couple of your team patrolling the hotel, just in case."

"Okay, I can do that."

"In the meantime, you and I need to run some scenarios for overnight and in the morning, because there is still one major issue here."

"What's that?"

"From what you've told me, I've got a feeling that Walker and Gonzalez do not have the merchandise that Stonor promised to deliver."

Taylor gasped. "Of course, which means whatever this *merchandise* is, it must still be in the hotel somewhere."

"Exactly."

38

THE HOTEL LOUNGE
SATURDAY, 11.15PM

Taylor left Banbury in the incident room, as he said he had several secure calls to make. She grabbed the SOCOs from the mobile lab and gathered the whole team in the lounge. She glanced briefly at Mellon, who was sat on reception as she walked past. He avoided her gaze.

She could sense the tension in the room. Brennan had told her what happened with the DNA sample, and he had ended up being a sympathetic ear for both Joshi and Chesters, who'd been distressed by Ablett and Spence's behaviour. She was ready for them.

She fixed Ablett and Spence with a firm expression, as they sat next to each other on one of the leather sofas, smugness washing all over them. "Right, I've been talking to the DCI from CTU, and whilst this investigation remains our lead, we have a significant CTU angle. This means that we need a tight, focused team that can be trusted to deal with highly sensitive information about a significant CTU case, whilst continuing to bring the perpetrator of our murder to justice. This means the team will need to be reduced in number with immediate effect."

Taylor tried not to smile as the look on Ablett and Spence's faces changed from smug to concerned, as they began to realise what she might be doing. She didn't waste any time in bursting their bubble. "Right, I don't need any sergeants on the team as CTU will be providing this resource. I can also reduce down to two SOCOs."

"You what!" exclaimed Spence.

Taylor kept icy cool. "You got a problem with that, Sergeant?"

"Well, yes. You need our expertise. Surely."

"And what specific expertise would that be, DS Spence? Are you an expert on counter terrorism cases?"

Spence spluttered, "Er, no, but what the fuck difference does that make?"

Taylor crossed her arms. "I think you are demonstrating with your little outburst that you don't have the maturity to be liaising with CTU colleagues on such a sensitive case. Please get your stuff and go home. Immediately. I will talk to you and Ablett later in the week when this case is under control."

Spence stood up, closely followed by Ablett. "Under control. What a fucking joke."

Taylor let the room settle for a second as the whirlwind of their exits played out. She turned to the remaining team members. "I'm sorry about that. I know a few of you have had to deal with the bad attitudes of our sergeants over the last couple of hours and I can assure you that I will be dealing with it in due course."

Joshi smiled. "Thank you, ma'am. I don't think I've ever come across police officers with such a bad attitude. They were completely undermining you."

"I know, and thank you for your loyalty. It means a lot."

She turned to the SOCO team. "Miss Chang, I'm happy to let you go, to enable Brennan and Whiting to keep the continuity on this case. If that's okay with you."

"Of course," replied Chang. "I'm glad I've been able to help in some way and happy to come back in if you need me."

Taylor thanked her and asked the team to go back to the incident room for a briefing with the DCI from CTU. There was a palpable change of mood in the group as the *bad boys* had been removed.

The stress and tiredness threatened to overwhelm, but she steeled herself for the next phase. Bed was a long way away.

*

Spence and Ablett grabbed their stuff and began to pace down the corridor towards the exit. Spence was fuming, every sentence laden with expletives and criticism of Taylor. Ablett fuelled the fire by agreeing with everything he was saying.

As they reached reception and the front door to the hotel, they glanced briefly at Jamie Mellon, who just glowered at them. Just as Spence was about to turn the large metal handle to open the door, he spotted something in the umbrella rack. He did an eye movement that urged Ablett to look at what he was seeing. Ablett's wide-eyed expression confirmed he saw what Spence was looking at.

Spence didn't waste a second and grabbed the item from the rack, whispering in Ablett's ear. "Let's see how the stupid bitch gets on with cracking the case without this."

39

BRIEFING WITH CTU IN THE INCIDENT ROOM
SATURDAY, 11.30PM

As Taylor re-entered the incident room, she was pleased to see that the hotel had replenished their coffee jugs and left a load of biscuits and pastries to keep them going. Banbury was still on the phone, his general demeanour suggesting that the call was not going his way.

Taylor encouraged the team to gather around the table as Banbury ended his call. He turned to greet the group, a forced smile on his face. "Welcome," he said, "I'm DCI Banbury from the Counter Terrorism Unit. I've been assigned to work with you on this case, as your DCI and I are now certain that we have a major crossover from your murder case with a long-term CTU op."

Taylor smiled, glad that he wasn't acting like Spence and Ablett, seemingly respectful of her rank and gender. She introduced Chesters, Joshi, Brennan and Whiting before opening the briefing with a pressing question. "Now, I know the DNA sample from Sanchez-Vicario has caused some stress in the team and has hastened the removal of

Spence and Ablett. However, I have authorised Brennan to process it as a non-chain-of-custody item. So, I'm on tenterhooks, Mr Brennan. Is there a match?"

Brennan smiled. "Yes, ma'am. The DNA sample from the glass that Sanchez-Vicario was seen drinking from matches the female sample we found in room 105."

Taylor nodded at Banbury and turned back to the team. "Wow. Well done, especially you, DC Joshi, the first one who spotted the possible connection."

"Thank you, ma'am."

"Right, now I know from a local police operation perspective this gives us enough probable cause to apply for and execute a warrant on Sanchez-Vicario. However, the CTU angle means that DCI Banbury and I need to consider a range of strategies before leaping into a potential search and arrest. We are now assuming that Sanchez-Vicario and our missing Mr Walker are the prime suspects in our murder case, but we also need them active to assist with the CTU case. I will let DCI Banbury explain."

Banbury explained the background to the CTU case, including the real identities of the gang of three that were at the hotel. He chose not to divulge Jamie Mellon's undercover identify, figuring that the fewer people who knew, the better. The team asked a few questions, and by the end of Banbury's briefing, they all understood that the case was now much bigger than a simple local murder.

"Okay," said Taylor, "I hope you can see that this case is much more complex than it first seemed, and whilst we do not underestimate the importance of solving this murder, we need to maximise the potential for cracking more than one case. I hope I don't need to remind you that DCI

Banbury has given you details of a confidential CTU op and therefore there is to be no discussion about this case outside this team."

She was met with compliant nods and determined faces.

"Okay, I know we are all tired, and I'm happy for you to use the room put aside for us if you need a power nap and to freshen up. However, whilst DCI Banbury and I work on the strategies for overnight and in the morning, I still have some taskings for each of you."

As the supportive manner of the team continued to pervade the room, Taylor couldn't help thinking how much easier this was without the misogynistic attitudes of Spence and Ablett. She pushed on. "Right, Chesters and Joshi. I want you to patrol the hotel throughout the night. As I've said, I'm happy for you to both have a break, but please ensure that at least one of you is always patrolling. Brennan and Whiting. Likewise, about the breaks, but do another sweep of rooms 105, 107 and Mrs Walker's room, 104. I know you think you have processed everything, but please check again. Any little advantage we can gain is vital if we are to get on the front foot. Finally, I know it's a long shot, but our Mr Young has clearly disposed of our victim's walking stick somewhere in the hotel. Keep an eye out for it as you are moving around the hotel."

The team grabbed some food and exited the room. Taylor blew out a breath. "Right, we'd better sit down and work out what the hell to do."

40

STRATEGIES
SATURDAY, 11.50PM

As Taylor wolfed down a Danish pastry, she noticed that Banbury still looked stressed. "Anything I need to know?"

Banbury shook his head. "No, not really. I was speaking to the super while you were with your team and this potential CIA interference has set some hares running. I'm waiting for him to call me back as it might put a different slant on this case."

"Ooh, intriguing."

Banbury just did a *huh* sound which Taylor took as a sign to leave it for now. "Okay," she said, "let's start with the scenario that Walker is still in the hotel and attempts to run in the night with Sanchez-Vicario in tow."

Banbury screwed up his face. "Here's the thing. If we believe that Sanchez-Vicario is Gonzalez, then she usually does this bit alone. You know, the delivery of the merchandise."

"But we think they don't have the merchandise."

"Exactly, which makes this scenario problematical. After the drop, I would normally expect Stonor and Walker to make a quick exit, leaving Gonzalez to do the onward transmission. We've never tracked this scenario, so I don't really know what they will do."

A thought suddenly jumped into Taylor's mind, and she found the piece of paper that Moretti had given her with the room details. "Hmm, I was right. The Walkers are due to check out in the morning, but Sanchez-Vicario and Young are here for another day, as well as our fake admiral."

"Fake admiral?"

"Yeah, Mr Morgan in room 112. Ex-Royal Navy Captain who seems to embellish his story each time he tells it, such as increasing his rank to admiral."

"Oh, you've checked him out then?"

"Yes, apart from bending the truth about his Navy career, he seems fairly unremarkable."

Taylor rubbed her forehead and refocused on the main suspects. "You see, why is Sanchez-Vicario staying for another night if the original plan was for Bush/Stonor to deliver the merchandise on Friday evening?"

Banbury squinted as he tried to kick his brain into gear. "Was Stonor due to check out in the morning?"

Taylor checked the list. "Yes, which adds weight to the theory that Walker and Stonor had planned for their bit to be done and were going to leave in the morning."

"So why is Sanchez-Vicario booked in for another night?" replied Banbury. "It must be a countermeasure, which might suggest that they are aware they are under surveillance."

"If they run, do you have assets in place to follow them?"

"Yeah. One of the things I was sorting with the super while you were out was a mobile surveillance team. They are on standby whenever we need them."

Taylor sighed. "Good. I'm not sure we can do much else with this scenario. I've got my DCs watching the room and patrolling the hotel, and you have your sergeant on reception."

Banbury nodded. "Agreed."

Taylor pushed on. "What about the morning scenario?"

"I'm not sure it's that different. Walker isn't going to suddenly show his face and check out with his wife, and we know Sanchez-Vicario isn't supposedly checking out anyway."

Taylor tutted. "Yeah, you're right. This is frustrating. What about us applying for a warrant and hitting them in their room now."

"Them?"

"Oh, as we've seen neither hide nor hair of Walker, I'm assuming he's hiding in Sanchez-Vicario's room."

"Oh, right, a good assumption."

"I'm guessing this isn't your favourite option though?"

"Well, yes and no. If we knew they had the merchandise, I would say a definite *no* to hitting them now, as I would want Gonzalez out in the wild, hopefully leading us to her contact. However, due to Stonor's murder, there just might be some value in confronting our suspects to see what we can shake out of them."

Taylor frowned. "The thing is, it's still bugging me where the merchandise is that was referred to in the conversation that was overheard by our guests. We assume Stonor was killed because he refused to give it to them, but my team hasn't been able to find anything in his room. The only thing that is unaccounted for is his walking stick, which was last seen in Young's room but has now mysteriously disappeared."

Banbury cocked his head. "Hold on. We haven't considered the scenario that Stonor actually had the merchandise on his person when he was meeting with them. When he refused to give it to them, one of them whacked him round the head and took the stuff from his dead body."

"Oh," exclaimed Taylor, "we hadn't considered that, but do we know yet what was actually stolen from Mrs Deveraux's safety deposit box, because that may determine whether that scenario is feasible?"

Banbury grabbed his phone and tapped away at the screen. "Er, no, doesn't look like it. I'll send a chaser to the member of my team that is liaising with the family."

Taylor looked at the incident board. "It's got to be money, surely."

Banbury stopped typing. "Well, yes, something with a high monetary value if these guys are involved, but it's just as likely to be jewellery or bonds, rather than actual cash."

Taylor didn't know whether it was the chronic tiredness or simply the fact that there were too many variables, but she was finding it difficult to order her thoughts. There was something about what Banbury had said that had tweaked a niggling feeling in her mind, but at the moment, she couldn't reconcile it.

As Banbury finished typing out his message, he looked back at Taylor. "This is a right dog's dinner. Whichever strategy we go with has no guarantee of success and may well let a murderer go free."

Taylor nodded. "My suggestion is that we wait. Let my team do their thing and see if our suspects do anything in the next hour. I'm going for a quick lie-down. I need to recharge my batteries if I'm ever going to keep my brain alert enough to make rational decisions."

Banbury smiled. "Agreed. Get some rest, and we'll reconvene in an hour. In the meantime, I'm going to find out what the hell this Yank is doing on my patch."

41

ROOM 116
SUNDAY, 12.30AM

Taylor had done a quick walk around, checking in with her team. They were still stuck to their tasks, none of them having taken up the offer of a rest in the hotel room they'd been allocated. She was relieved not to have to chuck one of them out. She knew that she should be setting a good example, but she was on her knees and tiredness was beginning to affect her thought processes.

The room was lovely. A large double bed was supplemented by beautiful furniture and lovely paintings on the wall. She went into the spotless, brilliant white bathroom, with fluffy towels and bathrobes hanging on the back of the door. She so much wanted to have a bath, but that was definitely not an option.

She walked back into the main part of the hotel room and lay on the bed. She closed her eyes, but for a while, her mind wouldn't settle, every scenario, every conversation, every piece of evidence swimming around her psyche.

The next thing she knew she was bolting awake. She

grabbed her phone which she'd lain on the bed next to her. It was 1.26am. She'd been out for about forty minutes. Her eyes were heavy, and she fought the urge to fall back to sleep.

As she tried to reorientate herself, the guilt washed over her. Why was she lying here as her team beavered away? Why was she relaxing when her husband was probably at home dealing with another one of Emma's wakeful nights? Why was she in this room as one, or maybe two, of her prime suspects in a brutal murder case were possibly sleeping under the same roof as her?

She sat up, rubbing her face vigorously, trying to get some life back into her tired, aching body. She went to the bathroom and splashed her face with water, not enamoured by the drawn face that was staring back at her. She dried her face and went back into the main part of the hotel room, smoothing over the bedcovers in case one of her team did decide to take a break.

She knew she should get back to it, but she needed this time. Some time to think, without all the dramas in her team, without all the stress of the case. She looked out of the window. The immediate garden was lit by modest lighting, but beyond that, it was pitch black. There was no light pollution, just Cotswold countryside clouded in darkness.

Her mind began to race through the evidence. She was confident that they had a substantial case against Sanchez-Vicario and Walker. They were both in room 105, and she was certain that one of them had struck the fatal blow. Mellon's admission that he had not been on reception the whole time on Friday evening cemented the notion that they had both moved the body to the lake. Her chief super had told her to work closely with CTU, but could she really allow one or more murder suspects to walk free in the morning?

Time was getting on, and she ran her fingers through her hair, trying to fluff it back up so it didn't look like she'd just got out of bed. Just as she was about to leave the room, she noticed movement in the garden. She peered out of the window. The figure had a padded jacket on, protecting them from the unseasonal cold spring night, coupled with a NYC baseball cap.

There was no doubt who it was. Young. He was speaking animatedly to someone on the phone.

She grabbed her phone and went down the steep stairs that led directly from the room to the main corridor. She ran along the corridor, trying to work out the fastest way to get out to the garden. She was next to a door that led to the front car park. The wrong side of the hotel, but at least she knew she wouldn't get lost in the rabbit warren of stairs and corridors that made the hotel so charming. She went outside, gasping at the cold. As she turned the corner towards the front door of the hotel and reception, Young came round the corner.

She moved fast to cut off his progress. "Mr Young. Can I ask what you are doing?"

He looked at Taylor, mildly amused at her question. "I was making a phone call to someone in LA. Reception's terrible in the hotel, so I came outside to do it." He glanced at his watch. "You see, it's late afternoon in LA."

Taylor knew she had nowhere to go with this but couldn't help herself but continue to *scratch the itch*. "Where's the walking stick, Mr Young?"

Young crossed his arms. "This is getting real boring, Inspector. I don't have a walking stick and never have."

"It was seen in your room."

"By who? That silly little maid. She's mistaken."

Another impasse. Young walked away and Taylor swore under her breath as she was left standing outside the hotel, having achieved nothing.

42

CIA REVELATION
SUNDAY, 2AM

Taylor had done a quick check in with her team. Brennan and Whiting had found nothing else in any of the rooms and she encouraged them to take a break. Chesters was keen to tell Taylor about Young leaving the hotel but was a bit crestfallen when she said she already knew. Joshi had been keeping an eye on room 101, where Sanchez-Vicario was apparently sleeping without any conscience as to what she'd done. Taylor was relieved that there had been no movement out of the room while she'd been asleep.

Taylor walked back round to the incident room to find Banbury on the phone once again, his conversation even more animated than last time. He gave her a quick eye raise as she entered the room but carried on speaking. It was obvious from the conversation that something was upsetting him. When Banbury finished the call, he swore and threw his phone on the table.

"What's up?" said Taylor.

He didn't speak for a moment, trying to stop seething before he spoke. He sighed. "You are never going to believe what's happened now."

Taylor gave him an encouraging expression.

"You were right about that Young character. He's bloody CIA. My super checked out what was going on after our initial suspicions. I was expecting him to tear a strip off our US liaison for failing to tell us if they had an active operation going on, but it seems like they weren't bothered about our views on the matter."

"Eh, so what's he doing here?"

"Well, here comes the real curveball. It seems that the CIA are investigating the same cyber terrorism ring that we are."

Taylor frowned. "What!"

"Exactly my reaction. There has been no liaison on this. No co-ordination with Interpol. Seems they've picked up something at the US end and decided to run an op under their own steam."

"Fuck, so Young is technically on our side."

Banbury nodded.

"Well," said Taylor, "that's a bit unfortunate as I spotted him outside a few minutes ago and challenged him as to what he was doing at such a late hour. He said he was calling LA."

"I guess that tracks," said Banbury, his mood now calmer and focused.

"Yeah, but I had another go about the walking stick, which he denied ever having."

"Oh, so we know he's lying to us."

"Yes, which is going to make any prospect of us working together a bit problematic." As Taylor's sentence drifted off, she could see Banbury's worry lines deepen, and he began to chew his lip. "Is there something else?" she probed.

Banbury grimaced. "I'm afraid so. The CIA's presence here is not just an annoyance. It signals something much more serious about this case."

"Oh, are you able to tell me what it is?"

Banbury paused but reconciled any doubt pretty quickly. "The one thing I didn't mention was how we've been tracking the big fish that I was hoping Gonzalez would lead us to. The intel we've collected on the wider OCG suggests that there is a woman running the whole operation. Based on the surveillance we've managed to get some results from, we gather she has a nickname. Medusa."

"Do you know who she is?"

"No, not exactly. Whilst our three amigos here have been pretty easy to identify and track, she's a ghost. The only intel we've got on her is when we had ears on a previous conversation between Walker and Stonor, when Walker was being a bit loose-tongued. It sounded like he never met this creature but was speculating about what he heard."

"Intriguing," said Taylor, her senses now completely in tune with what was going on, the tiredness suddenly a distant memory.

"Yes, he claimed that she is an older woman who gets away with running a major OCG by looking like your average grandma. No one suspects her, but he said she has a ruthless reputation for dealing with anyone who steps out of line."

Taylor cocked her head. "Hold on. So, how does that track with Young's presence here?"

Banbury went wide-eyed. "That's the thing. The one thing my super managed to glean from the US liaison is that the CIA are tracking her."

The implications of what Banbury had said hit Taylor like a tonne of bricks. "Holy shit. Are you saying that she could be in the hotel?"

43

MEDUSA
SUNDAY, 2.15AM

Taylor thought her head was going to explode with the implications of what Banbury had just told her. How was it possible that this so-called Medusa could be in the hotel?

She'd bolted out of the room to get some of her team back. She needed them to go back over everything they'd done so far on the hotel guests. Brennan was having a rest, but Whiting was still in room 105. Taylor asked if she could keep an eye on Sanchez-Vicario's room so she could get Joshi and Chesters back to help her with the task of finding out who Medusa could be.

Within ten minutes, the two DCs were back in the incident room. Banbury and Taylor explained what had happened. "Look at everything we've done so far on all our hotel guests that meet the profile, but go deeper," Taylor said.

Joshi had that determined look on her face that always made Taylor happy. A sharp focus on the task in hand. She was convinced Joshi had a bright future. She posed a sensible question. "Right, ma'am, so we are assuming that this Medusa is an older woman?"

"Yes."

"Okay, so looking through the list that the GM gave you, we should look at Walker in room 104, Kendal in room 106, Smith in room 110, Jennings in room 111, Morgan in room 112 and Li in room 113."

Taylor smiled. "That's right. As unlikely as this scenario seems, given how lovely and unassuming these people are, we have to consider the possibility that any of them could be our Medusa. If we believe the intel that CTU has gained, she gets away with being the leader of a ruthless OCG by looking like your grandma."

Chesters and Joshi began to tap away furiously at their keyboards. Taylor moved away from where they were sat to give them some space. She sat down the other end of the table with Banbury.

"What are we going to do about Young? Do we pull him in and get him to work with us?"

Banbury's deep frown lines reappeared. "Apparently not. My super said the US liaison was very clear that we are not to interfere in what Young is doing."

"Eh, can they do that?"

"No, not really, but the political ramifications of this will only get resolved by people at a much higher pay grade than you or I."

"But we know Young is lying to us and withholding vital evidence from our murder case."

Banbury shrugged. "Well, yes, based on what the maid told you but, from what you said, he voluntarily let you search his room and you found nothing."

"That's true, but he obviously dumped the evidence."

Banbury puffed out his cheeks. "Look, I'm not doubting your team's investigation, but do you really trust this maid? She's the only one who saw the walking stick in his room."

Taylor's instinct was to kick off at Banbury's challenge. She inherently trusted Eva Stimic. She had been valuable in the initial investigation and had seemed genuinely excited to help the police, but she had been a police officer long enough to know that his counsel was sound. "I don't know. I guess I'll have to park that for now, but politics or not, if I feel the need to confront Young about our investigation again, I'll bloody well do it."

Banbury smirked. "Fair enough."

Taylor knew she had to refocus her anger elsewhere and concentrate on finding this Medusa character. "Okay then. Have you done any profiling training?"

"Yes, I have," Banbury replied.

"Good. Give me your first instincts on a profile."

"Yes, ma'am!"

Taylor rolled her eyes. "Sorry, I know we're the same rank. I wasn't meaning to be all billy big boots."

Banbury laughed. "No problem. I'm just pulling your leg."

Taylor looked mildly embarrassed so was relieved when Banbury got back on task.

"Okay," he said, "firstly, she must be a sociopath. Able to fit in with normal people, normal conversations. Her behaviour will not raise any red flags with people. She will have a relatively normal domestic set-up. Husband, children, grandchildren, etc."

"Agreed. What else?"

180

"She'll be an adept liar. She'll have a life story that she sticks to religiously, but there is just the smallest chance she could be caught in a lie. I know from working with the really good profilers that this is often the only way that these people can be caught. A psychopath will always stick out, their behaviour will unnerve people, but this is not how our Medusa will be. I believe the gossip we overhead from Walker in that she acts and looks like your average Grandma. If we really believe that she is somehow one of the old ladies in this hotel, think about which one you feel was bending the truth or their stories were inconsistent."

Taylor stifled a laugh. Banbury looked hurt.

"Oh God, sorry, I wasn't mocking you, but when you said about *bending the truth*, one of the guests immediately came to mind."

"Really, who?"

"Well, it so ridiculous, but there's a woman called Mavis Kendal who was one of our witnesses to the shenanigans in room 105. She was revelling in the gossip mileage she was going to get from being involved. Loved the sound of her own voice that one."

"So, you think she's our Medusa?"

Taylor shook her head. "No, that is so far out there. I mean, I know she fits the profile, but I just can't see it. She is definitely the one whose stories get embellished every time you speak to her, but it just can't be her."

Banbury sighed. "But that's the point. If we believe the profile, it will be the most unlikely candidate."

Taylor looked back at the list of guests that fitted the profile. Her brain just couldn't reconcile it. How could any of these women be the head of an organised crime group?

44

SPENCE'S FLAT
SUNDAY, 2.15AM

Spence sat in his flat, sharing a beer with Ablett. His anger at how they'd been treated was still showing no signs of dissipating. He'd convinced Ablett to come back to his place so he could vent some more. There was no chance of him sleeping. He was so wired. So, a beer with a mate, slagging off the boss, seemed like the best plan.

"Are you going to do anything about her then?" said Ablett.

Spence snorted with derision. "What are we supposed to do? Sounds like she's gonna haul us over the coals as soon as she gets a chance."

"Can't you talk to her chief super? Tell him how incompetent she is."

Spence shook his head. "The problem is she's got SOPs on her side about that bloody DNA sample. If it comes down to it, they'll support her because I didn't follow procedure."

"What were you supposed to do? If you hadn't grabbed

that glass when you saw it, the hotel staff would have taken it and washed all the evidence away."

"Yeah, and she knows that. I took a risk to help the case, but because she's a fucking man-hater, she decided to call me out on it."

"She could have still processed it as a non-chain-of-custody item, at least to see if it matched the sample in the murder room."

Spence took a swig of beer and slammed it down on the table. "That's the thing. I bet that's exactly what that stupid bitch has done."

Ablett finished his beer. "That's all well and good, mate, but I think we've burnt our bridges anyway."

"What do you mean?" retorted Spence.

Ablett stood up and examined what they'd taken from the hotel. "Any forensics that might have been on this thing are well and truly fucked now we've touched it."

Spence shrugged. "I don't care. Yeah, we've done wrong, but when the shit hits the fan, I'm going to make sure the top knobs know that she's been using a civilian to search guests' rooms."

"Oh yeah, that maid."

"Exactly, fucking double standards, and she ain't getting away with it. When this is all played out, I'm going to apply for a transfer away from her team. She ain't getting another minute of my time."

Ablett patted Spence on the shoulder. "Fair enough, mate. Let her sink in her own incompetence."

Spence took another swig of beer. "You off?"

"Yeah, got a day off, so gonna sleep all day."

Spence watched Ablett leave; his anger was still

simmering. He picked up the walking stick and spun it round in his hands, feeling the weight and then swinging it like a sword.

He allowed himself a brief smile.

45

A BREAKTHROUGH IN ROOM 105
SUNDAY, 2.40AM

Taylor checked in with Joshi and Chesters. Having looked at the time, she was acutely aware that they'd been going for nearly twelve hours straight. She encouraged them to go and have a power nap, but they both respectively declined. They were focused on digging deeper into their Medusa subjects, and Taylor could only surmise that adrenalin, caffeine and sugar were keeping them going. She was secretly happy at their commitment. Whilst she was concerned about their welfare, the relentless movement of time was stressing her out. They had about seven to eight hours before a load of their potential suspects walked out of the hotel.

Banbury was back on the phone, liaising with his super about the CIA interference. Taylor was so pissed at Young. He was holding all the cards, but all she wanted to do was cuff him and let him stew in a police cell. As her emotions flicked between anger, stress and determination, the door to the incident room opened and Brennan beckoned to her.

"Ma'am, Whiting's having a break, so I've taken over the watch on Sanchez-Vicario's room whilst continuing to process the hotel rooms."

Brennan had an endearing habit of showing his excitement in a wide-eyed, childlike expression, which Taylor immediately picked up. "I assume you've found something."

"Yes, ma'am. In room 105. I wanted you to see it in situ."

Taylor gestured to Banbury that she was leaving, and he nodded his understanding. She followed Brennan quickly along the corridor and up the stairs to room 105. They glanced back at room 101 as they passed. It all seemed quiet.

Brennan carefully stepped over the precipice of room 105 and grabbed his torch. He knelt down by the right side of the bed, near where the blood stain was still prominent in the carpet. He shone his torch under the bed. "Look, here. Embedded in the carpet."

Taylor craned to see over Brennan's shoulder. "Let me have a better look."

Brennan stood up and gave her the torch. She knelt down and focused the torch back on the area. She double-took and looked up at Brennan. "Is that what I think it is?"

"I'd say so, ma'am. I wanted you to see it where it was, because of how close it is to the blood stain."

"Aha. So, you think that it may have been dropped by our victim?"

"I think that's a decent assumption."

Taylor stood up. "Right, get a picture of that and then bag it."

Brennan did just that. "Are we sure that is the only one?"

"Yes, Whiting said she'd been doing a grid search of the carpet in here but hadn't done under the bed. I took over about fifteen minutes ago and this is the only one I could find."

"Amazing. This might just be the breakthrough we need in terms of how our murder connects with the CTU case. I need to go and show this to Banbury."

Brennan looked pleased with himself and enthusiastically agreed to carry on the search of the three rooms, whilst keeping an eye on Sanchez-Vicario's room until Whiting returned.

Taylor took the evidence bag and rushed back to the incident room. She couldn't take her eyes off the evidence. If this was real, the tragic circumstances that took place on Friday evening and the CTU case began to make sense.

As she walked back into the incident room, she caught Banbury's eye. He was still on the phone but peered intently at the evidence bag she was holding up. As the realisation hit him at what he was looking at, he immediately disconnected the call and grabbed the bag.

His open-mouthed expression matched Taylor's first reaction. "Where did you find this?"

"Under the bed, in room 105. It was embedded deep in the carpet, which is why it took the team some time to find it. It was right next to the blood stain."

Banbury took in a deep breath. "Wow. I think we might have just found the reason for everything that's been going on here."

46

ONE STEP FORWARD, TWO STEPS BACK
SUNDAY, 3AM TO 5AM

The discovery of what could be part of the *merchandise* had temporarily lifted Taylor and Banbury. As one small part of what they hoped was a bigger haul, it gave them a working theory as to what had been stolen from Mrs Deveraux's safety deposit box and explained why Bush/Stonor had been killed, if he'd refused to hand it over.

At this point, they could only surmise that the single item they'd found was a sample that their victim had either used as evidence of his successful heist or was him skimming off the top. It raised the disturbing question of whether their prime suspects had removed the rest of the *merchandise* and were primed to move it out of the hotel in the morning. Taylor felt like smashing her watch in some perverse attempt to stop the advancement of time.

Banbury had immediately resumed his constant phone calls, badgering his team to find out from Mrs Deveraux's family whether what they'd found could have been in her box, but trying to progress an investigation through the early hours of the morning was understandably problematical.

Chesters and Joshi had finally relented, sheer exhaustion finally forcing them both to take a break and get their heads down for a short, refreshing sleep. They'd been digging deeper into the seven older women that fitted the working profile. They were looking beyond the basic checks that they'd already done, such as reviewing the police national computer system for any evidence of criminality. Their social media presence was patchy, reflective of that generation of people who often saw the internet and all its foibles as something to be feared. Spending patterns had been researched and phone logs were being pored over. It was mind-numbing work and was testing the resilience of the two DCs as every avenue was a dead end. Taylor had tried to keep their spirits up, but she knew they had to rest if she was going to keep them on the case. It wasn't helped by the complete implausibility that any of these *grandmas* could be the head of an OCG. She'd met and spoken to most of them. They were all lovely women of a certain age, enjoying their retirements and the freedom it gave them. Taylor just couldn't see how any of them could be involved. Her stomach flipped at the thought. Could they be working to a duff profile and wasting valuable resources on a wild goose chase?

Banbury had left the incident room, leaving Taylor on her own to contemplate her plight. She stood by the incident board, pen in hand. She began to circle the things that were unresolved. The murder weapon. It seemed like everything else had taken priority, but it niggled at her that they had found no evidence of a murder weapon. Whiting reported that the ME had concluded the victim was hit over the head with a large, blunt instrument. There were no spikes, indentations or marks on the victim's skull, which suggested the weapon was smooth, like a bat or club. Taylor asked if the walking stick could have been the tool of choice, but this was ruled out as being too small.

The thought of the walking stick immediately riled her up and she circled it several times, cursing through gritted teeth as she did so. Her patience with Young was running thin. Her team had found no evidence of the walking stick being dumped anywhere in the hotel, which either meant Young was hiding it or it had been discarded outside, the darkness stopping any attempts to search the grounds.

Next, she circled Martin Walker. Where the hell was he? His wife had not been able to contact him, but it seemed like that was not unusual. Taylor's team had found no evidence of him returning to his offices and this, coupled with no taxi bookings from the hotel on Friday night and CTU's insistence that he was still in the hotel, meant he had to be hiding…

Suddenly, Taylor took a step back from the board and gasped loudly, the thought hanging in the air. How could she have been so stupid? The assertion that Walker was still in the hotel was based on Mellon's surveillance. Now they knew that Mellon had been absent from his post during the night on Friday, that theory was shot to pieces. She'd focused so much on Mellon's absence being the explanation as to how the body had been moved out of room 105, she missed the possibility that Walker had then simply walked away. She knew the miles and miles of unlit roads and surrounding countryside made this theory improbable, but they must have had torches to navigate to the lake, so it was possible that he had simply used torchlight to make his escape. She knew she had to challenge Banbury about this possibility when he returned, because if the shit hit the fan, this one was on him.

Taylor blew out an exasperated breath. She fought back tears. The stress and tiredness were taking their toll, not helped by the thought that her daughter Emma would probably be awake any time now, meaning her husband was back on single-parent duties. As she continued to stare at the incident board, her agitated state was disturbed by Banbury coming back in the room.

Taylor looked at him, expectantly. "Anything?" she enquired.

Banbury shook his head. "No. Nothing."

Taylor closed her eyes and screamed out in frustration. One step forward and two steps back.

47

THE WALKING STICK (PART ONE)
SUNDAY, 5AM

Chesters and Joshi returned to the incident room and resumed their deep dive into the seven Medusa suspects. Banbury returned to his obsessive phone calls, acknowledging the potential mistake about Walker and promising to get one of his team to see if they could locate him away from the hotel.

Which left Taylor to stew on the two unresolved items. She made up her mind. She was going to resolve the problem of the walking stick. She checked in with Whiting and Brennan, who were still doing grid searches of every inch of the three rooms. She thanked them profusely, so impressed with their dedication and professionalism. She asked them to look further to see if they could find any evidence of a murder weapon and was pleased when Whiting said they had found some tiny splinters of wood in room 105, which were too small for forensic examination but could be matched to a potential murder weapon.

As she walked out of the room they were in, she couldn't help but be entirely energised by the prospect of banging on Young's door and waking him up at this unearthly hour. A classic police operation tactic. Catch the criminals while they sleep, although she knew she couldn't really label him as such. A liar, yes, an arrogant prick, yes, but technically on the right side of the law. She got to his hotel room and banged on the door. She knew she was probably going to cause Banbury some problems by doing this, but she wasn't bound by the same politics that he was having to deal with.

There was no answer. Maybe he was a heavy sleeper. She banged again. Nothing. The adrenalin she was running on seemed to suddenly dissipate and she felt light-headed. She put her hand against the wall and waited a minute for the feeling to pass. She banged on the door one more time, but there was no answer. She turned and walked out the door that was opposite Young's room. It led out into the car park. The sharp, cold air made her catch her breath, but it cleared the fog in her head. She stood for a second, taking in the freshness of the air, the darkness shrouding the limited lighting around the hotel building.

Just as she was about to walk round to the front of the hotel, she couldn't believe her luck. Young was walking round the corner, on his way back to his room. She was mildly amused at his facial expression as he clamped eyes on her. He tried to up his pace to walk past her, but she put out an arm to stop his progress.

Young glared at her. "I suggest you move that arm immediately, Chief Inspector, unless you want your career to go down the John."

Taylor decided not to be goaded by his attitude and went for a conciliatory tone. "Look, Mr Young, I'm not going to pretend that I'm anything but pissed off with you, but if you help me with one thing, I promise I won't bother you again."

Young's angry expression didn't change, but his eyes went from side to side, trying to evaluate Taylor's offer. He was breathing heavily, but after a tense few seconds, he calmed himself and relaxed. "Okay, Chief Inspector, one favour, and that's it. If you bother me again, I will report you through my hierarchy and make sure your chief constable has no choice but to haul your arse over the coals."

"Agreed."

"One favour," reiterated Young.

"Yes. Just tell me where you put the walking stick."

Young frowned but immediately turned back towards the front of the hotel. He walked through the front entrance and invited Taylor to stop in the lobby. As he closed the door, he looked left. He stood frozen in confusion.

"Something wrong?" enquired Taylor.

Young looked back at her. "It was here. I put it in this umbrella stand."

Taylor looked and shot an equally confused look at Young. "It's gone."

48

THE WALKING STICK (PART TWO)
SUNDAY, 5.20AM

"What time did you dump it?" Taylor tried to keep her tone calm, but she was steaming inside. She had to keep Young engaged.

"I... I don't know," he spluttered, suddenly losing the ice-cool persona that had wound Taylor up so much.

"Think, please, this is really important."

"I guess a little while after we spoke the first time. When I was walking back to my room, I realised your cryptic questions were related to the walking stick. I found it lying outside in the grass a little while after the body was discovered and just put it in my room. I wasn't sure whether it was significant, but when you started asking questions about it, I decided to get rid of it. I think we spoke after I'd had dinner, so I suppose around 8.30pm."

Taylor cursed under her breath. "That's not good. That means anyone could have taken it. Did anyone see you put it in here?"

"No, I don't think so."

Taylor's rage was bubbling to the surface, so she did the best thing she could and prepared to disengage with Young. "Right, favour delivered. In the spirit of co-operation, I'm going to ignore the fact that you compromised evidence in a murder case and call it quits."

Young's arrogant persona had returned, and he went to walk past her. Taylor couldn't resist one more question. "Oh, one more thing. I assume *your* cryptic comment about *looking for things hiding in plain sight* is related to the woman you have under surveillance?"

Young's face hardly flinched, but he tapped his nose. "One favour. Remember."

As she watched Young walk away, she couldn't help but notice Mellon staring at her. She began to wonder whether it was her, because it seemed like half the people who were supposed to be on her side were determined to piss her off. Her anger control was working overtime, but she approached the reception cubbyhole. "Mr Mellon. A question. During the time you've been on reception, do you recall seeing anyone hovering around the umbrella stand and possibly removing something?"

Taylor was relieved when he immediately engaged in the conversation. No arrogance. No attitude. "It's been pretty quiet in here since I've been around, but now you mention it, there were a couple of people who were doing exactly that."

"What?"

"Hanging around that umbrella stand. I thought at the time it was a bit odd, but they soon moved on."

"Who?"

"Your two sergeants."

The implications of what Mellon said hit her like a tsunami. She walked into the lounge and sat down, the light-headedness returning. She tried to dismiss the obvious thought but kept telling herself that it wasn't possible. They were police officers for God's sake. Committed to upholding the law. She sat for a moment staring into space, trying to reconcile it in her mind. The problem was that everything Brennan, Joshi and Chesters had told her about their attitudes when she called them out about the forensic sample, led her to a single, frightening conclusion.

She picked up the phone and dialled her chief super. She desperately hoped that he was already awake. She didn't need his anger as well.

"Price."

"Oh, sir, thanking you for taking my call at this unsocial hour. It's Taylor."

"This better be good, DCI Taylor. I presume you've made some progress on the case."

"Yes, sir, but what I'm about to tell you is not good, and I would not make this accusation lightly."

"I'm nervous."

Taylor sighed. "Sir, I have reason to believe that DS Spence and DS Ablett have removed a vital piece of evidence in our murder case. I need a massive favour from you. Can you organise officers to go to their houses and look for a walking stick?"

"You have to be joking."

"I'm not, sir. I called them out on a major procedural point during our initial investigations and I know it pissed them off so much that they started slagging me off to the rest of the team."

"Now come on, I can see that they might be a bit pissed off but breaking the law? I can't see it."

"Please, sir. I'm sure about this, but if I'm wrong, I will apologise to Spence and Ablett personally, in your office, without prejudice."

"Shit. You'd better be right about this."

49

TEAM BRIEFING
SUNDAY, 7.15AM

The stress and exhaustion had finally caught up with Taylor. Her body did that involuntary jump that happens when you are asleep, and you feel like you're falling. She opened her eyes, trying to work out where she was. Dawn was beginning to creep up from the horizon, streaming weak spring light into the room. She sat up. She was in the lounge. She looked at her watch. She must have dropped off, for almost an hour and a half.

She rubbed her face and got up quickly, embarrassed at what she'd done. She went upstairs to find Brennan and Whiting packing up. "We're done, ma'am," said Whiting. "We've combed every inch of the three rooms and found nothing else."

"Oh right," she replied, still trying to shake the fog from her head. "Can we just have a debrief before you go? I'll get everyone in the incident room in ten minutes."

The team had been on this for nearly twenty hours. Taylor felt guilty that the sleep had refreshed her whilst others were barely surviving on a power nap.

Taylor updated the team on the developments she was able to disclose. She'd agreed with Banbury that they would not divulge Young's identity, and she thought it prudent not to mention her suspicions about Spence and Ablett.

Whiting and Brennan updated on their work, adding the possibility of the murder weapon being a club or bat to the incident board as a result of the wooden splinter found in room 105. Taylor agreed to their departure but was pleased that they both promised to be on call for an immediate return to the hotel if something else developed.

Joshi and Chesters reported that they had a sniff of a trail on the Medusa subjects but wanted to do more work before they said any more.

But all these were minor details compared to the significance of what Brennan had found in room 105. As Taylor held the evidence bag up, the team seemed genuinely in awe of what they were being shown. "We think this item is part of a bigger haul and is the reason for everything that has been going on here this weekend and is almost certainly linked to the CTU case. DCI Banbury is trying to verify with Mrs Deveraux's family—"

Taylor's sentence was interrupted by Banbury's phone ringing. He apologised but urgently pressed the green button to connect the call. The whole team watched his facial expressions as he spoke animatedly to the person on the other end. When he put the phone down, he seemed to be frozen in shock, rubbing his mouth as he prepared to reveal what he'd just been told.

Taylor was stuck between excitement and annoyance. "What is it?" she probed.

Banbury's expression eventually changed to a broad smile. "That was my inspector, the one that has been liaising with Mrs Deveraux's family."

Taylor's patience was running thin. Was Banbury deliberately trying to wind her up with this slow reveal? "And?" she shouted.

Banbury's smile didn't fade despite Taylor's annoyance.

"They have just found insurance papers for what was in Mrs Deveraux's safety deposit box."

The dramatic pause almost made Taylor want to leap across the table and shake the information out of him, but she gritted her teeth and let him have his moment.

"It's a certificate insuring seventy-five solitaire diamonds to the tune of one million pounds."

50

SURVEILLANCE
SUNDAY, 8AM

The revelation that the single diamond found under the bed in room 105 was now almost certainly part of a million-pound diamond heist had injected new vigour into the team. Different theories as to where the rest of the diamonds could be were rehashed. Banbury and Taylor's previous theories about them either being with Sanchez-Vicario/Gonzalez, ready to be moved, or somehow stashed away by Bush/Stonor in a place that no one had yet found, were still the favourites.

Brennan and Whiting had offered to stay, but Taylor wanted to give them a proper break, so after the welcome arrival of breakfast items, provided by the hotel, they quickly refuelled and prepared to leave.

Moretti arrived back at the hotel and checked in with Taylor. He tried to maintain professional courtesies, but Taylor could tell he was beginning to lose patience with the fact they were still there, being provided with free food and drink.

Just as Taylor was about to fill her face with a bacon roll, the door opened and Eva Stimic stood in the doorway, looking sheepish but with a hint of excitement in her face. Taylor walked over to her.

"Is there anything you need me to do?" she enquired.

Taylor smiled. The realisation struck her. They'd been agonising all night about whether to get a warrant to search Sanchez-Vicario's room, but here was an opportunity for an unofficial search. "Yes, just one thing. When you go in and clean room 101, Miss Sanchez-Vicario's room, have a good look around. See if you can find evidence of anyone else staying in that room. A man, probably. Also, see if there is anything that wasn't in there yesterday."

Stimic's excitable expression heightened. "No problem. I'm on it. I'll do it now as I've just seen her go down to breakfast."

As Taylor watched her go, she realised she had the opportunity to observe Sanchez-Vicario. She spoke to Banbury and he too saw the potential of the situation. They told Chesters and Joshi what they were doing, but they barely acknowledged what they said, as they beavered away at whatever threads they'd found, helpfully fuelled by sausage butties.

Banbury and Taylor followed Brennan and Whiting out of the door and walked towards the restaurant. They had a discreet word with the head waiter and were shown to a table in the middle of the restaurant, with a good view in all directions. They could see Sanchez-Vicario sat on her own towards one end of the restaurant. They both got up to get items from the breakfast buffet, all the while keeping a discreet eye on their prey.

When they returned to their table, Taylor whispered to Banbury, "What do you make of that? She doesn't look like someone sitting on a million-pound haul, ready to move it out of the hotel."

Banbury began to spread jam on a piece of toast. "I agree. She looks incredibly cool, but then this gang are well known for their ability to blend in and disguise their criminal motives."

They both tried not to stare, but Taylor was slightly unnerved when Sanchez-Vicario caught her eye and smiled. It was a smile she'd seen before. The type of smile your average psychopathic killer gave when they talked about their crimes. It was unsettling and added to Taylor's concern that they were missing something. Taylor's heart began to race as she thought about Eva Stimic searching her room. This was made worse as Sanchez-Vicario stood up.

Taylor had a second to make a decision. She had to protect Eva Stimic. Banbury jumped as Taylor leapt up from her chair, banging the table and making all the cutlery, plates and bowls clang together. She intercepted Sanchez-Vicario at the entrance to the restaurant. She had to buy Stimic more time.

Sanchez-Vicario stopped, staring at Taylor with a disapproving look, the evil smile no longer a feature. "Something I can do for you?"

"I understand that you are not checking out this morning?"

"That's right. Why do you ask?"

"Just interested."

Sanchez-Vicario fixed Taylor with a fierce stare, trying to intimidate her. Taylor held firm. Sanchez-Vicario went to move off.

"We'll let you know if we need to speak to you again, Miss Gonzalez."

Sanchez-Vicario stopped for a second but didn't look back, walking quickly out of the restaurant.

Taylor walked back to the table.

"What was that all about?" enquired Banbury.

"I'm hoping I've just poked the bear."

51

A GRIM DISCOVERY
SUNDAY, 8.05AM

Brennan and Whiting loaded the last items into the van and reversed out of their space. Brennan yawned. "Bloody hell," he said, "you don't realise how tired you are until you stop."

Whiting nodded and looked at her watch. "Yeah, just an eighteen-hour stint."

Brennan huffed. "I guess the overtime will contribute to my next holiday."

"I feel bad about leaving her."

"Yeah," replied Brennan, "she's a good one that DCI, especially having to deal with those arsehole sergeants."

"Ain't that the truth," replied Whiting, shaking her head with disapproval. "I've a feeling they are going to regret crossing her."

Brennan smiled. "Let's hope so."

They got halfway down the long, snaking driveway that took them out of the hotel grounds, about eighty yards past the lake, when Whiting screamed for Brennan to stop.

He slammed the brakes on and looked at Whiting. "What is it?"

"Look," she exclaimed, pointing at a large compost heap. It was tucked behind a couple of small trees by the fence that separated the hotel from the field that was full of grazing sheep. It was inundated with crows bouncing around and screeching at each other as they squabbled over their quarry.

Brennan peered at the scene. "Holy shit. Is that what I think it is?"

They quickly parked up on the driveway and ran over to the scene. They shooed the crows away and stared at what they thought they'd seen. They both looked at each other as their suspicions were confirmed.

A single arm was poking out of the compost heap, pockmarked with wounds where the crows had been pecking at the dead skin. "Go and get the canopy, quick," said Whiting, "and get the DCI."

Within ten minutes, the canopy was around the scene and Brennan had returned with Taylor. As they entered the canopy, Taylor and Brennan saw Whiting's concerned face. She had carefully moved the contents of the compost heap to reveal the full identity of the body.

Taylor took a deep breath. "Makes sense," she said.

Whiting looked at her quizzically.

"That is Martin Walker. The maid has just cleaned Sanchez-Vicario's room and said there is absolutely no evidence of another person staying in there overnight. Now we know why."

Taylor's brain was once again racing with all the new possibilities, but her deliberations were interrupted by Brennan gesturing to Whiting. "What's that?" he said.

Whiting followed his eyeline. To the left of where Whiting was trying to examine the body carefully, without disturbing the scene too much, was something poking out of the bottom of the compost heap. She stopped what she was doing and carefully moved the debris from around the item. As she worked slowly but diligently, there were collective gasps from the group.

They revealed a baseball bat. Brennan took over, carefully removing enough of the compost heap to enable him to pick the bat up and examine it. "Huh, I think we've just found our murder weapon. There's a few splinters at what I reckon is the point of impact. I'm guessing that wood splinter we found in room 105 will match it."

As Brennan was speaking, Whiting had revealed enough of Walker's head to examine it. "I think we can be sure that is a double murder weapon. Look. He's got similar blunt force trauma to what was on the first victim."

Taylor looked at both of them. They picked up on her non-verbal signals. "Don't worry, boss," said Brennan, "what's another few hours between friends."

Taylor muttered a *thank you* as she tried to work out what had happened. "Do you have any immediate sense of how long the body has been here?"

Whiting sat back and looked over the body. "Well, based on lividity, I would say this body has been here over twenty-four hours."

Taylor frowned. "Eh, so this has been here the same length of time as the body in the lake?"

Whiting grimaced. "I'd say so, ma'am."

Taylor put her hand to her mouth. "Why are we only finding this now? Didn't we search this area?"

Whiting looked a little embarrassed. "I'm sorry, ma'am. We didn't. There was so much going on that I only did a search of the immediate area on the lakeside."

Taylor felt guilty for seeming to criticise Whiting and Brennan, given their dedication on the case. She tried to quickly move on. "No worries. At least we found it, which just adds fuel to my theory that Sanchez-Vicario killed them both."

"Ma'am?" enquired Brennan.

"Working assumption, but I think that they killed Bush/ Stonor in room 105. Walker helped her to move the body and then she knocked him off as well."

"Oh," replied Brennan.

"Yes, so Sanchez-Vicario or Gonzalez, whatever her name is, is cleaning up the trail, which means she must have the merchandise."

Taylor asked the team to process the new evidence as quickly as they could, as she ran back towards the incident room. She couldn't let Sanchez-Vicario leave the hotel.

52

ARREST
SUNDAY, 8.45AM

"Walker's dead."

Banbury stopped what he was doing and walked over to Taylor, who had just arrived back in the incident room. "You what?" he exclaimed.

"We've just found Walker's body. It was dumped in a compost heap about eighty yards away from the lake where the first victim was found. My team think he was killed at around the same time."

Banbury raised his eyebrows. "Well, at least our intel about him not leaving the hotel was right and got me and my sergeant out of an embarrassing situation."

Taylor's disapproving look was picked up by Banbury. "Oh shit, sorry, I didn't mean to sound selfish, but you know…"

Taylor didn't have time for his self-pity. "We need to arrest Sanchez-Vicario now and get a warrant to search her room. We also found the murder weapon: a baseball bat. My team are processing the scene and the evidence, which

I'm sure will put Sanchez-Vicario in the frame for both murders."

"Oh but—"

Taylor was in the zone. She wasn't going to take any shit. This was her investigation, and she was done having to pander to the CTU agenda. "No buts. We need to be able to properly process her DNA, and the only way I can do that is to formally caution her. I'm convinced she has the remaining diamonds. She's knocked off the rest of the team, either because she's going to do a runner with the goods or is on her way to deliver them to Medusa. I'm convinced her booking an extra night here is a red herring. She's leaving today, and I have to stop her."

Banbury stood there open-mouthed as Taylor shouted for Chesters to come with her. As both the DCs looked at her, Joshi came over with Chesters. "Ma'am, I think there's something you should see. We've been doing the deep dive you asked for on the seven Medusa suspects and we've found something."

Taylor was so focused on the task of arresting Sanchez-Vicario that she could barely process what Joshi was saying. "I... I can't deal with this now, DC Joshi. I need to arrest Sanchez-Vicario before she leaves, and I need you to go and find Mrs Walker. We need her to identify the body and hopefully this time it actually is her husband."

"Oh, okay."

Taylor practically ran out the door with Chesters in tow. As they stormed along the corridor, she turned to Chesters. "What's that all about?"

"We've got a thread on one of the suspects, which we need you to look at... but don't worry; it can wait."

Taylor frowned, not convinced that it really could wait, but she had to focus on the immediate threat. They reached Sanchez-Vicario's room and banged on the door. No answer. They banged again. No answer.

Taylor turned around and bolted down the stairs. "Find her!" she screamed at Chesters. Taylor went left at the bottom of the stairs and Chesters went right. She flew into reception. "Sanchez-Vicario. Where is she?" she screamed at the receptionist.

The alarmed receptionist managed to blurt out that she had just gone into the car park. Taylor rushed out of the door, to see Chesters running behind a white BMW. Taylor instinctively jumped in front of the car. The brakes squealed as the driver reacted to the unexpected obstacle.

Taylor stared fiercely at the driver. Sanchez-Vicario stared back at her. For a second, Taylor was concerned that she was going to drive right over her, but Chesters had caught up, yanked the door open and unceremoniously dragged her out of the car.

Taylor read her rights against a backdrop of screaming and expletive heavy abuse from Sanchez-Vicario that flipped between Spanish and English.

Taylor was annoyed that the arrest had occurred right outside the hotel, which had drawn a small crowd and the disapproving gaze of Moretti. A custody van had been called, but Taylor moved Sanchez-Vicario away from the scene and placed her in the back of her car while they waited.

"You have nothing on me, you English bitch," shouted Sanchez-Vicario as she was manhandled into the car.

Taylor looked at her. "We've found Martin Walker, Miss Gonzalez, and we know all about you. We'll get you checked into custody at the police station, and once you've organised a lawyer, you'll be interviewed under caution."

The mention of her real name stopped her talking. Ten minutes later, the custody van arrived. Taylor asked Chesters to accompany her to the station and check her in. He agreed to get back to the hotel as soon as he could.

Taylor walked back to the incident room, ready to face the music with Banbury. He was, as she predicted, not happy. "What have you done?" he said, a distinct anger in his voice.

"Look, I really appreciate your support on this, but I can't ignore two murders. I'm convinced we will be able to link her to both murders, and when we find those diamonds, you can take the credit for making a dent in your investigation. Gonzalez is being taken to custody as we speak, so you are welcome to come and interview her alongside my investigation."

Banbury's anger was simmering, and his eyes darted from left to right as he considered what Taylor had said. He shook his head. "You'd better be right about this, or you have potentially messed up ten months of CTU work with your little power play."

There it was. Taylor knew how to be like a rutting stag with people like Banbury. He'd played the game longer than Spence or Ablett so had learnt how to hide his misogyny, but when the chips were down, it always came to the surface.

The staring contest and battle of wills was interrupted by Joshi coming back into the room. She was alone. Taylor gave a questioning look.

"Mrs Walker's left, ma'am. Reception said she checked out about 8.20am."

"What!" exclaimed Taylor, the realisation hitting her immediately. "But that means she must have driven past the scene of the murder."

"Well, yes, ma'am."

"Don't you think that's odd? Her husband's missing and she's already been in our canopy once before. Don't you think she would stop and find out what's happening? I mean most people would. Wouldn't they?"

As Taylor poured her feelings out, she couldn't help but be distracted by Joshi's face. As she spoke, Joshi was chewing her lip. Something was on her mind.

Taylor tried to ignore it as other immediate priorities consumed her. "Get someone to find Mrs Walker and bring her back here ASAP."

Joshi frowned but walked away to do as she was asked.

53

INSECURITIES
SUNDAY, 9.15AM

The frown unnerved Taylor, but just as she was about to ask Joshi what was up, her phone rang. It was her chief super. She put her finger up to Joshi in a *wait a second* gesture.

"DCI Taylor," the voice on the end of the phone said, stern and businesslike.

"Yes, sir, how can I help?"

Her chief super put on the low, serious tone that she had heard many times. The kind of tone he usually reserved for press conferences when he had to deliver some grim news or appeal for help in a murder case. She knew this time it wasn't about that.

"I'm sorry to say, but your instincts were correct. I sent officers over to both Spence and Ablett's homes. They found the walking stick in Spence's flat. He wasn't even trying to hide it. I think seeing fellow officers at the door made him think he was being summoned back to the investigation. They tell me he was a cocky little shit until they announced their real intentions."

"I'm sorry, sir. I really didn't want to think that of them, but it was the only explanation for the missing evidence."

"Well, don't worry about it. It's not your problem anymore. I've suspended both of them and asked the Professional Standards Department to complete a full investigation into the circumstances behind this situation. Concentrate on getting your case closed down. That's all I need you to do."

"Okay. We've just found a second body and made an arrest. DC Chesters is bringing our suspect into custody. Can you get someone to give him the walking stick and bring it back to the hotel?"

"Oh, right. Of course. I assume CTU are aligned on this."

"Er, sort of, but don't worry, I'm sorting it."

Taylor disconnected the call. She stared at Banbury, who had resumed his incessant phone calls. A sudden pain in her stomach made her wince. She knew she was running on empty, and her body was complaining. She rubbed her face, doubt suddenly consuming her.

She was getting close to twenty-four hours on this case, with only a couple of power naps to sustain her. She began to wonder whether the chronic tiredness was affecting her judgement.

Why had Spence and Ablett taken that walking stick? What possessed them to break the law? Was she really such an awful person that she had driven them to such extreme actions? A PSD investigation was not good on anyone's record, and whilst she surmised that they would probably get off with a slap on the wrist, she felt weirdly guilty about being a part of their downfall.

The animated tone of Banbury's phone calls didn't help either. She'd reacted. Reacted to what she felt was important in her case. The CTU involvement had been fine, up to a point, but the prospect of a double murderer leaving the premises was too much for her to bear. She was waiting for the warrant to come through, and she hoped to God that her instincts about the diamonds were right. She was sure that Banbury had wasted no time in escalating her actions up his food chain, which meant the next call from her chief super was likely to be difficult. Her abrupt ending of their last phone call had probably already alerted him to her angst, but what could she do? She wasn't going to be anyone's puppet.

As the insecurities threatened to overwhelm her, she refocused on Joshi and shook off her self-persecution. "I'm sorry, lots going on."

"I know, ma'am. No worries. Do you want me to brief you on what Chesters and I have found?"

Taylor smiled. "Of course. I could tell by your face that you were itching to tell me something."

Joshi looked a little embarrassed but cracked on. "As you and DCI Banbury requested, we have done a deep dive on the seven women that potentially fit the Medusa profile. At first, we were hitting brick walls, which seemed to be consistent with the limited intelligence that CTU had been able to find about Medusa—"

"Or what they are prepared to divulge," interrupted Taylor.

Joshi smirked. "Yes, ma'am. Anyhow, despite extended checks on the seven, we found nothing. They all appeared to be squeaky clean. Good upstanding citizens."

Taylor's smile broadened. "Stop teasing me, I can tell from your face that you found something."

"Well, maybe. It's a really small thing, but we decided to look at the phone records of all our women and cross-referenced them with what we know of our suspects and victims in the CTU case."

"And?"

"There is one very strange thing. There is a phone number that was called by one of our women on Friday afternoon, which then made a call to Martin Walker about ten minutes later. The call that apparently called him back to work."

"Oh, which woman made that call?"

Joshi turned her laptop screen towards Taylor to show her who it was.

Taylor gasped. "Oh... my... God!"

54

Taylor could hardly process what she was looking at. She looked over to Banbury, who was inevitably still on the phone. She knew she had to share this. She caught his eye and gestured him over. He still had the pinched angry face as he disconnected the phone and walked over to the table.

"Look," said Taylor, "I know you're pissed with me, but Joshi here has found something about our potential Medusa suspects, and I think you need to review it."

Joshi explained what she and Chesters had done. Banbury listened but made no comment, which Taylor thought was odd. She'd given up treading on eggshells. "Well, what do you think? Have you had her on your radar, because quite frankly I'm gobsmacked that she could be involved?"

Banbury didn't respond, just rubbed his chin and stared at the screen. Taylor decided not to break the silence this time. Eventually, he spoke. "So, what's your theory here?"

Taylor gestured to Joshi to respond. "Well, sir, isn't it a bit strange that she makes a phone call to this number and then the same number rings Martin Walker ten minutes later?"

Banbury frowned. "I'm not sure that's much to go on."

Taylor's heckles immediately rose. "What? Has she come on your radar? Is there something you're not telling us about her, because to me, this is the only strand of investigation that we have on our Medusa subjects."

"We haven't had any reason to suspect her."

By now Taylor was so far away from the compliant, fawning-to-CTU person that she had been nearly twelve hours ago when Banbury turned up. She was probably already going to get a bollocking, so she went for broke. "DCI Banbury, I imagine that your intel analysts have access to information that my team could only dream about, yet you dismiss something that my DC has found in a few hours. You say you've been on this case for ten months, so why hasn't your team found anything on this woman?"

Taylor was getting used to the new, angry Banbury. He shook his head and walked away, straight out of the incident room door.

Joshi grimaced at Taylor. "Touched a nerve there, I think."

Taylor sighed. "This is so typical. When you get any of these national teams involved, it seems like you are constantly playing politics and doing your job with one hand tied behind your back."

"What do you want me to do with this?"

"I just don't know. I guess technically, our investigation is coming to a close. Whether CTU like it or not, I have a suspect in custody for our double murder, and that is arguably the limits of my jurisdiction. Finding this Medusa character is really up to CTU now."

Joshi wrinkled up her face. "Are you sure, ma'am?"

Taylor stood staring at Joshi's screen, unsure what to do. As her mind flipped between cutting off CTU and doing their work for them, her deliberations were interrupted by a notification on her phone. The warrant had come through.

"Okay, we're going to have to leave this. The warrant for Sanchez-Vicario has come through. As Chesters isn't back yet, get either Whiting or Brennan to help you with executing the warrant."

Joshi did as she was told, leaving Taylor staring at the laptop screen. She still couldn't believe that this lovely old lady could be Medusa.

Just as she was about to leave, to join the others in executing the warrant, Banbury came back into the room. He started speaking the minute he caught Taylor's eye.

"I'm done here. Now that you've removed the major suspect from our surveillance op and Walker is dead, my boss has closed us down. If you let me know when you are going to interview Gonzalez, I will join you. Needless to say, my boss is furious that our op has been compromised like this. You'd better be ready for some heat to come your way."

With that, Banbury left, leaving Taylor with no chance to respond. She gave a deep sigh and walked out of the incident room, hoping to God that they were about to find the missing diamonds.

55

EXECUTING THE WARRANT
SUNDAY, 9.50AM

Taylor arrived at room 101, to be greeted by Whiting and Joshi. Whiting had left Brennan to process the second murder scene. They'd decided to leave the body in situ until Angela Walker returned to identify him.

With Banbury gone, Taylor decided to muck in. To do some proper detective work instead of having to babysit CTU and play the politics. "Right, Whiting, go and search the car. Joshi and I will search the room. We need to find those diamonds, or I'm in deep shit."

Whiting departed for the car park, leaving Joshi and Taylor to start searching the room, but as soon as they stepped through the door, they knew it was going to be pointless. The room was empty. All of Sanchez-Vicario's belongings were gone.

Taylor sighed. "As I thought. She was doing a runner, which means everything will be in her car. Go and help Whiting as there will be much more to search through down there. I will still search the room because, unlikely as it may be, she still had this room booked for an extra night, and there is the outside chance she's stashed the diamonds somewhere in here."

"Oh," said Joshi, "you think she may have left them for this Medusa person to collect."

"I think it's a possibility we can't ignore."

Joshi left, leaving Taylor stood in the centre of the room. As she looked at the bed, the tiredness threatened to overwhelm her. She so much wanted to lie down and sleep, but she knew she had to keep going. She stood for a minute, not moving, taking in the surroundings, trying to work out where someone would hide diamonds.

Nothing leapt out at her, so she started to search. First, the obvious places, like drawers and under the bed. She lifted the mattress and searched all around and in the bed frame. She got a chair and searched on the top of the four-poster bed frame. She looked and felt up the small recess where the faux fireplace had once been. She went into the bathroom and looked in the toilet cistern. She felt along the bath panel to see if it came off, but it was solid and had not been moved. She got down on her hands and knees and felt along every inch of the carpet to see if a section had been cut out.

After twenty minutes of searching, she sat on the floor, leaning against the back wall. Beaten. She had found nothing.

As she prepared to leave, she took one last look across the room. There was nothing. The diamonds weren't here.

She flew down the stairs and into the car park, desperately hoping that Whiting and Joshi had been more successful. As they caught her eye, their faces told her that her hopes were being dashed. Whiting spoke first. "Nothing, ma'am. Joshi's been through every part of her luggage and found nothing. I've done a preliminary search of the car and also hit a blank. Ideally, I need to get this car back to the station so we can really do a piece on it. You know, rip the seats out, tear off all the upholstery. That sort of thing."

Taylor couldn't believe it. Her instincts about the diamonds had been wrong, and now she was deep in the shit. She acknowledged Whiting's point about doing a fuller search of the car, telling her to get it removed and back to the station as soon as she could but, in her heart, she knew it was pointless. Her mind continued to race through the possibilities. Had Medusa already taken delivery of the diamonds, assuming that one of the seven suspects in the hotel was actually her? Or, had Bush/Stonor somehow hidden the *merchandise*?

She left Whiting to finish off the car search and make the arrangements for its removal. With Joshi, she walked through the hotel and out to the back gardens to go and see how Brennan was getting on. As they neared the canopy, Chesters was walking down from the car park, the walking stick in a large evidence bag.

"Ma'am," he said as he approached, "the chief super asked me to bring this back. How did he get hold of it?"

Taylor looked at Joshi and Chesters. She knew she couldn't keep it from them. The gossip was probably already halfway round the station. "I'm sorry to say, but it seems that Spence and Ablett found the walking stick in the umbrella stand by the front door of the hotel and decided to remove it, in some perverse attempt to get back at me. They've both been suspended pending a PSD investigation."

Joshi and Chesters stood there open-mouthed. Chesters spoke first. "My God. What possessed them to do that?"

Joshi snorted. "I'm not surprised. Arrogant pricks, thinking they are above the law. Let's hope they get the appropriate sanction."

Taylor put on a weak smile, grateful for their support, especially as the doubts about whether her behaviour had contributed to Spence and Ablett's poor judgement continued to bother her.

As the conversation continued, Brennan popped his head out of the canopy. "Is that for me?" he said as he saw the evidence bag that Chesters was holding.

They all stopped the gossiping and walked over to Brennan. "Yes, it is," said Taylor, "but I'm afraid the forensics have been completely compromised." She repeated the story about Spence and Ablett, garnering a similar reaction.

"Well," said Brennan, "I need to go to the van to process this bat, so I will do what I can with the walking stick."

"Okay, thanks," replied Taylor.

As Brennan began to walk out of the canopy, he turned back to Taylor. "Oh, do you want me to get the body picked up by the ME?"

"Er, no. We are trying to get Mrs Walker back here to identify the body."

Brennan huffed. "Huh, second time unlucky."

Taylor turned to Chesters and Joshi. "We're basically done here. I need to let you two go and get some rest. Once we've removed the car and cleared this scene, there isn't much more we can do."

"But, ma'am," said Joshi, "what about the work we did on identifying Medusa?"

"DCI Banbury has left. His boss closed them down. Our priority is to secure a conviction against Sanchez-Vicario/Gonzalez. The Medusa stuff is up to CTU now. If Banbury decides to do nothing with what you found, then that's his bad. You two have been exceptional in difficult circumstances, but you have been going for over eighteen hours, and you need a rest."

Before there were any more protests, Joshi's phone pinged. "Oh, it's Mrs Walker. She's back."

56

The last thing Joshi and Chesters did before they left was to bring Angela Walker to the canopy. She was pale and drawn. Taylor thanked the DCs and fixed Walker with a sympathetic stare.

"I'm sorry to ask you to do this for a second time, Mrs Walker, but I'm afraid to say that I believe this is actually your husband."

Walker pouted. "Let's get this over with," she said, her voice cracking with emotion.

Taylor gestured for her to walk into the canopy that was shielding them from the horror. As soon as Walker walked in and saw the body, she gasped, immediately turned around and left the canopy.

Taylor followed her out. Walker turned to look at her. "Yes, that's him. That's my husband."

Taylor got on the phone to ask Brennan to come back down and get the body moved. She put her arm on Walker's shoulder and suggested they went back into the hotel. They went to the incident room, and she made her a coffee. Walker took tentative sips as she fought back tears.

Taylor eyed her curiously. There was something about her reaction to seeing her husband's dead body that wasn't sitting right with Taylor. The emotions displayed had been relatively consistent with what you would expect. The pale face, the gasp, the tremor in her voice and the tears, but for some reason, Taylor didn't think they were genuine. She didn't say anything as Walker continued to sip her drink, but she couldn't shake the feeling that she was putting on an act. A moment of self-doubt crept in. Was she being paranoid because half the people in this investigation didn't seem to be who they said they were? The wigs, the make-up, the disguises just added to her paranoia that everyone was acting a role, like some perverse real-life murder mystery weekend.

Taylor shook the doubts off and decided to go for broke. "Are you up to answering a few questions, Mrs Walker?"

She looked up, confusion etched on her face. "What about? Am I under arrest?"

"God no. It's just some loose ends to tie up now we've found your husband."

"Okay," she replied, her response accompanied with a deep sigh.

"Thank you. Can I first ask why you drove straight past our canopy this morning and didn't stop to see what was going on?"

Walker put on an incredulous expression. "Why would I? I didn't know that you had my husband's body lying there, and I'm sure you didn't need innocent members of the public getting in the way of your work."

Innocent members of the public. That sentence made Taylor's detective radar go into overdrive. It was a common theory amongst detectives that people who were keen to impress their innocence often had something to hide. "I guess because you'd seen the set-up at the previous crime scene and your husband appeared to be missing that it may have piqued your curiosity."

The tears had stopped, and there was now an unnerving steeliness to Walker's responses. "I'm sorry, Chief Inspector, but it didn't enter my head. I just wanted to get away from this hellhole of a weekend. And now the absolute worst has happened, don't you think it's reasonable for me to get away from this place and grieve the passing of my husband?"

Taylor was like a dog with a bone. She couldn't let it go. Something was up with Walker's reactions. She went for it. "Where are the diamonds, Mrs Walker?"

"You what!" she exclaimed, the volume of her voice rising.

"The diamonds. We know your husband was part of a major organised crime group that is responsible for major heists of cash, bonds and jewellery. We know that a consignment of diamonds was stolen from a safety deposit box a couple of months ago and they were due to be handed over to someone in this hotel, before someone started murdering people."

Walker's face was framed in shock, slowly turning to an amused expression. "Are you out of your mind? You threw my world into turmoil when you told me my husband was a crook and now you are trying to tar me with the same brush."

Taylor wasn't going to be put off her stride. "Does the name Medusa mean anything to you?"

There was a slight hesitation in Walker's response, but she quickly corrected herself. "What?"

"Medusa," Taylor repeated.

"I don't know. Isn't she that Greek god that had snakes on her head and made people blind when they looked at her?"

"Did you ever hear your husband use that name?"

"No!"

"Okay, Mrs Walker, can you explain why you made a phone call on Friday afternoon to a phone number that ten minutes later contacted your husband? The call he apparently took that asked him to go back into work."

Walker stared at Taylor, any emotion from seeing her husband's dead body now well and truly behind her. "You're delving into areas you don't want to go."

Taylor recoiled. "Really. Don't you want me to find out who killed your husband?"

"It's private and nothing to do with my husband's death."

"I think I need to be the judge of that."

Walker said nothing for nearly a minute. Taylor stared her down. She was not going to let it go. It worked.

"I'm having an affair. The call was to the man I'm seeing."

Taylor was not expecting that but kept focused. "Why did he ring your husband?"

"He's a work colleague of Martin's. They work on the same projects. I guess he was the one that asked him back to work."

Taylor's short-lived confidence in her line of questioning was rapidly falling apart. The phone records that Joshi and Chesters had found, coupled with Taylor's sudden suspicion about Walker's reactions to her husband's death, had convinced Taylor that she was the mysterious Medusa.

But, if she believed the answer that Walker had just given, her suspicions were way off the mark.

Walker picked up on her hesitation and stood up. "I hope we are done here. I'm going to ignore your outrageous allegations and concentrate on laying my poor husband to rest. When can I get the body for burial?"

Taylor was poleaxed. "Erm... yes, I'm sorry. We need to do a post-mortem, but after that, the coroner will contact you."

As Walker began to walk out, she turned back towards Taylor. "If you don't mind me saying, dear, you look like you need a rest. Tiredness is affecting your judgement."

Taylor stared at the door as Walker walked out. She was right. For a moment, she was convinced Walker was Medusa, but the exhaustion was leading her to illogical conclusions. What made it worse was that Banbury's apathy at what they found on Walker had now been condoned. It was a small thread which had ultimately led to a reasonable explanation. The rational part of Taylor's brain told her *it figured* as CTU analysts had found very little on Medusa in ten months of investigating.

Taylor knew she had no choice. She had to close the incident room down, get home and have some rest. Her suspect was in custody, and she could stew in a cell until the morning.

She went and found Whiting and Brennan. He had already got the mortuary van arranged and Whiting agreed to close the incident room down and get the car back to the station.

Taylor contacted the custody sergeant to advise him that she would be interviewing Gonzalez in the morning and to make sure that she had her legal counsel sorted. She messaged Banbury the details but wasn't sure that he'd turn up.

Her last act at the hotel was to speak to Moretti, thanking him for their hospitality and confirming that all the hotel rooms could now be handed back to him for guests to stay in once more. He seemed relieved to get rid of the circus.

She got in her car and drove home. Tomorrow was another day.

57

THE INTERVIEW (PART ONE)
MONDAY, 9.30AM

Taylor had slept for twelve hours straight. When she got home, she fussed over her husband and daughter, made them dinner, read Emma a bedtime story and generally tried to make up for her absence. She completely flaked out as soon as Emma went to bed.

Her husband woke her up at 7.30am and they had fast, frantic sex. The stress release was just what she needed and, after a hearty breakfast, she was back on track.

She arrived at the station just before 9.15am and checked in with the custody sergeant. He confirmed that all the arrangements were in place for the interview and that Gonzalez's brief had already arrived. As she began to organise the interview room, Brennan popped in, a huge smile on his face.

"We've got her, ma'am. The official DNA samples we took match with the female sample found in room 105 and the ones found on the handle of the bat. We can place her at the scene of both murders and have her DNA all over the murder weapon."

Taylor read the forensics report. "That's amazing. Thank you so much. It's going to make this interview so much more interesting."

"I'm afraid the walking stick was useless though. The forensics were completely compromised by Spence's actions. I will say, though, that it's very nice with excellent craftsmanship and a little bigger than your average stick. It's handmade from hazel, with a gold-plated handle and footing. It also had the initials CMS engraved in gold on the shaft, which I assume stand for Charlie Michael Stonor."

"That's odd," said Taylor, "given that he was trying to be Mr Bush."

"I know, which makes me think the stick was a very precious item to him."

Brennan left Taylor pondering the mystery of the walking stick. A few minutes later, the door opened again. It was Banbury. "Oh, you came."

"Yes, my super thought it was the right thing to do. I'll just observe though. You can ask all the questions."

At half past nine, the custody sergeant brought in Gonzalez and her brief. There was an uncomfortable vibe between Taylor and Banbury, but she couldn't let that distract her.

Introductions were made and the recording of the interview commenced. Taylor launched in. "Okay, let's start with your identity. I am conducting this interview on the assertion that you are Maria Gonzalez and not Maria Sanchez-Vicario, the fake identity you used to book a hotel room at the Cotswold Manor Hotel."

"No comment," Gonzalez replied.

"To confirm that you have been charged with two counts of murder, against Mr Martin Walker and Mr Charlie Stonor on the evening of Friday, 13 April and the morning of Saturday, 14 April. I assert that you killed Charlie Stonor in room 105 and, with the help of Martin Walker, moved his body to the lake in the grounds of the hotel. You then proceeded to kill Martin Walker by the lake and dumped his body and the murder weapon in a compost heap about eighty yards away from the lake."

"No comment."

"You killed them both by hitting them over the head with a baseball bat. As I said, we found this murder weapon discarded in the compost heap next to Martin Walker's body."

"No comment."

Taylor leant forward, allowing time for a dramatic pause. "Hmm, interesting," said Taylor, "your no-comment approach seems to be founded in misplaced confidence that I don't have any evidence to support my accusations."

Gonzalez shrugged.

"You see, Miss Gonzalez, my colleague here is from the Counter Terrorism Unit and has been tracking you for over ten months. We know that you, Walker and Stonor have been part of an OCG that has been executing large heists of cash, bonds and jewellery. We know that Bush, or Stonor, stole seventy-five solitaire diamonds from the safety deposit box of a Mrs Deveraux and was due to deliver them to you this weekend at the hotel."

"No comment."

"So, what went wrong that made you kill them both? Did they get greedy and refuse to hand over the goods?"

"No comment."

"The thing is, we have your DNA in room 105 and on the handle of the murder weapon."

This time, Gonzalez did not respond. She just looked at her brief, who shook his head. There was a brief silence before Gonzalez spoke, garnering a concerned look from her brief.

"Impossible," she said.

"What's impossible?" replied Taylor.

"The DNA. I wasn't there."

"That's not what the forensics are telling me."

Her brief whispered something in her ear and then addressed Taylor. "Could I request a short recess so I can consult with my client?"

Taylor glared at Gonzalez. She didn't want to give her a chance to reset now she had her on the ropes, but she knew that it would not look good when it came to trial if she didn't agree.

"Okay, you have ten minutes."

58

THE INTERVIEW (PART TWO)
MONDAY, 10AM

"I want a deal."

Taylor looked at Banbury, who raised his eyebrows at Gonzalez's opening gambit.

"Why?" said Taylor. "Are you admitting to these two murders?"

"If I am given full immunity against prosecution, I will tell you everything you need to know."

Taylor looked at Banbury. "Can I say something?" Banbury said, seemingly respectful of the boundaries. Taylor nodded.

"Okay, Miss Gonzalez. My colleague here has you bang to rights for two murders which will get you two life sentences. My team can place you squarely in the middle of an organised crime group that is funding cyber terrorism across the world. You must have a whole lot to tell us if you honestly think we can agree to waiving all that criminality for total immunity against prosecution."

Gonzalez shrugged. "It's up to you."

Taylor looked at Banbury, who gave her a wide-eyed response. "No deal," Taylor replied. "The best we can do is promise that we will ask the judge to take into account your co-operation when he sentences you, depending on what you can reveal to us."

Gonzalez sighed and looked at her brief. He gave an encouraging nod. "Okay, deal. What do you want to know?" she said through gritted teeth.

Taylor was surprised by how quickly she folded but didn't lose any time in restarting the questioning.

"Did you kill Charlie Stonor and Martin Walker?"

"Yes."

"Why?"

"They failed to deliver. My boss decided it was time to cut them off. I did as I was told."

"You mean this mysterious Medusa character?"

Taylor noticed the involuntary twitch in Gonzalez's face as she mentioned Medusa.

"How do you know that name?"

"As I said, Miss Gonzalez, my colleague here has had your team under surveillance for over ten months. They have heard conversations referring to this Medusa character as being the big boss of your outfit."

Gonzalez dipped her head and muttered something in Spanish. Taylor surmised that she was now under more stress based on the tone of what she said.

"Who is she?"

"I've never met her."

"Really," exclaimed Taylor, "you expect me to believe that?"

"It's true. All contact was by burner phones. She left me

instructions on where to leave the packages and I was paid on delivery."

"Was she at the hotel over the weekend?"

"No, not that I'm aware of. I was originally supposed to deliver the package to a warehouse lock-up near Dover yesterday but, as I said, they failed to deliver."

"So, you don't have the diamonds?"

"No."

"And you have no idea where they are."

"No, it was Stonor that caused the problem. Walker was his handler, and they were supposed to meet me in room 105 and hand them over."

"What happened?"

"Stonor said he was fed up with doing all the dirty work and being paid a pittance. He said he'd stashed the diamonds away somewhere safe and was going to use them as his retirement fund. He wanted out."

"So, you killed him."

"Well, yeah. The minute I knew he'd betrayed us, I knew he had to die. The boss always made it clear that anyone deviating from the plan had to be dealt with."

"Okay, your confessions will be taken into account, but I'm assuming my colleague here will need much more before we can even consider making representation on your behalf to the judge."

Banbury picked up on the queue. "Thank you, DCI Taylor. You are indeed correct. I'm gonna need a whole lot more about the OCG for you to be granted any clemency."

"Fire away," Gonzalez said.

"I need Medusa. Are you still in contact with her?"

"Er, well, I still have the burner phone for this operation

and a number to contact her on. Now that the diamonds have not been delivered, I don't know whether she will have closed this down."

"But you're willing to try?"

"Of course."

"What about the US set-up?"

"I've never been there."

"But you can confirm that is where the cyber terrorism hub is working from."

"She gave very little away, but she did mention New York many times."

"Anything else?"

"Yes, she shipped most of the packages by sea."

"How do you know that," enquired Banbury, "if she didn't tell you much?"

"I'm not stupid. I knew I had to have a backup plan if this ever went... how do you say... pear-shaped."

"Which was?"

"I put a tiny GPS tracker in each package to see where they went. In all cases, they went via dockyards in Dover, Poole or Southampton. I worked out that she was moving the goods in large packing containers, which always ended up in the US."

"How far could you track the packages?"

"They were all picked up from dockyards in the US and mostly the signal ended in a hotel in New York, which, as I've already said, is a place she often mentioned. I assume that was when she opened the package and discarded the wrapping where I'd put the tracker."

Taylor could see Banbury was on a roll and let him continue.

"What did Medusa sound like?"

"British. Very well spoken. Hard as nails."

"Young? Old?"

"She sounded old. Her voice had that lived-in sound, if you know what I mean."

Banbury whispered to Taylor that he was done and began to type frantically on his laptop. She took this as a cue to take back over the interview.

"If you knew Stonor had the diamonds, why did you kill him? Surely it would have been better to beat the information out of him."

"We cut our losses."

"You cut your losses on a million-pound payday!"

"That's what the boss told us to do if any operation didn't go to plan."

Taylor was not convinced by that part of the story but had her confession and decided to end the interview for now. She summarised what would happen next and said she would be in touch with her brief about the arraignment.

As the custody sergeant dealt with Gonzalez, Taylor was surprised to see her chief super poke his head round the door.

"A word," he said, "with you both. Upstairs in my office. Now."

59

THE CHIEF SUPERINTENDENT'S OFFICE
MONDAY, 10.50AM

Chief Superintendent Adam Price was one of the good ones. Taylor liked him. He had the great quality of being a firm but fair leader, with a clarity of message and a humility to realise he had to surround himself with people who had the different skills he needed to succeed. He never once exhibited any signs of misogyny and in fact was a major mover and shaker in the force's diversity, equality and inclusion work. That he wanted to speak to Taylor was not unusual, but his tone was.

She walked up the stairs to his office, Banbury in tow. When she entered his office and was introduced to the guest sat in one of his visitor's chairs, she realised why he was grumpy.

"DCI Taylor, this is Detective Superintendent Sharpe from CTU. I think you've already spoken on the phone."

"Oh, yes, good to meet you, sir."

Price wasted no time in launching in, seemingly aware of who Banbury was, which made Taylor suspicious that this was not the first time they'd met that day.

"The thing is, DCI Taylor, Superintendent Sharpe here is not happy with your actions and is seeking an explanation from us about the operational decisions you made over this weekend."

Taylor closed her eyes briefly and put her head back to calm herself. She wasn't surprised at the scrutiny but felt ambushed by the circumstances. She didn't stand on ceremony and poured herself a coffee from the pot that was in the middle of the meeting table, not offering to pour the others one. She wasn't going to give them the satisfaction of re-enforcing any archaic gender stereotypes by being *mother*.

Eventually, she spoke. "What do you want to know?"

Sharpe took over. "I understand from DCI Banbury that you did not consult with him before you made the arrest of Gonzalez."

"That's correct."

"Why? Up to that point, he said you had been working side by side, developing strategies that benefitted both your murder inquiry and our OCG case."

"That's true, but once we found Walker's body and the murder weapon, everything changed."

"How so?"

"We were both convinced Sanchez-Vicario, sorry Gonzalez, had been involved in the murder of Stonor, but we didn't really know whether she had the diamonds so agreed to wait to see what she did. When we found Walker's body, I surmised that she must have them and had killed Stonor and Walker to clean up loose ends. I reacted quickly because it struck me that her booking that room for an extra night was a ploy to put us off the scent and that she was in fact leaving that morning… and I was right. My DC and I intercepted her as she was driving out of the hotel car park. I took the decision to arrest her on the spot as I needed a way to formally process her DNA now we had some potential additional evidence to convict her."

Taylor noticed a subtle, supportive smile from Price. A smile telling her she was doing well and to keep going. A smile that was apologetic at the situation but also resigned to the fact that Price had to play the politics. She took this as a good sign, as Sharpe's questions got more accusing.

"You were wrong though. She didn't have the diamonds."

"I know. I took a gamble."

"A gamble," exclaimed Sharpe, his voice beginning to rise in pitch and volume. "A gamble that removed the possibility of us being able to track her to Medusa."

Taylor frowned. "With the greatest of respect, sir, Banbury and I have just got a confession from Gonzalez for both murders. She's confirmed that Stonor and Walker did not deliver the diamonds and she has no idea where they are. She told us that her instructions were to kill anyone who stepped out of line and walk away if the case was compromised."

"And you believe her?"

"Yes, I do. It didn't take long for her brief to realise we had her bang to rights for both murders with the DNA evidence we had. They went straight for a deal but didn't flinch when we renegotiated the terms. She's peddling backwards like she's on a pedalo trying to get away from a shark attack."

Sharpe didn't seem to get or appreciate the shark analogy. "All the same, we've now lost a major thread on identifying Medusa."

Taylor was fed up with being criticised and continued the respectful defence of her actions. "It seems to me, sir, that we've closed down a major UK cell by what's happened this weekend."

Sharpe glared at her. "Are you trying to do my job, Chief Inspector? Are you suddenly an expert on counter terrorism work?"

"No, sir, but this must surely put a dent in their operation."

Sharpe sighed. "You have no idea what you're talking about. Taking out a few foot soldiers like this is tantamount to taking the tip off an iceberg. You're still left with a whole lot of danger you can't see."

Taylor wasn't going to be beaten. "Hold on, what about Young? You say he's CIA. He was clearly watching someone and not giving us any co-operation. If you're right, he wasn't worrying about our small fish. He was looking for Medusa too. We used your profiling to identify some of the women it could have been. Why don't you ask your CIA buddy who the hell he thinks it is?"

Sharpe shook his head. Arrogant and disrespectful. "Oh yeah, Banbury tells me you thought Angela Walker was in the frame, but she explained away your little phone call trail as nothing more than a chat to her lover."

Taylor rolled her eyes. "Whatever. My team worked bloody hard on that Medusa profiling, but I guess, as you so eloquently reminded me, it's not really anything to do with me. I'll just get on with convicting a double murderer."

Taylor was relieved that the barrage from Sharpe subsided, and Price took the opportunity to close the meeting down. Sharpe and Banbury left with no further comment.

Price turned to Taylor. "Well done for standing up for yourself. I'm sorry I couldn't warn you about that but, as you could tell, he was making a lot of noise, and I thought it better that we dealt with it immediately."

"What happens now?" enquired Taylor.

"Oh, don't worry about it. I'll smooth the politics over with the chief. She'll be happy that you've cleared up two murders on her patch, so quickly, and CTU will probably treat us like yesterday's chip paper before we know it."

"Sir, do you think I did the right thing?"

"Look, Chloe, you know from your command training that we are judged on the rationale behind our decisions and the operational circumstances in which they are made. Your decisions stand up to scrutiny."

Taylor smiled. The use of her first name was a tactic that he used when he switched from command mode into the humble, supportive leader that she had grown to greatly love and respect. She was glad that he supported her decisions and felt vindicated in her view that she should not let a double murderer walk free.

She walked back down the stairs to the CID office on the ground floor. She'd asked the team for a quick debrief and now felt happier that she could stand in front of them, with her head held high.

60

TEAM DEBRIEF IN THE CID OFFICE
MONDAY, 11.55AM

Taylor walked into the office. Chesters, Joshi, Brennan and Whiting were sat there drinking coffee. She immediately felt the awkwardness of Spence and Ablett not being there.

She launched straight in. "Team, I just wanted to gather you together this morning to thank you for your incredible work over this weekend and for the ridiculously long hours you've endured to ensure we can get these convictions. Maria Gonzalez, the lady we know as Maria Sanchez-Vicario, has confessed to both murders in exchange for helping with the wider CTU case."

"Are you okay, ma'am?" said Brennan. "I gather you were called up to the chief super's office to meet with the CTU top brass."

Taylor stifled a laugh. "I don't think I would call their superintendent *top brass*, but yes, I was being held to account in that meeting for the rationale behind the decisions I took. He wasn't happy that we compromised the CTU strategy."

"What did the chief super say?" asked Brennan.

Taylor smiled. "He was cool. When they left, he explained that he had to play the politics but was completely behind the actions we took. He said the chief would be happy that we've cleared up two murders on her patch and that was all down to your collective professionalism."

The team seemed happy, but Taylor couldn't help noticing that Joshi had the distracted look on her face that she'd had when she was on the Medusa work and Brennan had the nervous twitch which normally meant he wanted to tell her something. She tried to ignore her instincts and cracked on.

"Okay, so we can consider this case as drawing to a close. Please make sure that all your evidence and statements are properly catalogued for the CPS file. I'm just waiting for the date of the arraignment, so we need to make sure we are ready to prosecute this case."

Taylor was expecting them to disperse, but they all sat there. No one moved.

"What's up?"

She'd not been wrong about Brennan's nervous twitching. "I'm afraid we can't do that, ma'am."

"Why?"

"Well, because the body we found in the compost heap is not Martin Walker."

"What! How is that possible?"

"The thing is, we compared the DNA samples from the toothbrush that Angela Walker gave us with one of the male samples from room 105, and they matched, so we assumed it was Martin Walker's."

"Well, yes. Everyone said he was Martin Walker, even CTU who've been tracking him for ten months."

"But that's the thing. When I loaded the samples into the forensics system and ran them against the national database, the samples came up as someone else."

"Who?"

"A man called Richard Snelling."

"Who is he? Is he known to us?"

"Oh yes," said Brennan, "he's a nasty piece of work. A record longer than my arm. Robbery, violence, perverting the course of justice. He got out of prison about fourteen months ago and is almost certainly back to his old ways, including being part of the OCG."

"So, he's been impersonating Angela Walker's husband all this time, even during the CTU surveillance period."

"I think that is a good bet because all the CTU intel has him down as Walker."

Taylor recoiled. "This is blowing my mind. How on earth is this possible? Where's the real Martin Walker and what does Angela Walker…" The realisation struck Taylor as her sentence remained unfinished. "Holy fuck. So, Angela Walker is involved. Were we right? Is she Medusa?"

Brennan glanced at Joshi with a broad grin over his face.

"Oh, it's better than that. Walker is her married name. Her maiden name is Snelling. Richard Snelling is her brother."

61

NEW THEORIES
MONDAY, 12.10PM

Taylor started pacing the room, manically waving her hands in the air as she tried to process what she was hearing.

"Quick, one of you get a board and write down what I'm about to say."

Chesters and Joshi jumped to it and got the portable whiteboard. Taylor gave them a stressed smile.

"Right, so Snelling has been impersonating Martin Walker. I'm guessing since he came out of prison. Which means Walker is probably dead. See if you can find any John Does in the mortuary system or find out what the real Martin Walker was doing around fourteen months ago. I'm guessing he's clean, which is why they didn't hesitate in using his real name. His criminality only came to the fore when CTU started watching him."

Chesters and Joshi were doing a great job writing up Taylor's thoughts as she continued to talk at an electric pace, like her brain needed to offload everything at once.

"Now, Angela Walker, née Snelling, is obviously cut

from the same cloth as her brother but has been hiding her criminal persona, including, we assume, being this Medusa character, within the respectability of a retired home counties woman living in the suburbs. I reckon she saw an opportunity to recruit her brother to the OCG when he came out of prison and decided to get rid of her law-abiding husband."

She looked wide-eyed at the team, who gave her nods of encouragement to carry on.

"So, this weekend, Angela Walker and her brother checked in as husband and wife... eww... and proceeded to put on a performance, like every other bastard we seemed to come across on this case. I remember the maître d' saying that it was obvious they were having an argument all through dinner and that they made a point of reacting to the fake Mrs Deveraux, aka Sanchez-Vicario, aka Gonzalez, when she gave her little performance in the restaurant. It was all designed to be noticed, possibly so it got back to us."

Joshi put her hand up, and Taylor allowed her to break her ramblings. "The thing is, ma'am, at dinner, nothing had actually happened. If we believe what Gonzalez says, she didn't know that Bush/Stonor was not going to deliver the goods later that night. How would Walker have known that the police were going to be called to the hotel?"

Taylor's face wrinkled in concentration. "A good point, but here's the thing. I don't know what Walker's done with her husband, but I reckon she may have already decided to knock her brother off after this job was done. I bet she saw an opportunity to use a career criminal like him for this one job and then dump him. If she is Medusa, everyone says she has a ruthless reputation for getting rid of people that don't toe the line. In this case, it seems that family ties don't mean much, and she was setting up the scenario in case she needed it."

Joshi put her hand up again. Taylor nodded to her to speak. "There's something else about that phone call she made to her so-called lover. I just couldn't let that go, so I did some more work on it this morning. She was lying. I checked the two calls we originally tracked with the mobile phone suppliers, and they confirmed that both calls could be triangulated to the mobile phone towers within the five-mile radius of the hotel. It means that both calls were almost certainly made and received by people in the hotel."

Taylor stopped and put her hand to her mouth. "Of course," she exclaimed. "Angela Walker made the first call to either Bush or Sanchez-Vicario, sorry Stonor or Gonzalez, to initiate the meet. Whoever she called then contacted Snelling to tell him to go to room 105 later that evening."

Chesters interjected. "But, ma'am, what about Mrs Kendal saying she saw Walker outside room 105, and how does her room being ransacked come into this?"

Taylor nodded. "Yes, good point. I think one was reactive and the other planned. If we've got the timeline right, she'd already told Gonzalez to kill anyone that stepped out of line. I think she was genuinely curious as to what was going on in the room and went to earwig. I think what Mrs Kendal saw, in terms of how Walker reacted, was all part of the performance. Mrs Kendal isn't the most subtle character, and I reckon Walker probably saw her snooping out of her bedroom door and decided to put on a performance, once again relying on it getting back to us. I mean, think about how quickly Walker was on to us when we first examined the crime scene. She wasted no time in telling her story and painting her husband as a bad person, even dropping the hint about hearing his voice in that room."

"What about the room ransacking?" probed Chesters again.

"Ah, now that was the planned bit. When we revealed that we suspected her husband of being a criminal, she played the part of the poor, neglected wife who was now suffering at the hands of her nasty husband. She knew by this point that the diamonds were missing, so she pretended that someone had ransacked her room looking for them, adding weight to our theory that her husband was involved."

Whiting joined in what seemed like some perverse Q&A. "What about the body identifications, ma'am?"

"Yeah, she played those well. Made sure that both times she was in and out of the canopy quickly, meaning we only saw what we thought was an understandably shocked woman, who didn't want to linger at the sight of a dead body."

The manic energy in the room suddenly subsided. Taylor sat down. "My God. If this is all true, Angela Walker is one hard-nosed bitch. She's clever. She set several things running this weekend to cover a number of scenarios. She had us running around to her tune and got two problematical people out of the way. If we believe Gonzalez, she protected her identity, making sure that the two of them never met, despite them sitting hardly twenty yards apart in the restaurant on Friday night. She is ice-cool and dangerous."

"What do we do now?" said Joshi.

Taylor took in a deep breath. "Well, the right thing to do would be to hand this over to DCI Banbury."

"But you're not going to do that. Are you?" said Brennan.

"No, I'm not. I want this part of the investigation locked down to this team. Follow up on these leads and get this written up and catalogued as a separate part of the case file. I think it's about time that the country bumpkins showed CTU how real detective work is done."

62

DECISIONS, DECISIONS, DECISIONS
MONDAY, 1.30PM

Taylor did not consider herself to be a maverick. She normally played things by the book, one of the many reasons why she'd fallen out with Spence and Ablett, although she knew she was being a bit of a hypocrite with the way she'd been using Eva Stimic. Her decision to keep this latest intel from CTU was a further step away from the standards she held herself and others to, but there was something about this case that was taking her places she didn't want to go. She wasn't sure whether she had become complacent as a result of the chief super's support, but she knew she was going to test his loyalty if she couldn't see this through.

Her brain was still struggling to comprehend that the *lovely old lady* persona that Angela Walker played so well, could really be hiding a major international terrorist. Sharpe had been right about one thing. She wasn't an expert at counter terrorism, but she knew enough to know that Walker's cover was genius. The problem she now had was that Walker was aware of her suspicions. It didn't matter that CTU had brushed her theories aside, she sensed that Walker would still be on her guard. Taylor wasn't sure whether Walker would give her enough credit to follow up on her answer about the phone call. In the moment, it had been a cool, considered response that Walker probably thought would get the police off her back. The one thing it confirmed was that Walker had an ice-cool persona, which re-enforced Taylor's assertions that she really could be Medusa.

She'd left her team beavering away at the new leads, which left her pondering her next move. She really wanted to pull Walker back in, but she knew that would be difficult if she continued to keep CTU out of the loop.

She finished her lunch and made a decision. She went down to the custody suite and asked to see Maria Gonzalez. The custody sergeant got them an interview room. Taylor leapt straight in.

"Miss Gonzalez, this is not an official interview, and it won't be recorded. It's just that something has come up and I wondered if you could help us. I understand if you would rather your brief was present."

Gonzalez eyed her up for a second, before giving her a sweeping hand gesture. "What do you need to know?"

"Martin Walker. He was one of your team. Correct?"

"That's right. He was Stonor's handler. I would get the brief for each job from the boss and pass it to Walker. He would brief Stonor and make sure the job was executed properly. We would then arrange a meet to drop off whatever the haul was, you know, cash or jewellery usually, and then I would move it onwards."

"Okay, so how long have you known Walker?"

"Er, I don't know. Maybe about a year. A year and half."

"And he introduced himself as Martin Walker."

"Yes, why?"

"That wasn't his real name."

Taylor was slightly perturbed as Gonzalez burst into laughter. "Something funny?"

"Oh, Detective, I was beginning to like you. I thought maybe you were better than the rest of these idiots."

"What's made you change your mind?"

Gonzalez sat back in her seat, an exasperated look on her face. "Do you really think that anyone in our line of work uses their own name? I mean, for fuck's sake, haven't you been grappling with multiple identities throughout your investigation?"

Taylor was embarrassed. Gonzalez was right. She tried to recover. "Sorry, yes, obviously we know about most of the fake personas, but we have reason to believe that the real Martin Walker may be dead. The man that was impersonating him is a career criminal and has some interesting links with other suspects in your OCG."

Gonzalez pulled a pinched expression. "Well, what I can say. We kept the chit-chat to a minimum. We used whatever names worked for each scenario and never got into anyone's life story. The less you know about each other, the better. All I can say is that he knew his way around a good robbery, and no one in our group is scared of terminating problems."

"You mean murder."

"You know what I mean, Detective. Haven't I already given you my confession?"

Taylor brought the informal interview to a close and thanked Gonzalez for her help. She was still surprised how co-operative she was being, given she was facing life in prison. If she kept helping them, Taylor decided she would do all she could to reduce her sentence, but her moral compass still held her to the principle that she had to go away for a long time. She was a cold, calculating killer ready to do whatever she was told without a shred of remorse.

Taylor went back to the CID office. The team were still deep in their work, following up the new leads. She decided to leave them to it and went and picked something up from her office desk. In all the furore of the last twenty-four hours, there was one person she had forgotten to thank.

She drove back to the hotel. She arrived just before half past two, desperately hoping that Eva Stimic had not left. As she walked into reception, one of the receptionists who had been at the first scene was on the desk. "Oh, Chief Inspector. Is there something wrong? I thought you'd finished your investigations here."

Taylor tried to give a reassuring smile. "We have. I just wanted to come back and thank someone for their help."

"Oh," said the receptionist. "Can I get them for you?"

"No, it's fine. I can find them, if you're happy for me to walk around the hotel."

Taylor didn't wait for the agreement, proceeding to walk up the stairs. She found Eva Stimic cleaning one of the rooms.

Eva immediately looked flustered. "Oh my. What are you doing here? Mr Moretti said you had finished your investigation."

"We have, but everything was a bit crazy on Sunday morning, and I didn't get a chance to thank you for everything you did."

"Oh, that's no problem. I was glad to help. Did you sort it? I understand a second body was found down near the lake."

"We did make an arrest."

"What! Someone staying in the hotel?"

"I can't really discuss this with you."

Eva gasped and gave a wide-eyed expression. "Miss Sanchez-Vicario. In room 101. It has to be. That's why you wanted me to check her room on Sunday morning."

Taylor smiled, without confirming Eva's perceptive insight. Eva seemed pleased that she had almost certainly got it right.

"Actually, Eva, there is one more thing I'd like your opinion on. Was there anything in Mr and Mrs Walker's room, 104 I think, that struck you as odd?"

Eva cocked her head to one side, thinking. Suddenly, she gasped again. "Actually, not odd exactly, but when I was dusting the round table in that room, I saw a small wallet, you know the type that contains flight tickets."

Taylor's stomach fluttered with excitement. "Go on."

"It was a single ticket in her name for a flight to New York."

Taylor thought her heart was going to burst out of her chest. She grabbed Eva's hand. "This is really important, Eva. Can you remember the date of the flight?"

Eva's eyes darted from left to right, trying to recall. Suddenly, she smiled. "Yes, 18 April. That's this Wednesday, isn't it?"

63

As Taylor began to drive back to the police station, her new-found confidence that she could keep CTU out of the loop began to wane. Now that she knew Walker had a flight booked to New York in two days' time, the chance of her being Medusa had just ramped up another level. Gonzalez had confirmed that the packages she tracked went by sea and usually rendezvoused with Medusa in a New York hotel. Taylor didn't believe in coincidences. She was now certain that Angela Walker was somehow the international terrorist, Medusa.

Her brain cycled through the options. If her team could prove that she had knocked off her husband, she had a stronger case for conspiracy to murder, due to the association with her brother and the little charade they pulled over the weekend. That scenario could be placed squarely in her jurisdiction as it related to the two murders in the hotel. If she could also get her for the murder of her husband, as a linked case, then so much the better.

The problem was, the minute she began to dabble in the Medusa case, she was going to struggle to justify that being within her jurisdiction. Gonzalez's confession was premised on her ability to help identify Medusa, but she knew that Banbury would assume that was all on his side of the fence. The fact that he didn't appear to know that Martin Walker was not who he said he was, added to the angst about boundaries. She knew he could accuse her of withholding evidence if she didn't tell him soon what the team had found that morning.

She screamed at no one in particular as she navigated the twisty roads across the beautiful countryside. She was gripping the steering wheel so tight her knuckles were turning white. She pulled into a lay-by and took in a deep breath. If she wasn't careful, she was going to have an accident.

She looked at her phone. She had no choice. She had to share what she knew with Banbury. She dialled his number and he answered within a few seconds.

"It's DCI Taylor," she said.

"Oh, what do you want?" His manner was rude and abrupt.

"My team have found some interesting things about the Walkers."

"DCI Taylor. I thought it was made quite clear to you by my super in this morning's meeting that you no longer have any remit to be involved in the CTU case. You've got your murder confession because Gonzalez is going to help us find Medusa. You compromised our op by your actions and have probably made Medusa go to ground, so please just butt out."

Taylor was gobsmacked but had the presence of mind to cover her arse. "So, can I be absolutely clear what you are saying. You are not the least bit interested in any intelligence my team may have found about the Walkers as it may pertain to your Medusa case."

"That is correct. You are barking up the wrong tree with Angela Walker. She has never been on our radar for this, and we've just had a breakthrough with our US liaison. Young is going to share his intel with us, in particular what he was doing at the hotel. Despite your attempts to shaft this case, we are now confident that a joint UK and US taskforce can get this thing back on track."

"So, you've found the diamonds?"

"No, and I'm not sure what relevance that has to this conversation."

"Just a question. Whatever you and your US pal think they know, the fact remains that a million pounds' worth of diamonds are still missing, and it's obvious Gonzalez has no idea where they are, so good luck with all that."

Taylor wasted no time in terminating the call, glad that she had kept her cool against such horrendous arrogance and got in the last word.

She started up her car and recommenced the journey back to the police station. Her self-confidence returned. She was going to prove to everyone that her team could not be ignored.

64

WALKING IN A DEAD MAN'S SHOES
MONDAY, 4PM

When Taylor returned to the CID office, the team were still hard at it. As soon as she walked in, Joshi spoke. "We've found him, ma'am. Martin Walker, I mean."

"Oh, how?"

"Well, it was actually pretty simple. They didn't do anything too complicated. Richard Snelling was pronounced dead a couple of weeks after he got out of prison. Victim of a stabbing, down some dark alley in South London. Because he was a career criminal who'd just got out of prison, it doesn't seem like the police did much more than a rudimentary investigation, putting it down to a criminal vendetta. The thing is, we know it wasn't Snelling, but it seems like they identified the body from documents he had on his person. We can only assume that things like his driving licence must have been faked to contain a picture of Martin Walker, because we are certain that it was Walker who was actually murdered, and they don't look a bit like each other. But what really cements this theory is that Angela Walker is recorded as identifying her brother's body."

Taylor put her hands against her temples. "Holy shit, so we are right. Walker set this up as soon as her brother got out of prison. I agree that it sounds like they set it up so Martin Walker was found with fake documents and then she did her poor grieving sister bit to remove any doubt. Jesus, that woman is colder than an iceberg." Taylor began to absentmindedly chew her nails, suddenly stopping in mid-gnaw. "Hold on. Can we prove this?"

Whiting had left but Brennan was still there, working with the two DCs . "Way ahead of you, boss," he chimed. "Martin Walker's body was cremated, which I guess is no surprise, given that they want to hide the evidence."

"Oh, so we're fucked?" replied Taylor.

"Not necessarily. If you can sign this request for a court order to exhume his ashes from the crematorium plot they so lovingly arranged for him, I can test the ashes to see if I can get a DNA sample."

"Is that likely to be successful?"

"I'm not going to lie. We probably have less than a five per cent chance that there is anything left that we can get a DNA sample from. The cremation process kills all DNA around soft tissues, organs and hair, stuff like that, but the one substance in the body that can sometimes survive the inferno is enamel. So, if he still had his own teeth, there is a chance."

Taylor quickly signed the document and sent Brennan off to do that as a priority, which left her with Chesters and Joshi. Chesters gave a conspiratorial grin and said, "I assume we are still not telling CTU about this?"

Taylor looked at them and sighed. "Actually, I lost my nerve on that one. I phoned CTU on the way back from the hotel."

Joshi frowned. "The hotel, ma'am. What were you doing back there?"

"I went to see the maid, Eva Stimic, because I realised we'd left rather abruptly yesterday morning after finding the second body. I just wanted to thank her for all her help."

"Oh," said Joshi, "how was she? Still trying to do our work for us?"

The comment from Joshi tweaked Taylor's conscience about her actions with using Eva, and how they would be seen, but she shrugged it off quickly. "Actually, she did tell me something else. Something that made me realise I had to share our growing theories about the Walkers with CTU. She remembers seeing a plane ticket in Mrs Walker's name. It was a flight to New York, leaving on Wednesday, this week."

Taylor let that information sink in. Chesters got there first. "Ah, so you think that's more evidence of her being Medusa. She would have been on her way to pick up the goods had the diamonds not been lost."

"Well, yes. It does seem to fit."

"What did CTU say?" probed Chesters.

Taylor shook her head. "This is where it gets interesting. I assumed that the revelation about Martin Walker and Snelling, coupled with Angela Walker having a flight booked to New York, would be enough for CTU to change their attitudes about our theories—"

Joshi interjected. "I can tell by your face that they didn't."

"Too right. As I said, I lost my nerve about keeping this from them, so I called Banbury. He was rude and dismissive of what I had to say. I even made him say it out loud that he had no interest in any intel we had on the Walkers, as it pertained to the Medusa case. He basically told me to butt out of their case, all because that bastard Young is apparently now talking."

Chesters blew out his cheeks. "Wow. What are we supposed to do now?"

Taylor fixed them with a firm stare. "Nothing changes. Keep chasing down these leads and cement not only our own case but bloody well prove that we are right about Walker being Medusa. CTU and CIA can play about down their dark alleys…" Taylor paused for dramatic effect, "…we are going to find the truth."

65

CRACKING THE CASE
MONDAY, 4.30PM

Taylor put her feet up on the desk and pushed herself down into her comfy office chair, thinking. She briefly looked at her watch. She'd promised her husband she'd be back by 6pm, which meant she had about an hour to sort out her thoughts.

She was optimistic that Brennan and Whiting would come through on Martin Walker's ashes, meaning she had a clear case against Angela Walker for conspiracy to murder. As CTU did not have her on their radar for Medusa, she wouldn't necessarily be criticised for further compromising their op, even though she was absolutely convinced that Walker was who they were looking for.

She pondered how they honestly thought they were going to track Medusa down. If Banbury was right, that her actions had made Medusa go to ground, it surely meant that Gonzalez had nothing to offer them. All Gonzalez had was the burner phone for that job. It seemed extremely unlikely that Walker would have left those lines of communication open, but the thought galvanised her, and she messaged Whiting asking her to bring the phone up from evidence. An idea was forming.

Angela Walker's flight intrigued her. Would she go now? If she was right that this was Walker's scheduled trip to pick up the diamonds, surely she would cancel the trip if there was no merchandise to collect. A moment of self-doubt crept in, and she could just imagine Banbury gloating if her theories were wrong and Walker was simply going on holiday to the Big Apple.

She shook it off. She'd learnt to trust her instincts. Her thoughts turned to the diamonds. Where could they be? Her team had scoured every inch of all four rooms that had been part of the weekend shenanigans. Apart from that single diamond under the bed in room 105, there was nothing. Taylor was convinced that Stonor would have kept the diamonds close to him. The fact that he appeared to have a single diamond on his person during the failed exchange suggested that he had maybe used it to goad them. Showing them the goods that he was refusing to hand over. Stonor had clearly misjudged the mood. If their theories were right, Stonor was never going to survive the betrayal.

Taylor shut her eyes and tried to envisage what was in Stonor's room and what possessions he had on him. The room was unremarkable. The team had searched it extensively and there was no evidence of any hidey-holes where he might have stashed the diamonds. Taylor knew there was a chance he'd stored them somewhere away from the hotel, but her instincts kept nagging at her. He would have kept them close.

The only other thing Stonor had was that damn walking stick. The piece of evidence that Spence had inexplicably compromised with his arrogance and poor judgement. She began to think about Brennan's description of the stick. Handmade. Larger than your average walking stick. Expensive. Inlaid with gold. His initials engraved in the shaft, even though he was pretending to be Mr Bush. It focused Taylor's mind. That walking stick was special to him. So special that he risked bringing something to a major criminal drop that had his real initials on it. She drummed her fingers together. There had to be something in that. The walking stick was key, if she could only work out why.

As Taylor agonised over the significance of the walking stick, Joshi brought in a full packet of digestive biscuits, smiling and raising her eyebrows as she removed the empty packet of custard creams. Taylor picked up on Joshi's vibe. "Don't judge me. I always eat when I'm stressed. My mother always used to call me hollow..." Taylor bolted up, making Joshi jump. "Oh my God. That's it. Hollow legs."

Joshi recoiled. "What on earth are you on about, ma'am?"

"Hollow legs. I eat all the time but never put on weight. My mother used to say I must have hollow legs."

Joshi pulled a face. "You're still not making sense, ma'am."

"I've cracked it, DC Joshi. Go and get that walking stick out of evidence. I know where the diamonds are."

66

THE WALKING STICK
MONDAY, 4.50PM

Taylor called the whole team into her office. Brennan and Whiting brought the phone and the walking stick in their respective evidence bags, as requested.

They lay on Taylor's desk as the team all took a seat in a semicircle formation. Taylor looked at the exhibits and then up to the team, nervous excitement coursing through her. "I want you all to be witnesses to this. If I'm right, we've just cracked this bloody case. If I'm wrong, at least I'm only embarrassing myself in front of you lot."

There were a couple of confused faces staring back at her, but she ignored them and pulled on a pair of forensic gloves. She picked up the evidence bag containing the walking stick. She looked at the SOCOs. "Right, you two. We're satisfied that this has been processed and me examining it will not compromise our case any further?"

Brennan and Whiting nodded in agreement.

Taylor let out a deep breath and unsealed the bag, slowly inching the walking stick out. Four pairs of eyes were fixed on what she was doing. She began to examine the stick, feeling up and down the wooden shaft. She stopped at the engraved letters, the gold inlay catching the light as she moved it around in her hands. She looked at the gold-plated footing. "We confirmed this matched with the indentation in the carpet in room 105?"

"Yes, ma'am, even though most of the forensics were compromised, we did manage to confirm the match and get a small blood sample ingrained in that footing. It placed the stick and Bush/Stonor in room 105."

Taylor nodded and turned the stick back up the right way. She shook it. There was nothing. She frowned, her eyes constantly darting up and down the stick. "Are you okay, ma'am?" said Joshi.

Taylor didn't answer. She was fixated on what she was trying to find. The wooden shaft was fully intact. One piece of quality wood, crafted into the main body of the stick. The footing was well made but essentially was just stuck on the end. Which left only one possibility.

Taylor began to examine the handle. Again, it was well made with more gold plating evident in the sturdy metal construction. She pulled at it. Nothing happened. She looked at it closely, focusing on where the handle met the wooden shaft. There was a reverent hush in the room as she worked slowly and methodically.

Suddenly, the team noticed a wide-eyed expression form on Taylor's face as she put one hand on the wooden shaft and another on the handle. She turned her hands in opposite directions. Nothing happened. She tried again.

Taylor let out a loud gasp as the two parts of the stick began to move. She turned her hands some more. It moved a bit more. She stood up, trying to gain more leverage. It worked. She turned her hands a couple more times. The handle and the stick separated. The stick had a hollow inside. *Hollow legs.*

Taylor stood there open-mouthed. The team looked at her, expectantly. She closed her eyes for a second, revelling in the moment she hoped would prove her theory right.

She put the handle down and smoothed out the evidence bag to make a receptacle. She carefully turned the walking stick over in a pouring action. Everyone held their breath. Nothing came out.

Taylor cursed under her breath, a deep frown forming. "Quick, get me a torch," she shouted at Chesters. He ran back into the main CID office and retrieved one.

Taylor shined it down the hole, her angry face turning to a beaming smile. She shook the stick, trying to move the small bag that she could just see at the bottom of the inlet. It was slow work, but the bag began to move at each shake. Eventually, a small velvet bag was close enough to the top of the opening that she could grab it out.

She placed it on the evidence bag and the whole team stood up to get a closer look. Taylor opened the bag and poured out the contents.

Diamonds.

67

Banbury and Sharpe sat round the table opposite Young. Sharpe took the lead. "I understand from our CTU US liaison that you are finally happy to speak to us."

"Yes, I'm Special Agent Young, CIA. It seems we stumbled into each other somewhat."

Banbury took over. "I think you stumbled into a local murder case first. We were only called because one of the suspects the local DCI was processing happened to have a warning marker in the crime system. When we realised she had one of our main players from a local terrorist cell in her investigation, we were over there like a shot."

Young nodded. "Yeah, she was a little bulldog that one."

Banbury smirked. "Uh huh. She didn't like you."

"The feeling was mutual."

"So come on then," Banbury probed, "why were you there?"

"We've been working through a large amount of intel on a cyber terrorism group based out of New York. We

273

think we've identified where their tech team are working from and have had the place under surveillance for several months. We've been tracking a woman who has been making regular flights from London to New York, checking into the same hotel and always visiting the premises we have been watching. This character that I think we all know as Medusa."

"So, you know who she is?"

"Well, we have a pretty strong theory. I was asked to come to the UK to track this woman's movements. I've had her under surveillance for about six weeks because we were tipped off that another job was going down. We had her booked into that hotel over the weekend with a flight out to New York on Wednesday."

Banbury's heart began to sink as he listened to Young but tried to remain calm. "But the diamonds were never handed over. Despite our annoyance at that DCI arresting Maria Gonzalez, she confessed to two murders at the hotel. It seems that Stonor and Walker, the gophers in our little terrorist cell, betrayed her. No one seems to know where the diamonds are."

Young pulled a pinched expression. "I don't know. We assumed that everything had gone to plan and that Medusa was going to be on that flight as planned on Wednesday."

Banbury's tone turned more aggressive. "Well maybe if you'd worked with us over the weekend instead of pissing off the local DCI, we might have been able to co-ordinate things better. I mean, didn't you find Stonor's body?"

Young rode the jibes. "Yeah, I was there when that American couple found him in the lake. I wasn't in any position to identify myself at that stage. I found his walking stick in the grass when I was walking back to the hotel. I kept it for a bit as I wasn't sure whether it had any significance. In the end, she kept badgering me, threatened to arrest me, so I had to declare my diplomatic immunity. I think you two worked out who I was so, in the end, I told her what I did with the walking stick to get her off my back. At no point did I know that the drop had gone wrong."

Banbury didn't want to ask the inevitable question. His phone call earlier in the day with Taylor came back to haunt him. He couldn't believe how wrong he'd potentially been, but he was right in his conviction that his team had found nothing about the woman he was sure Young was about to reveal as Medusa. He couldn't leave it any longer.

"Come on then, Young. Who is she?"

Young smirked, leaving a brief pause to add to the tension. "It's Angela Walker."

68

THE PLAN TO CATCH MEDUSA
MONDAY, 5.15PM

They all stared in awe at the glistening diamonds that were now laid out on top of the evidence bag. "Thank fuck for that," exclaimed Taylor.

"How did you work out the diamonds were in there, ma'am?" said Chesters.

"I just couldn't believe that Stonor had stored them somewhere else. I was convinced he must have them with him, especially when we found that one diamond in room 105. I kept going over why we hadn't been able to find them, and when it was clear that Gonzalez didn't have them, I went back over what Stonor had in his possession. What secured my theory was when you, Brennan, described the stick to me. I realised that this wasn't some ordinary walking stick. This was special to him, and the killer clue was that it had his real initials on it. I mean, why would he risk bringing something to a drop with his real initials on, when he was trying to disguise himself as someone else? It led to only one conclusion: that he must have somehow hidden them in the walking stick, although thank you, Joshi, for bringing back the trauma of my mother calling me hollow legs."

There were some impressed nods from the team. Whiting cut across the reverence. "What do we do now? Have we got to declare these to CTU?"

"No," replied Taylor, a bit abruptly. "I'm going to make damn sure that we can link this to the local case. I shall use all of this evidence to arrest Walker on three counts of conspiracy to murder, using the diamond heist as the catalyst for her crimes. Once our case is secure, it's up to CTU if they want to take her conviction further by charging her with terrorism offences linked to her little Medusa persona. No, I'm fed up with all these arrogant pricks thinking we are just some backyard country coppers. We did the hard work, and I'm damn well sure that we are going to get the credit."

"Are we just going to straight out arrest Angela Walker then?" asked Joshi.

Taylor picked the evidence bag up that contained the phone. "No. I want to run a sting operation. I want Walker to come to us."

"How?" replied Joshi.

Taylor unsealed the evidence bag that contained the phone and turned it on. It leapt into life. "I know it's a long shot," Taylor said, "but if Walker still has this burner phone active, I have an idea how we can catch her."

The team looked at her expectantly as she scrolled to the call log. Only one number had been called, consistent with the intel that Gonzalez had given them.

"Now," said Taylor, "my plan is only going to work if we are sure that Walker does not know that we arrested

Gonzalez. Are we sure that Walker had left the hotel before our little floor show out the front of the hotel?"

There was a brief pause before Joshi spoke. "It's okay, ma'am. I remember we found out that Walker left early, something like 8.15am, because you remember we questioned her as to why she drove past the crime scene when she left. You didn't arrest Sanchez-Vicario, sorry Gonzalez, until nearer nine."

"Okay, that's good enough for me." Taylor started to construct a text message.

I know where the diamonds are, but I don't have them yet. I can't make the original drop but will let you know when I've got them so we can make a new arrangement.

She showed the text to the team. They all nodded in agreement.

Taylor held her breath. "Well, here goes." She pressed send on the message. They waited a few seconds. Taylor cocked her head. "I think it's gone through," she exclaimed.

The team stayed silent as they all waited with bated breath, desperate to hear the ping of a returning message. Five minutes passed and nothing happened. Taylor nervously devoured a couple of digestives as everyone waited. Ten minutes. Nothing. Just as the team were about to give up hope, the phone pinged, thirteen minutes after the original text had been sent. Taylor almost dropped the phone in excitement. She opened the message.

Where are they?

Taylor responded straight away. *Can't say in case someone is monitoring the messages.*

These are burners. No one is monitoring these phones. Now tell me where they are.

Taylor began to get nervous. She had to keep her onside. She decided to go for the truth. *Stonor hid them in his walking stick. I know how to get hold of it.*

There was an agonising pause as the person on the other end of the phone didn't respond straight away. Again, Taylor jumped out of her skin when the phone pinged again.

Okay. Get it done quickly and message me as soon as you have them.

Taylor let out an excitable scream. "My God, I didn't think that would work."

The team were pumped. Taylor tasked Whiting and Brennan with resealing the evidence bags, taking photos of the deconstructed walking stick and sealing the diamonds and the velvet bag as separate evidence. She tasked Chesters and Joshi with finding a suitable location for the drop. She wanted it to be within the county so there would be no doubt about jurisdiction. Somewhere open and good for surveillance.

As the clock rolled round to 5.30pm, Taylor prepared to leave. She was still pumped with adrenalin but needed to get home and focus on her family. She'd just set up the biggest potential result of her career, but she had to distract herself. She had to sleep on it and make sure that she could work with the team on a foolproof sting operation with a clear, rested head.

As she began to walk out, her phone rang. She frowned at the caller ID. It was Banbury. She reluctantly answered it, and Banbury spoke without delay.

"I think I owe you an apology."

69

MEETING WITH BANBURY
TUESDAY, 9AM

Taylor made Banbury wait. They'd had the briefest of conversation the previous evening as Taylor was walking out the door, but she was determined not to lose any more family time. She arranged to meet him the next morning and here he was, sat opposite her, looking ashen-faced.

To his credit, Banbury wasted no time in repeating his apology and then tried to explain. "That Young character. What an arsehole. Seems he's been tracking Angela Walker for over six weeks and didn't think it merited a call to the UK intelligence agencies to share this nugget of wisdom. Seems like they've found what they think is the tech centre of this operation and have observed Walker going into the building on a regular basis."

Taylor left an uncomfortable pause after Banbury's opening gambit. She couldn't resist milking it for all it was worth. She eventually relented. "I agree, he was a total arsehole."

"He didn't like you."

"The feeling was mutual."

"That's what he said."

Taylor stifled a smile. "Well, as I said to you when I called you yesterday, we have some new intel on the Walkers that, if you'd bothered to listen to me, may have avoided this embarrassment for you."

Banbury shook his head. "Look, I'm done apologising to you. I didn't lie when I said that Walker had not come onto our radar, which is why I'm so pissed that the CIA apparently suspected her of being Medusa months ago. We had Martin Walker in the frame, but not her."

Taylor leant forward. "But here's the thing. The person you were tracking was not Martin Walker."

"What!"

"Yeah, surprised us too. When we processed the second victim, assuming it was Martin Walker, we were shocked to find the DNA came back as another person."

"Who?"

"A guy called Richard Snelling, who just happens to be the career criminal brother of Angela Walker."

Banbury put his hand over his face. "How did we not know that?"

"Well, for what it's worth, it was a strange thing for Walker to do. She tried to put us off the scent by pretending he was her husband, all over the weekend, and then identified the body. She must have known we would find out his real identity so I can only assume that she felt forced into getting rid of him."

"Where's the real Martin Walker?"

"She killed him. He was stabbed down some dark alley in South London and then she covered up the real story by somehow convincing the police that it was her brother who had died. Her brother immediately adopted Martin Walker's identity just before you started tracking him. You had no reason to think he was anyone else but Walker."

Banbury pulled a confused expression. "Hold on. We would have verified Walker's ID by facial rec."

Taylor shrugged. "I don't know what to say other than Angela Walker is clearly well connected and well resourced. It wouldn't surprise me if she's paying people off to hack into our systems and change the records, so we are none the wiser."

"That's impossible. Our systems are totally secure."

"Are you sure about that?"

Taylor could see Banbury was steaming with the realisation that, system hacks or not, he'd been played for over ten months by a fake Martin Walker. She decided to crack on. "My team are currently in the process of getting a court order to exhume Walker's ashes to see if we can get a DNA match from it. It's a long shot but, if we get a match, it will add evidence to my charges of three counts of conspiracy to murder."

"You've arrested her?" exclaimed Banbury.

"No, not yet, because there's something else you might want to know." Taylor couldn't help but revel in the blows she was landing.

"What?" Banbury said, a hint of spoilt child appearing in his manner.

"We've found the diamonds." Taylor watched with amusement as the open-mouthed expression threatened to freeze on his face. "They were hidden in the walking stick that belonged to Stonor. It was hollow and he stuffed them inside, contained in a velvet bag."

Banbury's face was crumpled with stress lines. "This changes everything. I need to get back to my team and plan what we're going to do."

"No," said Taylor, a firm, assertive tone evident in the delivery of the rejection of his statement.

"What do you mean *no.*"

"I'm sorry, but we are in the process of arranging a sting operation. I'm going to use the discovery of the diamonds to lure Angela Walker out and prove that they were the catalyst for the killing of her husband, her brother and Stonor. Once I've got her bang to rights for her involvement in killing her husband and all the shit that's gone on over the weekend, you can do what you want with the Medusa stuff."

Taylor continued to be amused as Banbury began to turn a deep shade of red as his spoilt child routine threatened to turn into a full-on bout of screaming abdabs. "You... you can't do that. You have to stop and let us take over."

"Too late, it's already in motion. We've got the burner phone that Gonzalez was using to communicate with Walker. I took a gamble and sent a message to the phone, saying the diamonds had been found. I wasn't sure whether Walker had closed the lines down, but we got lucky. She responded. We are in the process of arranging a new drop using the walking stick as bait."

Banbury's apology now seemed like ancient history. He was reeling, but his arrogance and false superiority was never far away. Taylor was having none of it.

"So, you have a choice. You either help me with this op or butt out until I have her in custody."

70

ARRANGING THE STING
TUESDAY, 10.30AM

Taylor focused the team on getting the sting op organised and executed. Banbury had left the meeting with no decision either way. Taylor knew the politics would start raging again, and there was a distinct possibility that she would be told to stop by someone higher up the food chain. She briefed her chief super straight after the meeting with Banbury and he was his usual supportive self. Taylor had outlined how all her actions were linked to the local murder cases, and he found it difficult to argue with her operational plan. They both knew that it might not be enough.

Chesters and Joshi were there. "Right, we need to get this plan executed quickly before the powers that be lock this down. Tell me your ideas as to the location of the drop."

Joshi took the lead. "Three suggestions, ma'am. One. Could we use the hotel? Two, use the large park in the centre of Cheltenham. Three, use the upper floor of the indoor shopping centre in Cheltenham, around the food places."

Taylor huffed. "I'm not sure the GM of the hotel will cope with us being back there, so maybe we'd better look at the other two options. The problem I can see with both of them is lots of escape routes, which we can't cover with just the three of us. How are we doing with getting more manpower?"

Chesters took over. "I've spoken to ops, and we reckon we can get another eight officers to help, provided the chief super signs off the operational plan and prioritises the resources."

"At the moment, he's on board, but we can't wait as CTU might wield their sword and get us shut down. So, let's go with the park. I don't like the shopping centre option. Too many people, too many shops she could disappear into. Whilst the park is wide open, we can at least have better surveillance, and with nearly a dozen of us around the site, we should be able to track whatever goes on."

"What about Gonzalez?" Joshi said. "I assume that Walker will be watching for the drop to happen and will be expecting to see Gonzalez."

Taylor smiled. "Well, my brilliant detective, that's where you come in. You are about Gonzalez's height and build, and remember she is the master of disguise. With a hoodie and some dark glasses, I'm sure you can pull it off."

Joshi grimaced at the thought but agreed to give it a go.

They rapidly put the finishing touches to the operational plan and Taylor made a point of printing it off and taking it directly to the chief super for sign-off. He complied, and they were both relieved that nothing had happened with CTU.

As Taylor got back to the office, she called Joshi and Chesters in. "Right, we are ready to go. Chesters, get the resources organised. I want an operational briefing at 3pm. Joshi, get your disguise organised and be kitted out in time for the briefing. Also, liaise with Brennan and Whiting. I want the walking stick back out of evidence as we are going to leave it at the sting site as bait. Get another velvet bag and fill it with some fake gems, in case she chooses to examine the merchandise at the drop site. I need her to think that she has the real thing, and we can't have the walking stick empty."

They both nodded their understanding as Taylor got out the burner phone. "Right, I'm going to set this up for 5pm." She spread out the map of the park they'd printed off on her desk. "Based on the topology of the park, we are going to use this bench. It's nice and central and far enough away from all of the park exits to help us manage the live situation."

Chesters and Joshi examined the map and took photos of the drop site.

"Joshi, I want you to walk to the bench, sit down for about a minute, holding the walking stick in plain sight. Then, lean the stick against the end of the bench and walk away. Chesters, we'll cover this in the briefing, but I want one officer on each park exit. We will be close to the drop site, watching what is going on. Make sure everyone's comms are working well before we are on the ground."

They both confirmed their understanding of the plan and their tasks.

Taylor blew hard and began to type a text message. "Here goes nothing."

Will be at Pittville Park, Cheltenham at 5pm. There's a bench in the centre of the park, just past the lake. I'll be sat on the bench for a few minutes with the walking stick. The diamonds are still inside. You need to twist the handle to open it up. I'll lean the stick against the end of the bench and walk away.

She hit send and they waited.

It seemed like forever, but ten minutes later, the phone pinged. It was on.

71

PITTVILLE PARK, CHELTENHAM
TUESDAY, 5PM

The team had been briefed. The resources were in place at 4.30pm, manning all the exits. Taylor was stood by a kiosk selling coffee, sipping a latte and trying to blend in. She had an uninterrupted view of the park bench. Chesters was nearer, sitting on another bench about thirty yards away from the drop zone.

Taylor glanced at her watch. It was a few minutes to five and she spotted Joshi walking towards the bench with the walking stick in her hand. Taylor cursed that someone else was sat on the bench, but they had luckily left enough space for Joshi to sit down.

Joshi got to the bench and sat at the opposite end to where the man was. She had her hood up and dark glasses on, which didn't look too out of place as the late spring day was mercifully bright and warm, not making Joshi's get-up too conspicuous.

Taylor couldn't help but take a look around, searching for Angela Walker. She couldn't see anything. She got on the comms and checked everyone was in position. They all responded that they were.

Taylor checked her watch. It was 5.01pm and time for Joshi to make her move. But, as Taylor watched her, she realised she'd reacted to something. They could hear everything that was going on. The man on the end of the bench was talking to Joshi. The audio of his voice was a bit distant, but it sounded like he was telling Joshi to leave the stick and walk away.

Taylor couldn't believe it. She reprimanded herself for assuming it would be this easy. If she hadn't got wrapped up in her own complacency, she would have realised that Walker would not come herself. She got straight on the comms.

"Alert. Op is changing. Walker has sent a man to pick up the walking stick. He's talking to Joshi now and telling her to leave the stick and walk away. He's tall, dark hair, wearing shades and has a blue sports top and black jeans on. As soon as he's mobile, keep onto him. Do not lose him!"

Taylor's heart was racing. She couldn't let this go wrong. She told Joshi over the comms to comply with his request. She held her breath as Joshi got up and leant the stick against the end of the bench. The man immediately got up and moved to the other end of the bench, discreetly grabbing the stick and leaning it against his leg. Taylor gave a running commentary on the comms. The man didn't move from the bench but eventually grabbed the stick and began to twist the handle. Taylor's heart felt like it was going to burst out of her chest. If he checked inside the bag, there was a chance he may realise they were not the real thing. He twisted the handle off and looked inside. He nodded and twisted the handle back on.

Taylor let out a huge sigh and, just as she was about to give an update on the comms, she felt a hard object being pushed into her back. "Don't look round, Detective, or I will shoot you."

Taylor stiffened at the voice and what she assumed was a gun in her back. "Angela Walker, I presume."

"Hmm, you think you're clever, don't you, but you have absolutely no idea who you are dealing with. Now get on your comms and tell all your officers to walk away so my man can get out of here without any interference."

Taylor played for time. "I'm not going to do that."

"Suit yourself. I won't have any hesitation in killing you. Do you think your husband and daughter will think you've been a hero, or will they curse every day since you were killed wondering why you were so stupid?"

Taylor's mind was racing. The mention of her husband and daughter was an obvious but unnerving tactic. The fact Walker knew about her home life was concerning and dangerous. "Okay, okay, I'll do it," Taylor said. She had no desire to die today but wasn't about to give up. Her mind was processing all the possibilities as she got back on the comms.

"Er, change of plan. All assets need to stand down. I repeat, all assets need to stand down and leave the park. The op is compromised."

Taylor could hear confused chatter at the other end. She cut across it. "Please, everyone. Do it now."

The gun was shoved harder in her back. "Good girl. Now my man is going to move and if I see anyone approach him or he has any trouble getting out of the park, you're a dead woman."

Taylor stood still, scanning the park. Joshi and Chesters had moved out of sight. The man began to walk away, going towards the east exit of the park. The gun was still pushed hard into her back, and she could feel Walker's breath on her neck.

Taylor thought about fighting back. Could she swing an arm, digging her in the ribs, giving her just enough time to disarm her? Just as she was deciding whether to stick or twist, Taylor felt a sharp pain in her neck and fell to the floor.

Her world went black.

72

CHELTENHAM GENERAL HOSPITAL
TUESDAY, 8.30PM

Taylor's eyes fluttered open as she tried to orientate herself. She saw the concerned face of her husband staring back at her and heard the excitable shouts of her daughter.

"What happened?" she said.

"You've been drugged. Seems you were injected with something. Your boss tells me you were on an important operation."

The realisation of what happened made Taylor come to properly and she tried to sit up. "Hey, hey," her husband said. "You need to rest."

Taylor let out a frustrated scream, regretting it the minute she saw the concerned face of her daughter. She cupped Emma's face. "I'm sorry, darling. Mummy's just a bit angry with herself."

They fussed over her for another fifteen minutes or so before her husband said he really needed to get Emma to bed. Taylor let them go.

Five minutes later, there was a noise at the door to her room. Chief Superintendent Price came in with Chesters and Joshi. Before they could say anything, Taylor blurted out, "I'm sorry."

Price gave her a sympathetic look. "It happens. We probably underestimated how clever Walker is and CTU dragging their heels didn't help."

"CTU?" exclaimed Taylor. "What did they do?"

"Just as the op was about to be executed, I got a call from Sharpe. He was furious and insisted I call it off."

"Given the time, I refused, and he slammed the phone down, saying he was deploying his team to the park."

"What happened?" said Taylor, a sense of dread in her voice.

"They were too late. By the time they got there, our team had done what you asked and disengaged. They found you slumped on the floor with no sign of Walker or her accomplice."

Taylor repeated her apology and grimaced at Joshi and Chesters. "Are you two okay? I'm sorry my incompetence cocked it up."

Joshi and Chesters both protested at the same time, giving her kind platitudes that she felt she barely deserved.

Price got back to business. "Look, it's a setback and yeah, there's now lots of politics raging, but the chief has our back. She is defending our operational plan based on it being linked to our local case. Your governance on this one was sound and has helped us to save face. She's meeting with the top brass at CTU, and it now seems as though the CIA have decided to play ball."

"Oh, sir, I really didn't mean to cause you or the chief this much aggravation."

"Look, stop wallowing in self-pity and focus on what we can do. Firstly, make sure the case against Gonzalez is watertight so we can prosecute her without any problems, although her usefulness and therefore co-operation may be lessened now we know who Medusa is."

Taylor glanced over to Chesters and Joshi, and they gave her a reassuring nod.

"Secondly, regardless of the politics, we now know for sure that Angela Walker is Medusa. In ten months of investigation and sophisticated surveillance, CTU never got anywhere near that, so you and your team should congratulate yourself for making a significant contribution to a national terrorism case, even if the sting went south."

Taylor gave a pained smile.

"Thirdly, I understand that if we ever catch Walker, you have a pretty strong case for three counts of conspiracy to murder, including her poor husband."

Taylor allowed herself a more complete smile. "Well, yes, if Brennan can get DNA from his ashes."

Price nodded. "And lastly, although Walker knows we are onto her and has gone to ground, we still have the diamonds."

Taylor frowned. "Yeah, I guess, although she is going to be pissed when she realises the walking stick didn't contain the real thing and I'm concerned about what she might do."

Price put on a questioning look.

Taylor fought back tears. "When she had the gun in my back at the park, she mentioned my husband and daughter. I don't know how she found out about them, but she is a cold, calculating killer, and I'm concerned for their safety."

Price immediately turned to Chesters and asked him to liaise with the control room to get patrols deployed around Taylor's house.

Taylor tried to sit up but clutched her head, the pain and wooziness still debilitating her.

Price reprimanded her. "You need to rest. They are going to keep you in for observation overnight. All your vitals are fine, but you need to let the drugs get out of your system. If you feel up to it, I'll see you back at work on Thursday."

The three of them exited the hospital room. An officer remained outside her room, keeping guard in case Walker sent someone to finish the job.

Taylor was exhausted and sleep was calling her. She drifted off, hoping that her family were safe and that Price and the chief really did have her back.

Today had been a bad day.

73

CID OFFICE
THURSDAY, 9.30AM

Taylor walked into the CID office. Physically, she was fine. There had been no ill effects from whatever Walker had injected her with and she had benefitted from a long day of rest. But mentally, she was all over the place. She felt lost. The one thing that wound her up about several of her male colleagues, their arrogance, had been her own undoing. Everyone had treated her like some backyard country copper, and she hated it. She'd allowed herself to get wound up and ended up making poor judgements. The chief super had been his usual supportive self, but she knew whatever he and the chief were doing to smooth this situation over would go against her if she ever went for promotion to Superintendent.

The team continued to back her to the hilt, and their smiling faces cheered her up as she poured a coffee and sat down with them in the main office.

"Come on then," she said, "tell me the worst."

Chesters spoke first. "We've got the CPS file done for the two murders, although Gonzalez has suddenly changed her tune and is insisting she was coerced into a confession. She's made a second statement stating that she had nothing to do with the murders."

Taylor's heart sank. "Oh, for fuck's sake. The chief super said that her usefulness had waned now we know that Walker is Medusa. I guess Gonzalez realises that and is back-pedalling."

Chesters tried to be positive. "It's fine, ma'am. We have her DNA on the murder weapon and can demonstrate clear motive and opportunity. We'll get her."

Taylor sipped her coffee, hoping that Chesters' optimism was not misplaced.

Joshi piped up. "We've also been putting together the CPS file against Walker for conspiracy to murder. Maybe the case against her is not so tight, but one way we might be able to bring Gonzalez back around is to get her to testify against Walker."

Taylor huffed. "But she's never met her."

Joshi smiled. "Ah yes, but she's heard her voice. If we can get a sample of Walker talking, we might be able to get Gonzalez to confirm she is the person that she has been speaking to."

Taylor sighed. "I don't deserve you two, and I'm sorry if my enthusiasm isn't matched by yours, but despite what the chief super says, I think I'm in the shit."

Joshi frowned. "Now come on, boss. This isn't like you. We can get both of these cases to a successful conclusion and, anyway, Brennan is going to be here shortly with the DNA results from the review of Walker's ashes. If they're positive, the case is much stronger."

Taylor drained the rest of her coffee. "I'm sorry. You're

both right and great work. We just have the small problem of trying to find and arrest Walker. I may have exposed her as Medusa but if it's made her go to ground, we might be waiting a long…" As Taylor's sentence drifted off, she bolted out of her seat, almost sending her coffee cup flying. "Oh my God. Did anyone check whether she got on that flight to New York yesterday?"

Chesters looked grim-faced. "Sorry, ma'am. We did. She was a no-show."

Taylor slumped back down in her chair. "Hmm, figures."

As the self-pity show threatened to get out of hand, Taylor's mood was lifted as she saw the familiar, excitable puppy that was Brennan.

Taylor didn't need to ask. His face said it all. "We got it? The DNA matched?" she said.

"Oh yes it did," replied Brennan. "We've got her now."

74

THE COTSWOLD MANOR HOTEL - ROOM 113
THURSDAY, 10AM

Eva Stimic worked diligently, pleased that the person who was in the room for the next few days had left the *please service my room* sign on their door. Getting a few rooms done early meant that she had a fighting chance of getting away a bit earlier.

She made the bed, cleaned the bathroom, putting out a fresh set of toiletries and replacing the bottled water. She took away the dirty towels and replaced them with clean, fluffy ones, the freshly laundered smell something that always made Eva happy.

As she began to dust the round table in the room, she stopped. Lying on the table was a notebook. A leather-bound notebook with three initials monogrammed on the front. She took a step away from the table, staring at it. Her brain was trying to process why she had reacted to its presence.

It was one of the things she'd prided herself on. Her observation skills. It was why she was so stoked to be asked by that detective to help her with that horrid affair the previous weekend.

Suddenly, Eva gasped. That was it. Thinking about the kind detective had made her realise where she'd seen the notebook before. The initials, AJW. The W was for Walker. The lady who had been in room 104 over the weekend, with the husband who had been murdered in the grounds of the hotel. The one the detective was asking about when she came back to the hotel earlier in the week. The one who had the plane ticket to New York.

Eva put her hand to her mouth. She didn't know what to do. A thought came to her, and she checked the room list. She moved her finger down to room 113. The name of the guest was Miss Serena Bellingham.

She recoiled. What the hell was going on? She began to doubt herself. She was being paranoid. The previous weekend must have spooked her more than she realised, and she was seeing danger and conspiracy at every turn.

She shook it off and continued to clean the room. The notebook lay there, like some Pandora's box. She finished the cleaning by vacuuming the room. She got all her cleaning stuff together and placed it outside the door, taking the sign off the door and hanging it on the inside of the handle.

She took one last look around. The place was gleaming. The notebook still lay there. Eva stood for a minute, staring at the quarry. She sighed and walked towards it. If her instincts were right, there was something off about this situation. The detective seemed agitated about Mrs Walker, and when she'd told her about the flight to New York, it seemed like the information had been a breakthrough in the case. Eva couldn't reconcile it at the time, because although she only met Mrs Walker for the briefest of moments, she seemed like such a kind old lady. She'd asked for an extra pillow when she arrived and even gave Eva a tip for bringing it up to her.

Eva's hand hovered over the notebook. Her heart was pumping. She picked it up, unclipping the clasp that was wrapped around the notebook to keep it securely closed. She tentatively opened it, scanning the writing on the first few pages. She frowned. It was full of numbers. Some looked like dates; others were just random numbers. She turned a few more pages. They were just the same. As she went to turn the next page, she jumped a mile as the door to the hotel room opened, making her drop the notebook on the table.

Eva gasped as the face she'd seen before came into the room, shutting the door behind her. Eva wanted to scream as Mrs Walker stared back at her. She'd changed her appearance: her hair was different, and she had much more make-up on. But it was the eyes that did it. The eyes that Eva had thought were so kind were now boring into her skull, an unnerving steeliness to the expression.

Walker looked down at the notebook and then up at Eva. "Well, we seem to have a problem here. Don't you think?"

75

LIFE OR DEATH
THURSDAY, 10.10AM

Taylor had been idly scrolling through her emails for about twenty minutes, unsure what to do next. Her brilliant team were wrapping up the case files. She should have felt a sense of satisfaction at having two strong cases to present to the CPS, but not having Walker in custody was niggling at her. She was trying not to self-persecute, but she knew her poor judgement with the park sting had contributed to Walker getting away.

She started scanning the morning briefing. The chief super had tasked her with a new case. A single man found dead but with no obvious trauma. The first responders had reported inconclusive evidence of an assault, leading to the notes speculating about suicide, manslaughter or murder. Just as Taylor was about to call the team in to task out the initial investigation, she heard a beep. She instinctively picked up her phone but was confused when there weren't any notifications on the screen. It took her brain a second to realise it was the phone they'd confiscated from Gonzalez.

Taylor gasped with shock. There was a text message on the phone from the number they'd been using to communicate with Walker. Her hand began to shake as she went to press on the message, adrenalin surging through her body. As she read the message, fear gripped her.

Hello, DCI Taylor. Yes, I know it's you sending me messages and not my little lackey. You thought you had me, didn't you? I'm always one step ahead of you... but now we have a problem. A maid has violated my privacy, which just can't happen. I have a gun to her head and unless you bring my diamonds to the place this all started, she will be dead by noon. Text me when you're close. Her life depends on it. AJW

There was a second message straight after it.

Oh, and come alone. If I see any of your team, she's dead.

Taylor's heart froze. Walker was at the hotel, and she was holding one of the maids hostage. Taylor couldn't process what was happening. Was it Eva, and if so, how had she got herself in this position? She wondered why Jamie Mellon hadn't flagged it but realised that CTU had probably withdrawn him from his undercover assignment.

She read the message over and over. The sensible thing to do was to flood the hotel with police resources, but they would be sacrificing the maid's life just to land Walker. Taylor shook her head. She just couldn't do it. The decision was made.

She walked out of her office, trying to act normally as Chesters and Joshi looked up. "Er, just popping out for a bit. We need to have a briefing on a new case when I get back."

Taylor didn't wait for a response but couldn't help noticing their concerned faces. She wasn't sure she'd pulled it off. She shook it off and went down to the evidence store.

She explained to the officer on the desk that she needed to check out some evidence, trying to stop her hands shaking as she filled in the form. She avoided eye contact and walked out the second he gave her the velvet bag containing the diamonds. As she made it outside into the station car park, she stopped and leant against a wall. She was hyperventilating and had to catch her breath.

"Are you okay, ma'am?"

Taylor jumped a mile. It was Whiting. "Oh, yes, fine. I think maybe I'm still feeling the after-effects of that drug I was injected with."

Whiting looked concerned. "Where are you going with the diamonds?"

Taylor winced, looking down at the evidence bag in her hand. "Oh, er, CTU have asked to see them. They want to verify that they are the real thing, so they can close down the safety deposit box robbery."

"Really," her tone evidently telling Taylor that she didn't believe her.

Taylor bent over and took in some deep breaths, trying to distract Whiting from the web of lies that she was building.

"I think you'd better go and sit down, ma'am. Can I take the diamonds to CTU for you?"

Taylor stood up straight. "No, no, I'll be fine in a minute. Don't let me keep you. I'm sure you've got more important things to do than worry about me."

Taylor was relieved when Whiting finally left her to it. She wasn't convinced that Whiting believed a word she'd told her, but she had no time to worry about it. She looked at her watch. It was already 10.40am and it was at least a half hour drive to the hotel.

She got in her car and sat for a second. Her breathing was nearly normal, and the light-headedness was passing. She started up the car and set off.

When she was about five minutes away from the hotel, she stopped and texted Walker back. She got an immediate response. *Room 113 and you'd better be alone.*

Taylor parked up away from the main entrance. She wanted to enter the hotel without being seen by any of the staff. There was at least one thing she'd learnt from her weekend at the hotel: all the different ways you could get in and out of the main building.

She walked across a grassy area from the car park that was next to the tennis court. She went in the back entrance that led into the lounge. A couple of people were sat there drinking coffee, but she sped past them and straight up the stairs, not daring to look right at reception, in case she was apprehended. She scoured the top floor, before realising that room 113 was down the other end of the hotel, nearer the room where they managed the weekend incident from. She walked down the steep stairs and into the main ground-floor corridor. She kept her head down, hoping that no one recognised her. She got to the end of the corridor without incident and went down the stairs by the room they'd been in. She checked a couple of doors. Panic began to set in. Where was room 113?

She walked through a connecting door. There were stairs immediately to her left leading up to a single door. She strained to see what the number was. She was sure it was the right room. She nervously crept up the stairs. Cleaning supplies were still outside the door. This was it.

Taylor tried to slow her breathing and lightly tapped

on the door. She heard a faint voice from the other side. It sounded like she was being told to come in.

She pushed at the door, and it gave. As she tentatively entered the room, her worst fears were confirmed. She was greeted with the terrified face of Eva Stimic, tears running down her cheeks, her mouth gagged and a gun pointing at her head.

76

Whiting rushed into the CID office, garnering concerned looks from Chesters and Joshi. "I've just seen the boss. Is she alright? She was acting really weird."

Joshi looked at Chesters. "I don't know," she said. "She left about twenty minutes ago saying she had to go somewhere and would be back to brief us on a new case in a bit."

Chesters frowned. "She did seem a bit agitated."

Whiting rubbed her forehead. "Something's not right. She had the evidence bag with the diamonds in. When I asked her what she was doing with them, she said she was taking them to CTU."

"What!" exclaimed Joshi. "Why would she be doing that?"

"Exactly, they don't have any business with the diamonds while we have them logged as key evidence in our two cases."

"Oh my God," shouted Chesters, "are you saying she's doing a runner with a million pounds' worth of diamonds?"

"No, no, nothing like that. Not Taylor. No, she's in trouble. She was practically keeling over with the stress of what she was doing. Struggling to breathe, stuff like that."

Joshi jumped up and ran into her office. She scanned around as the others followed her. "What is it?" said Whiting.

"It's gone. The phone we were using to contact Walker."

Chesters gasped, a wide-eyed expression on his face. "No, surely not. She hasn't gone somewhere to meet Walker, has she?"

Joshi frowned. "Why would she?"

Chesters put his hands on his temples. "Think about it. The phone's gone. She's taken the diamonds. Walker's got something on her or… oh no, she's got one of her family and is threatening to kill them unless she gets the diamonds."

Joshi and Whiting looked horrified. "That can't be true, surely," said Joshi. "She would have asked us to help."

"Not necessarily," said Whiting. "If Chesters is right, Walker probably told her to come alone."

"We have to tell the chief super. Now!" shouted Chesters.

77

THE COTSWOLD MANOR HOTEL - ROOM 113
THURSDAY, 11.20AM

Walker stared at Taylor as she entered the room. "So, we meet again, Detective Chief Inspector. I can't say it's a pleasure. You've been a thorn in my side these last few days, and it's got to stop. I'm glad you finally made a sensible decision and brought my property."

Taylor had no plan but knew she had to keep her talking if she had any chance of working her way out of this situation. She tried to give Eva a reassuring nod, but the poor girl was terrified.

"It's not your property. You're just a common little thief."

Walker cocked the gun, making Eva scream from behind her gag. "I don't think you want to be upsetting me, Detective, if you want this pathetic creature to be alive in the next few minutes. Although, I suppose at least she won't have to be the one to clean her spattered brains off all the surfaces."

"What do you want?" said Taylor with a steeliness that she didn't feel inside.

Walker screwed up her face. "What do I want?"

"Yes," replied Taylor. "I mean, what's your plan here?"

Walker pushed the gun harder against Eva's head. "My plan is for you to give me those diamonds and then I'm going to kill you both."

Taylor had been scanning the whole time they'd been talking, looking for something that she could use as a weapon or a distraction. A large wardrobe was to her left, but otherwise there was a large gap between her and where Walker was holding Eva.

"Come on," shouted Walker, "I haven't got all day. Throw the diamonds on the bed and then kneel down."

Taylor's life began to flash before her. Images of her husband and daughter flashed into her mind. The loyal faces of her team who would probably be cursing her for being so stupid for coming here with no backup. The chief super, with that kind but slightly disapproving expression he tried to hide when she'd messed up again.

She only had one option. She opened the evidence bag, Walker's eyes boring into her. She took out the velvet bag, pushing her finger into the hole to loosen the drawstring. She poured a couple of diamonds into her hand and held it out, so Walker could see they were the real thing.

Walker's face softened as she saw the gleaming gems, catching the morning light that was streaming through the window. "Good," she said, "I'm glad you are not trying to trick me this time."

As Walker's sentence drifted off, Taylor threw the diamonds in the air, towards Walker. It had the desired effect. Walker instinctively stepped forward to grab the flying objects, as the remaining diamonds began to spill out of the bag in mid-air. Crucially, she took the gun away from Eva's head.

Taylor took the opportunity and lunged forward, pushing Walker hard. The gun went off in the melee, but it had fired straight into the ceiling, as Walker fell back, losing grip of the gun as she fell. Walker recovered her position quickly, despite her aging years, and pushed hard against Taylor from her prone position. Taylor lost a bit of momentum but soon recovered as she punched Walker straight in the face. Taylor was surprised how she rode the blow and grimaced as one of Walker's legs kicked out hard at her own. Taylor's leg buckled as she fell forward, giving Walker the opportunity to shove her backwards, sending Taylor sprawling back onto the floor.

Walker managed to stand back up and grabbed the gun as Taylor scrambled to get up. Walker pointed it straight at Taylor, her face screwed up in fury. "I'm gonna enjoy this, you fucking bitch."

Taylor froze, waiting for the inevitable, but as she was about to let out a frustrated scream, Eva had pulled herself together and swung a bottle of water hard against Walker's head.

The blow landed. Walker seemed to be in limbo. The blow hadn't knocked her down, but she stood there, dazed. Eva dropped the bottle and ran into the bathroom, sobbing uncontrollably. Taylor lunged forward, connecting a kick right in her stomach. Walker went down.

Taylor's brain was full of fog. Walker was still a danger, but she had to save Eva and protect her own life. As Walker began to sit up, rubbing her head, Taylor couldn't help but feel like she was in one of the *Terminator* films. Walker just wouldn't go down. She just wouldn't stop.

As panic set in, the next few seconds seem to play out in slow motion. A sudden commotion at the hotel room door. The door flew open and heavily armed officers stormed into the room, surrounding Walker and aiming their automatic weapons at her head and torso. They kicked her gun away, as they quickly manhandled Walker and cuffed her.

As the armed officers dragged Walker out, Taylor was suddenly confronted by a sea of concerned faces. Chief Superintendent Price, Joshi, Chesters, Whiting, Brennan and Moretti the hotel manager, who clearly thought he'd seen the last of her.

A medic came in and checked Taylor, but she was more concerned about Eva. Joshi and Moretti went into the bathroom. They found Eva curled up in the corner, crying hysterically. They coaxed her out of the room and passed her into the arms of a second ambulance crew.

Taylor looked at Price. "I'm sorry. I'm sorry," she said. "I didn't know what to do."

Price shook his head. "Let's not worry about that now. There's plenty of time for all that."

"How did you find me?" said Taylor, fighting back tears.

"Your team thought you were acting strange, so they tracked you by your radio. When they realised the phone you've been using to communicate with Walker had gone from your desk, they put two and two together. They spoke to me, and when we realised you were at the hotel, we decided to throw everything we had at it. It was lucky that one of the staff saw you going up to this room, or we may not have got to you in time."

Taylor tried to apologise again, but the tears began to flow. An ambulance crew took her away.

78

SIX MONTHS LATER

Taylor sat in the coffee shop, nursing a steaming cappuccino. She'd been through the ringer. The chief constable and Price had given her a three-hour grilling a few days after the final hotel showdown. Every step of the investigation was reviewed. Every decision she made was scrutinised. Her judgement had been called into question several times, and Taylor didn't try to make excuses for the things that had gone wrong. Spence and Ablett had dobbed her in about the use of Eva as an unofficial search hound, a fact that had not gone down well.

Taylor surmised that the only thing that had saved her from a full PSD investigation and probable disciplinary action was the fact that Walker had been caught and the politics with CTU had been smoothed over. They had a successful conclusion to a ten-month operation, and it seemed as though the CIA were also happy. The successful prosecution of Maria Gonzalez on two murder charges also helped, and Taylor was hopeful that she would also get conspiracy to murder charges against Walker when the whole complex case against her finally got to court.

The chief told Taylor that her team had given their full backing to everything she'd done, which just made her feel worse. Spence and Ablett had been disciplined and moved back to reactive patrol. Their time on CID not likely to be repeated. The chief was passionate about weeding out the bad apples, and she complimented Taylor for her actions around the errant sergeants, in the middle of a challenging case.

It all added up to a slap on the wrist, coupled with a certain amount of respect from the chief, in particular, who knew what it was like for female officers to survive in the volatile environment that was modern policing. That said, they encouraged her to take some leave immediately after their conversation. Taylor knew it was their way of avoiding the need to suspend her.

Taylor was grateful for their leniency and used the time to reconnect with her husband and daughter, enjoying a pleasant spring break in a cottage in Cornwall.

She hadn't heard any more from the hotel. She wasn't sure that *Murder at the Manor* was really going to be a PR strapline that they were going to use any time soon. As she smiled to herself at the thought, the person she was meeting bounded into the coffee shop, a beaming smile crossing her face as she spotted Taylor.

"Eva," Taylor said, "you look much better since the last time I saw you."

Eva Stimic sat down and ordered a latte from the enthusiastic waitress who was offering her services before Eva could even sit down.

She grimaced. "Thank you. I feel much better. Mr Moretti gave me a month off on full pay after the incident.

314

He is a very kind man. I've been back to work for a while now, and although going into some of those rooms still gives me the *heebie-jeebies*, I'm just about okay."

Taylor smiled. "That's good."

"What about you?" enquired Eva, a caring, concerned expression on her face.

"Oh, I'm fine. Like you, I had a bit of a break afterwards. I was held to account for everything that happened, but I think I got away with a bit of a slap on the wrist."

Eva shivered. "God, I still can't believe that Walker woman. How could someone seem so normal and then turn like that? I don't think I've ever been as frightened as when she caught me in that room. Her eyes. They were so evil."

"Oh, yes of course. You were looking at that notebook when she caught you."

"That's right. I realised I'd seen it before and was trying to place where. When I saw the monogrammed initials on the outside, I realised it was over the weekend in Mrs Walker's room. I was confused, because when I checked the guest list, it was a different name."

"Yes, for some reason, she decided to hide out in the hotel, after my botched operation at trying to catch her. She used a false name so no one would spot her, but she didn't account for trainee detective Stimic now, did she?"

"Oh, I don't know about that," said Eva, an embarrassed look over her face.

"Hey, don't underestimate how important your brilliant observations were. That notebook had all the details of the jobs she'd pulled off, with dates and the money that had changed hands. The counter terrorist team managed to use it to solidify the case against her. They were delighted to get it and are confident it is the key piece of evidence that will win them their case."

Eva still looked embarrassed. She pulled a stack of papers out of her bag and handed them to Taylor. "I'm sorry, but I don't think I can apply to be a police officer. You've been very kind to me, but I just don't think I can bring myself to fill in the application papers you gave me. I've never been so scared in my life as when she had that gun pointed at my head. I just don't think I could handle that day in and day out. I don't know how you do it."

Taylor leant forward and rubbed Eva's arm. "It's not always like that, but I completely respect your decision. But you let me know if you change your mind, and I'll fast-track you onto my team."

They carried on chatting and drinking their coffees as they changed to lighter subjects. As their time together was drawing to an end, Taylor's phone beeped.

She picked it up. It was a message from Joshi asking when she was going to be back at the station. Taylor smiled. It was time to solve another case.

ACKNOWLEDGEMENTS

As always a huge thank you to my family for their unwavering support with my writing career. Special thanks to Jacky Wade, Hannah Wade, Karen Warner and Anthony Cooper for continuing to be my alpha readers. Also thanks to friend and fellow author, Tony Guntrip for his brilliant editorial support and brutal scrutiny of my writing.

A huge appreciation must go to my growing readership who continue to support my writing by purchasing and enjoying my books, plus the local independent bookstores in Oxfordshire who continue to stock my books.

Thanks to the Book Guild for their support in getting this novel produced and published.

And finally to all the brilliant people I meet as a result of my author work, who inspire and motivate me at every turn.